THE TURNCOAT
PRINCE

AMELIA SMITH

ISBN-13: 978-1-941334-16-4 (paperback)

ISBN-13: 978-1-941334-17-1 (ebook)

Published by Split Rock Books

Cover and book design by the author

Cover image is a detail of "The Hunters in the Snow " by
Pieter Bruegel the Elder, ca. 1565.

The title font is Canto Brush Open, and the text is set in
Starling Book, both by The Font Bureau.

Table of Contents

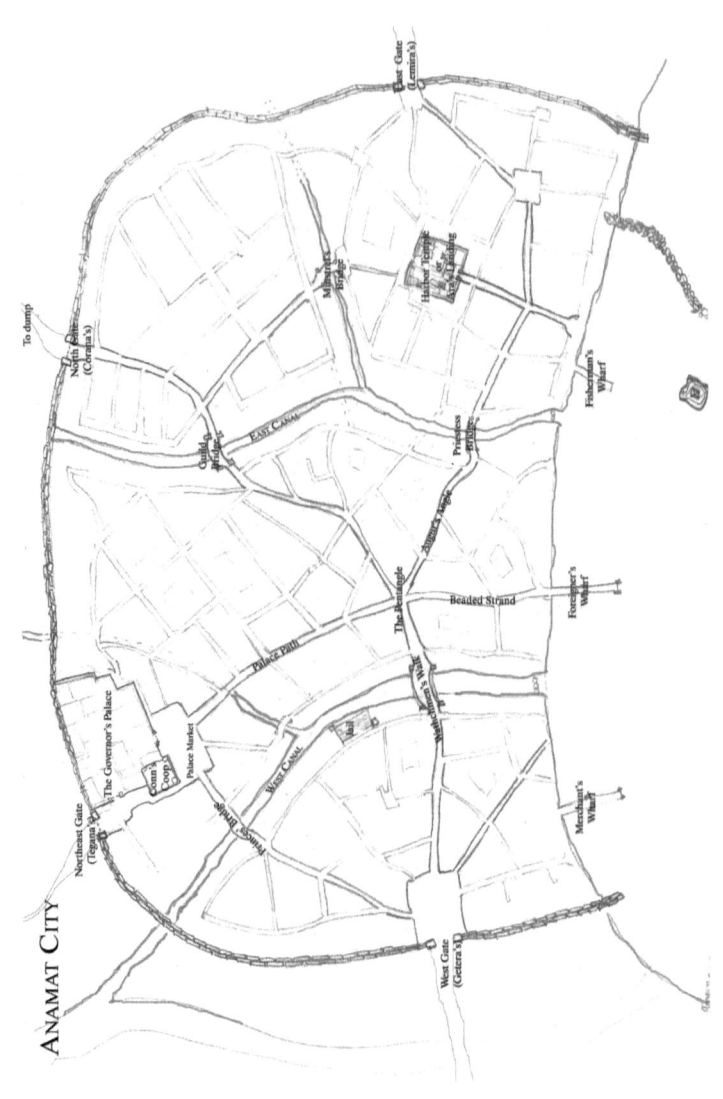

ANAMAT CITY

East Gate
(Lorrin's)

Miller's
Bridge

Harbour Temple
or Archgardens

To dump

North Road
(Cloraka's)

Fisherman's
Wharf

Guild's
Influence

EAST Canal

Princess
Bridge

Palace Path

The Promenade

Beaded Strand

Foreigner's
Wharf

Shipka's Ways

Waterfront Walk & Esplanade

The Governor's Palace

Coin's
Corner

West Coast

Palace Market

Temple Street

Merchant's
Wharf

Northeast Gate
(Teguna)

West Gate
(Gadeza'ul)

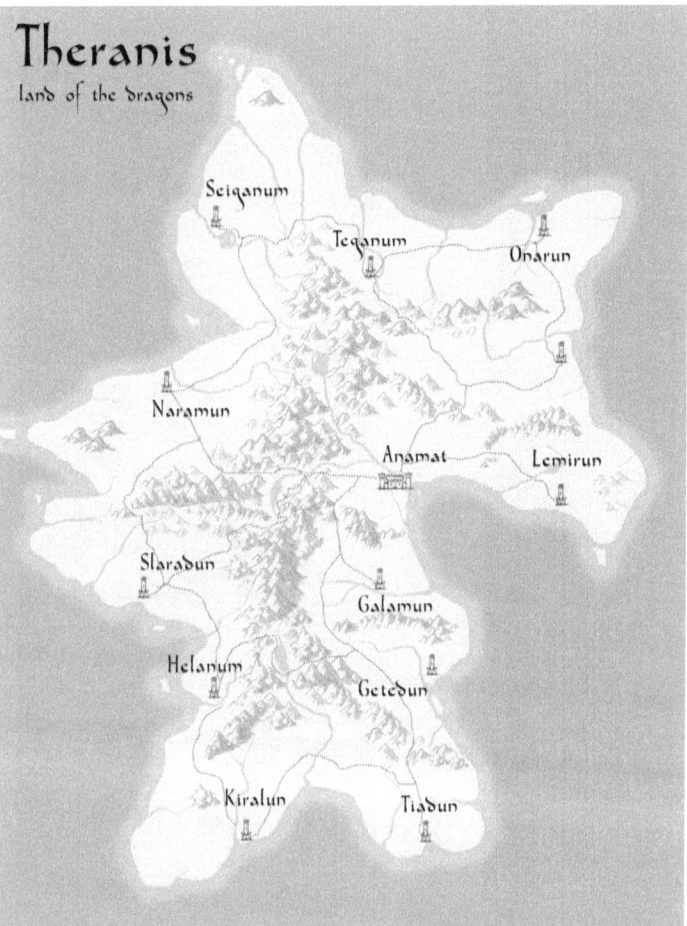

Theranis
land of the dragons

Prologue

At the moon before Midsummer, dignitaries and princes of the provinces set out on the road to Anamat. The princes rode in, all but the prince of Tiadun, whose body had gone down to the dragons' realm in spring. His brother, murderer, and presumptive heir led his caravan across the mountains, while Gallia, his bereaved mistress, fled across the hills and sailed to Anamat with traders from a neighboring province. As soon as she reached the city, she presented herself at the governor's palace.

The governor of Anamat and his mistress, Tiagasa, reclined on their couches, a table of delicate sweetmeats spread before them. They were young and giddy with power. Gallia remembered that feeling. She would be drab before them even if she hadn't just stepped off a tilting ship.

"Our Lady of Tiadun," the governor's mistress greeted her, lifting her head ever so slightly. "You come to us at last." Her manner was cool. She must have heard that the prince was dead, or perhaps she was only displeased that Gallia had not come to pay tribute to her before.

The governor cut in before Gallia had a chance to explain why she had stayed away since the old governor's death.

"Please, do sit." He indicated the padded stool opposite his couch and snapped his fingers for wine. A glass was set before her in an instant. "I trust your journey was pleasant." He smiled, but he must have known that she hadn't come to Anamat simply for the markets and festivities.

"The sail from Getedun was swift, at least," Gallia said, sitting up as straight as she could on the proffered stool, which set her a full head below the governor. He had done this deliberately, to remind her that his power extended beyond the reach of the princes and their kin...not that she was one of them anymore.

"I heard that you arrived by ship," Tiagasa said. Her voice dripped like honey, clouded, sticky. "How curious that you did not travel with your caravan, with your servants. You precede your prince?" She spoke as if she resented the loan of a maidservant in this season, when half the peasantry in the valley was pressed into service at her palace to provide for the noble visitors, important visitors. Perhaps she was not one anymore. She'd hoped that she would still be honored for her former position.

"My prince is dead, blessed one," Gallia began. She was taken aback by the sudden snarl of Tiagasa's lips, but she pressed on. "Yes, you and I have both been priestesses. I came alone because I feared for my life."

The governor snorted at that. "Your life can be in no such danger unless you take up hunting."

"I see that the news of Terenet's death has reached you. This hunting accident was all too convenient for Calar, and although I do not hunt, there are other kinds of accidents which can be arranged as easily."

The governor made a shooing motion. "Even if there's something to your allegations, why would he trouble with you? You aren't bearing an heir at your advanced age, or are you?"

Gallia shook her head.

"I doubt that Calar had any hand in his brother's death, but even if he did, your departed lover was barren and had no heirs. Calar's sons would be next in line to the throne, if for any reason Calar himself is unsuitable. The succession is clear, and Calar is—" He hesitated, pursing his lips. "Calar is well-known to his fellow princes." He didn't say "unlike you," but those unspoken words hung heavy in the air.

Tiagasa laid a hand on the governor's arm to stop him from speaking further.

"I would think that you would hesitate to condone a murderer's rule," Gallia said, rising from her stool.

"Nothing can be proven against him. We have our intelligences. Without an heir, you have no claim."

"It's true that I have no heir, but I have other news of a child of his," Gallia said. "Everyone believed that Terenet was barren, myself included. He never told me. Some twelve years ago, he learned that he had sired a child. It was only I who was barren from so many years of drinking the priestesses' tea."

Tiagasa drew her breath in sharply but said nothing. She'd left the temple almost eight years before but had yet to bear the governor an heir. She knew what it was like. She should have been sympathetic, but she was not a compassionate woman at the best of times. She would not want to appear weak before her husband. Gallia backtracked.

"It does not affect all women so. Unbeknownst to me, Terenet had gone to the rite with a priestess in one of the village temples, who then bore a child. The girl looked like him, the same red hair, the same scowl. I am told that she fled to Anamat and became a priestess here, at Ara's Landing." She turned to Tiagasa. "She would be about your age, perhaps a little younger. You might know of her."

"I don't know. I might. Red hair, you say?" Tiagasa had gone very still, her eyes narrowed. She knew something of this girl.

"Is this so?" the governor asked. "Why have I heard nothing of this? Why is this daughter of his not in Tiadun?"

"She wished to leave, and he did not stop her. Even then, Calar was scheming. Perhaps Terenet feared for his daughter's safety. She had been raised among peasants, then with the priestesses."

Tiagasa's eyes were narrowing. She knew this girl; Gallia was sure of it.

"If you will help me find her, she and I would challenge Calar's right to inherit his brother's throne. He is a murderer."

The governor stood. "I have no reason to doubt Calar's honesty and I intended to seat him as prince at our councils this year, but if you can present this girl, then of course we must have a trial for the succession."

"You will help me find her, then?"

Tiagasa shook her head and the governor followed her lead.

"I have pressing business to attend to with some of our foreign traders," the governor said, looking uneasily toward the door behind him. "If you do not trouble me with this further, we may delay confirming Calar's inheritance until next Midsummer, saying that it is a period of mourning. If you can present this daughter of Terenet's, we will hear your case in the council next year."

Gallia took a deep breath. She had just over a year to seek this child of her lover, this young woman. She had hoped for more help, and less power to Calar in the meantime, but this would have to be enough. She could still see him telling his guards to let her die in the mountains. "If Calar is regent, you should appoint one of your people to oversee him, to ensure that he does not overstep his rights."

"Consider it done," Tiagasa said. The governor startled and frowned at his mistress for a moment, then turned his bland, still-youthful smile back to Gallia. "Do not think that I know of this young woman," Tiagasa continued. "You may not find her. I am quite certain that she left the temple some time ago."

Tiagasa did know her, then, but had not considered her useful and wasn't sure that she would be useful now.

"I thank you for your consideration," Gallia said. "I will depart to the temple in the morning."

"As you wish," Tiagasa said, "but as I said, you will not find her there."

§

Chapter One

Darna reached for her tunic. Tevan tried halfheartedly to pull her back into the bed, but she shook him off and crossed to the far side of her room.

"You're brilliant," he said. It was one of his usual empty lines of praise, something he said so often that it had lost all its meaning.

For at least a year or two, she'd intended to ask him to stop visiting her, but she had no other prospects, nor any real reason for her discontent, so she'd never gotten around to it. Now he was about to leave for the bleak western province of Slaradun. There was no need to ask him to go anymore. She would have her bed back to herself in a few days' time. When he came back, well, that was something she could manage next Midsummer.

"If you hadn't trained for a priestess all those years, I think you'd have surpassed me by now at the guild," Tevan said. He didn't really mean it; she knew that he thought more of himself than he did of her.

The guild master did praise her work, which was all well and good, but Tevan was Anamat-born and related to half the members of the higher guilds. If he'd been younger than she was, which he wasn't, and dull-witted, which he also wasn't, the guild master still would have favored him.

"Of course, I'm glad you did have your time in the temple," Tevan said, finally sitting up and facing her. "Now you're my own personal priestess."

It was things like that which irritated her, that possessiveness undermining every bit of flattery, as if the only reason any of her qualities mattered was the questionable fact that he had them in his hands. She counted the days until he would leave, three more nights. Now he was looking out the window again, ignoring her.

"Looks like you have a visitor. Another lover?" he asked.

"I don't have another lover and you know it," Darna said. How did he still manage to be so jealous? She had a crooked gait and red hair, and she scowled half the time. Not the kind of woman to attract many lovers, especially when the most beautiful priestesses in the known world were at the temple just downhill. Although she'd been inside those walls herself, she'd never been a beauty.

"Whoever it is, she's probably just looking for the healer." One of Darna's neighbors was the second-best herbalist in the city outside of the temples.

"He," Tevan corrected. "Handsome fellow. Guardsman. I think I've seen him around the palace."

Darna tensed. Thorat knew where she lived, but he'd never come to visit her. They usually met at Myril's rooms whenever he was in the city, or over jars of ale at Ink Pounders. Yes, that was his step on the stair, confident yet light.

"I'll just tell him where to find the herbalist," Darna said as casually as she could manage.

She went out onto the landing. There he was, climbing her own stairs. Sometimes, she had dreamed that he would come, had fantasized that he would take her in his arms and forget Iola for a little while. She knew that would never happen. Even if Thorat lost his ardor for Iola, which would probably never happen, he was far too handsome for her, as Tevan would no doubt point out.

She did count Thorat as a friend, and he looked worried.

"Did you hear me coming?" Thorat asked.

"My friend saw you on the street." She pulled the curtain aside to let him in.

Thorat hung back. "I need to talk to you alone."

"I'll just tell him to go," Darna said.

"I'll keep watch," Thorat said.

It was an odd thing to say, but before she asked him what was wrong, she had to shoo her indifferent lover away. Tevan had already pulled his tunic on over his head and was picking up his sandals.

"It's an old friend from my scrappling days," Darna said. "He seems to have some news he wants to tell me alone."

"Surely, it's not so personal as that," Tevan said. "We can all share a cup of tea, maybe invite in some foreign sailors, too."

"It's not like that." Darna ushered Tevan to the door and brushed his tunic down fiat. "I'll see you tomorrow."

Tevan shook his head. "Not tomorrow. I have meetings with the prince of Slaradun and his suppliers all day, and they'll probably go into the night. But the next day?" He smirked and reached out to pull her in close. His warm breath wafted across her face. He did like her, gracious about it or not.

"The next day is Midsummer Eve," Darna said softly.

"And I'll be here. All day and night if I can." He hugged her closer, wedging his thigh between hers, and kissed her. "Remember that," he said.

"I'll have to go to the temple for the vigil."

"All afternoon, in that case." Finally, Tevan let her go. On his way out, he gave Thorat a smug look, as if to remind Thorat that he'd claimed Darna first.

Thorat ignored him. Once inside, he went directly to the window, looking up and down the street before he said anything. Darna went to his side and watched Tevan emerge below, then walk down the street and around the corner. Some revelers were piling up wood for a bonfire at the square. One of them had a drum that he tapped tentatively, as if trying to remember the chants. Thorat looked sharply around the room, then drew the curtains shut.

"Was that your lover?" Thorat asked.

"For now," Darna said, as if Tevan hadn't been pursuing her since before she left the temple, for entirely too long. For all that, he'd never met her oldest friends in the city. He'd never wanted to. "Do you want a cup of tea? I have some warm already," Darna offered. It was the dregs of the pot, but it *was* still warm.

"I think you'd better sit," Thorat said.

Darna hesitated. She had two stools beside her writing table, but she sat down on the bed instead. Thorat took the closer stool and sat down facing her. He took a deep, shaky breath. He seemed nervous, but Thorat was never nervous. He always seemed unerringly sure of himself, but now he glanced worriedly at the gap between the drawn curtains.

"This place isn't safe for you," he said. "I think you should go stay in the temple."

"Don't be ridiculous; I've lived here for years." Darna looked over her shoulder and drew the curtains across that last gap. "Is it something to do with Tiadun?"

Thorat nodded. "Was the prince of Tiadun your father?"

"I don't know." He might have been. After all, her mother had been a priestess and might have lain with any number of men, including the prince of their province, but no man was supposed to claim a priestess's child as his own, though they did when it suited them. The prince *had* tried to claim her. He'd sponsored her priestess training, possibly because she'd stood as proof that he could sire a child, although a girl child wouldn't normally inherit the throne. He'd needed that, not that it had done him any good in the end.

"He's dead now, so it doesn't matter."

Thorat shook his head. "That's the trouble. It does matter. Calar, his brother, your uncle, he found out about you. He wants you dead. He's offered a land grant, a rather large land grant, and a share of the Cerean trade in dragon stones to the man who kills you."

"Kills me? Me?" Darna's voice squeaked. "Why?"

"I don't know all of it," Thorat said, running his hand through his hair. His hand looked strong, competent. He had a good longsword which he knew how to use. Maybe he would protect her, not that she'd ever needed protection before.

"You don't know all of what?" Darna asked. If she was going to be murdered, she'd like to know why.

"He had your father murdered."

"I don't *know* that he was my father." The idea that Calar had killed his brother, the prince, was not at all surprising.

"The prince looks like you. Looked like you. He had the same expressions. I believe he was your father, even though you're not like any other princess I've seen."

"I wasn't raised to be a princess."

"You weren't raised at all. You're half-wild."

"Exactly," Darna said, "but now I'm also a full initiate of the Guild of Planners."

"Congratulations. I didn't know that."

"They blessed my masterwork this past winter, just before Tiada was killed." Tiada was the dragon and guardian deity of her home province. Dragons were supposed to live forever, as long as the land, so now her homeland was dead. The death of the dragon meant far more to her than the death of a man ever could, even if that man had sired her, and that was far from certain. Thorat had been there at Tiada's death. That much she knew, though the details of why he'd been there were not entirely clear.

"You know about that?" Thorat asked.

"Iola thought I should know. She said that Tiada had joined the deepest stream, and that that was different from death, though it looks the same to us on the surface. She knew that I was Tiada's child." Darna had sensed the absence of the dragon before Iola had told her about it.

"And not the prince's," Thorat mused.

"I have no interest in being connected to the prince of Tiadun," Darna said. "He had nothing that I wanted. Everyone knows that. Besides, it wouldn't make any difference. Why would Calar want me dead?" She did know her alleged uncle's name. She kept track of what was happening in Tiadun, just in case. "I'm no threat to him."

"But he thinks you are, and he's right," Thorat said. "You could walk into the province, marry any chieftain or prince's kin, and challenge him for the throne, even if he hadn't killed his brother, or had him killed. The priestesses and the villagers could put you on the throne as mistress of your own keep. You could cause trouble for Calar whether or not you try to take the throne yourself. Half his claim rests on the idea that his brother was barren, which he wasn't, not if you're the old prince's daughter. The armsmen at the keep are resigned to Calar's command, but people don't like him, not in the keep town and not in the villages, either. He brought the Cereans in and had them led to the gate."

If she were to avenge Tiada's death, then she would have to challenge Calar, not to mention the Cereans. The thought had some appeal, but she had no way to do it. Calar had a small army of guardsmen and a battalion of Cereans at his back. She had only herself, her limping self with her measuring tools and scrolls. It wasn't a fight she could win as a simple guildswoman, or as a presumptive princess, not alone.

Thorat frowned at the floor. "The old prince, for all his vole-slaughtering worship of Farseer..."

"What about him?" Darna prompted.

"He wasn't dragon-blind."

"He must have been," Darna said. No one who'd seen Tiada could turn to foreign gods, could they?

"He wasn't at the end. My apprentice was in the camp and overheard him say that he was seeing dragonlets."

"Your apprentice?" Darna asked. "And what *were* you doing there? Working for my uncle who wants to kill me now?" It was all just absurd.

"I left before that," Thorat said, crossing his arms over his chest.

Darna frowned. Thorat was as secretive as a priestess, maybe more so. She felt that he wasn't just a simple guardsman. Myril and Iola knew more, more that they'd never shared with her. She only knew that there was something else to him, that it had something to do with why he'd been in Tiadun at the death of Tiada, not that he'd been able to save her. He was, after all, only a man.

"Stay with me," Darna said. "I'll be safe here if you stay with me."

"I can't," Thorat said. He gave her a pained look. "I would if I could, honestly I would, but I think maybe you could be safe in the temple. Calar has half his guardsmen here in Anamat, and that price he's put on your head is enough to tempt almost anyone."

"Does it tempt you?"

"Of course not."

Darna felt petty for asking. She knew better than to doubt Thorat, even if he was too good for her.

"We have to figure out how to keep you safe," he said.

Darna nodded. Since she'd left the temple and the dancing teachers had stopped badgering her with exercises, her old limp had reasserted itself. She could walk fast enough with a cane, but she wouldn't be able to outrun a skin-and-bones scrappling, let alone a fit guardsman with a sword or an archer's arrow. She wasn't ready to die, and it wasn't worth the risk to try to talk her so-called uncle out of his ill-conceived assassination attempt. If he'd had any sense, he wouldn't have considered her a threat to begin with, but clearly, he didn't, and if there was one thing she'd learned in her years as a guildswoman, it was that you couldn't talk sense into someone who'd started off with none. Calar was almost certainly dragon-blind. He couldn't see what his so-called foreign allies were doing, elbowing him out of place, as their tradesmen were displacing the guilds of Anamat.

In any case, Calar had betrayed the dragon who had saved her from death after that boar had gored her as a child. The dragon had always meant more to her than her human parents had, and now her father was dead and her priestess mother was long gone into the hills. Darna couldn't remember her mother's face, and chances were she was dead too.

Calar had had Tiada killed, and now it seemed that he wanted to end Darna's much-less-significant life, too, all so that he could rule a barren land, a land with no dragon, with that bloodthirsty pack of Cereans behind him, daggers poised to stab him in the back, which was no less than he deserved. She would leave them to it. Tiada would be avenged, after a fashion.

"I could take you to Myril's instead," Thorat suggested, dragging her back from her musings. "It's almost dark. If you pull up your cloak, no one will see your hair."

"It's too hot," Darna said. "No one wears a cloak this time of year. I'd be less conspicuous in an Enomaean head wrap."

Thorat snorted at that thought.

"Just put on a cloak," he said. "You can carry whatever you need for the next few days underneath it, and I'll come fetch whatever else you need later. Everyone's probably too drunk to take much notice, anyway."

Darna looked out the window. She heard a crash and someone shouted, then the familiar festival smell of spilled ale wafted up from the cobblestones. "You're probably right. I suppose I could go to Myril's, then." Myril would hear any threat coming from far away – she would know when she had to hide. It would be safer than being alone.

She wrapped up her best drawing and measuring tools in a leather satchel, along with two clean tunics and a little parchment for notes. Thorat paced while she packed, looking out the window every three strides and sometimes checking the landing.

"What do Calar's henchmen know about me?" Darna asked him.

"They know that you're in the city, and I don't think it will take much for them to find you here. They know that you have red hair, that you look like kin to the prince, and that you have a limp. Some of the older men might remember you from when you were a servant at Tiadun Keep, before you left for Anamat."

"I doubt it," Darna said. "No one noticed me then, or if they did, it was only to tell me to get back to work, or to get out of their way."

"It can't have been that bad," Thorat said, in the manner of someone who has always been liked by everyone he met. "Tiadun Keep wasn't my favorite place, but while they're not the best of men, some of them are all right. They must have felt some sympathy for a child made to work too much."

"I was good at escaping work when I wanted to," Darna said. "Even if they had seen me then, which they didn't, they'd hardly recognize me without my old mud and ashes."

Thorat frowned. "Surely, some of them remember," he said, sounding a little less sure of himself. People had always noticed him, with his bright smile and shining eyes. "But you're right; people at that keep are dirtier than most, what with not having a public bath. The guardsmen have to make do with a bucket in the stableyard there most of the time."

"I doubt that any of them would know me," Darna said.

"It would only take one man who wants that land," Thorat said. "In any case, they know you were at Ara's Landing, at the temple, and that you left."

"But they don't know I'm with the planners' guild?"

"I don't know, but it would be easy enough for them to find out if they ask the right questions."

He was right. Most of her fellow priestesses – former fellow priestesses – understood that she didn't like to be bothered, and wouldn't be likely to tell a stranger where she'd gone. Then again, there was Tiagasa, the governor's mistress. That one would play whatever advantage she could find, and she wasn't alone in that. If Calar asked Tiagasa, the temple wouldn't be a safe haven for long. Men weren't allowed to bring in swords or knives, but there was always choking or poison. Any priestess with a rudimentary knowledge of simples could poison her. Darna had no particular enemies in the temple, but Tiagasa had ways of making other people fall in with her schemes.

Darna pulled her cloak up and set out for Myril's place with Thorat and his good sword guarding her back and her stick to clear the way, if she needed it. She tried not to use it: they would be looking for a woman with a limp, and her cloak alone was suspicious enough. No one was paying attention to her, though. Everyone on the streets had a jar of ale or stronger drink in their hands. They were too busy shouting out Midsummer greetings or dancing to badly played music to sink a hidden dagger in her back as she scurried across from one hidden alley to the next.

Myril's place was on the soothsayers' street, halfway up the hill from the old bridge in the middle of the city. Darna hoped that Myril would dye her hair again, not that dye would disguise her for long at the temple, where everyone knew her. She would be stuck like a bug on a pin, just waiting for them to find her, and in the meantime, she'd go mad with waiting to be killed. She cursed Calar as a fool, but then, her father had been a fool too. He'd been too charitable to his blood relations. Maybe Calar was simply trying to avoid making that mistake.

Soon, they climbed the narrow stair to Myril's always-welcoming room, with its bundles of herbs drying on the rafters and its jars of potions on clean and carefully tended shelves. An old farmer passed them on the stair, clutching his bag of remedies. Darna's neighbor was only the second-best herbalist outside of the city's temples – Myril was the best, outside the temples or in, and among the best cooks, too, when she had space on her stove for a purely culinary broth.

"I heard you coming," Myril said as they entered. "I sent one of the boys from the bridge to bring supper from the tavern down the canal."

Darna dropped her satchel of finely made tools on the floor and leaned her back against the door, slamming it firmly shut. Her heart galloped. She took a couple of shallow breaths. Her hands were shaking.

Myril peered at her. "What is it?"

Darna gulped. She couldn't find her voice, so Thorat explained.

"Darna's uncle, the one who killed her father, the prince of Tiadun, has put a price out on her head," he said.

Myril nodded, rather too calmly, Darna thought. "I should have expected that. I was delivering a few scrolls to the palace this afternoon when I heard a rumor that Gallia plans to challenge Calar's succession. To do that, she'll need you." She took Darna gently by the elbow and led her to the window seat.

"She wants to find me too?"

Myril nodded. Darna didn't have the energy to pretend ignorance of who Gallia was. Gallia had been her father's mistress since probably before she was born. He'd loved her, so much so that he hadn't taken another mistress when he knew that she was barren, even though it had led to all of this; the allegations of his impotence, his untimely murder. If he'd had a known son, it all would have been different, but it was too late for that now.

"What if Gallia finds me?" Darna asked. "Can she stop these assassins?"

"I don't think so," Myril said. "She came to the palace alone, without a single servant. She wasn't in the habit of coming to Midsummer Council, not since Parnet became governor, so she has no particular friends in the city, unless they're from long ago. She may have gone on to the temple."

"The temple is safer than the palace," Thorat said.

"Not safe enough," Darna said. Her heartbeat had slowed but her hands were still shaking. Three guardsmen were walking down the street below Myril's window, idly chatting as they went but looking around as if searching for someone or something. This street was the first place anyone would go looking for a former priestess. "Maybe I'd better sit further out of sight."

She started crying. She never cried, curse it all. Thorat and Myril helped her to the dark corner bed where Myril's patients sometimes slept. Darna shook her head at herself and tried to say something, but it didn't work; she just burst into tears again and buried her face in Myril's soft, strong shoulder. Myril smoothed Darna's hair and stroked her back. Eventually, her sobs subsided.

"You can dye my hair," Darna said at last.

Myril shook her head.

"Anything to disguise her, anything at all, will help," Thorat said.

Myril got that faraway look in her eyes.

"Don't prophesy," Darna begged. She hated it when Myril looked into the future. It left Myril shaken even when it wasn't a crossing time, even when she wasn't haggard from too much work as she was now.

"Dyeing won't do," Myril said in her half-tranced voice. "You have to leave Anamat. This is where they're looking for you, isn't it? They won't think to look in the provinces." By the time she finished speaking, she sounded ordinary again. The fact that she hadn't gone into full trance was a small reprieve.

"I can't go to the provinces," Darna objected. "I can't walk that far."

"You'll have to," Myril said.

"You could go into the hills," Thorat suggested. "The bandits aren't... They aren't as bad as I always thought they were. You could be a hermit priestess."

"I'll be no kind of priestess at all," Darna said. "I can't go to the provinces, and I certainly can't go to the hills. I'm staying in Anamat!"

"They'll find you here," Myril said patiently. "It's where they're looking. I could dye your hair, but too many people here would know you anyway. Almost everyone knows you, and you can't trust all of them."

Darna looked down the hill to the golden spires of the temple, still glowing in the last light of sunset. She and Myril had been novices there together, then priestesses for a season. The novitiate had been stifling, the priestesshood not much better. True, it had been comfortable, luxurious, but the walls were so confining, the gossip just as bad.

"The temple is the first place they'll look," Myril said.

Darna sighed. Myril always spoke the truth, but usually it wasn't so hard to hear. She'd lived in Anamat half her life, the much better half of it. She'd come as an almost-grown girl, become a woman in the temple, and joined a guild. Here she was, a master of her craft at last, and now she had to leave the city, to pretend... She couldn't think what she would pretend.

There was a sound outside Myril's door, and in a flash, Thorat had his dagger out.

"Put that away," Myril said. "It's only the boy with our supper. You'd better go now too. Darna and I will be safe here for tonight."

§

Darna woke late the next morning to the sound of Myril telling someone to come back after Midsummer.

When Myril saw that Darna was awake, she poured two cups of sweet tea from the earthenware jar sitting by the window and handed one to Darna. Myril took care of everyone. It was impossible to feel afraid in her domain.

"Thank you," Darna said.

"It was no more than you would do for me."

Darna shrugged. She wasn't so sure about that. If Thorat or Myril needed her, she would try her best to help them, but she would never have this warm, safe place, and she would never be like Myril. Myril would have been a truly great priestess if the trance hadn't taken her so hard that she'd almost lost her mind in those depths. It didn't help that she had no innate interest in lying down with men, not even in the rite, where they had no claim on her. Iola's presence made matters worse, too, always reminding Myril of what she couldn't have. She'd come to the fortune-tellers' row, within sight of the temple but outside its bounds, to be a chronicler and a healer, to measure out her talents in careful, safe parcels, at arm's length.

Despite the danger, Darna moved to the window to look out. Up the street, a prince's train was making its procession down to the harbor temple to pay its annual tribute to the ambassadress before her journey to the dragons' realm. Some prince was there, and he would lie with Iola where Myril could not, go in to the rite and not understand half of it, and leave some of his riches to Iola and the dragons.

"Do you think I'll die?" Darna asked.

Myril looked into her cup. "No. Not this year, and not the next year, but that doesn't mean you should stay here and wait for someone to try to change your fate. You need to leave Anamat; I'm sure of that much."

"Maybe I could go to that farm on the Western road that Thorat's always talking about," Darna said. That wouldn't be too far, only a short walk to the city walls. She could manage that much except on days when the pain was at its worst, and she didn't have those more than a few times a year.

"To Raina's place?" Myril raised her eyebrows. "I don't think so. The children would drive you mad, and besides, it's too close. You can't stay in the valley. Besides, I won't have you bring your danger to Raina's doorstep, not with all those children there and her other work."

Darna sighed. "Then what can I do?"

"I don't know yet," Myril said. "Did you have any prophetic dreams?"

It was a ridiculous question. Myril was the one who had prophetic dreams, not her. Still, she tried to remember what dreams she'd had, if any. The only thing that came to her was an image of a horse, trudging along like a pack animal. She was on its back.

"A horse? I think I was riding a horse in my dreams."

Myril shuddered. She didn't like horses; no priestess did. They were foreign animals who shied at dragonlets.

"I can't see you going to Enomae, but I can't see anything else, either." Myril stood up and went to her door, opening it a crack as if she had a visitor. Darna didn't hear anything until Myril said, "Thank you," and closed the door again.

Myril leaned against her door and looked at Darna. "The Aralel will be in her chambers until midday. I'm going to see if she can help."

"Help with what?" Darna asked, half knowing the answer already.

"She might know which provinces are safest for you, and where they would welcome a new priestess without too much question."

"I don't want to go back to priestessing at all, much less in one of those kinds of temples." The thought of hiding on her back with a succession of foreign sailors and pig-headed farmers between her bent legs had no appeal at all.

Myril sighed. "It's all I can think of, though the winged ones know I wouldn't choose it for myself, or for you." She crossed over to a carved cabinet by the window and took out a small bag on a string – one of her protective amulets. She hung it around Darna's neck. "I'll be back soon," she said. "Stay away from the window, and don't open the door to anyone but me."

Tears threatened to well up in Darna's throat, but she stuffed them back. She hugged Myril and let her go. "Don't be long."

§

Darna sat alone in the darkest corner of Myril's room and tried to read a scroll, but it was a dry old text about the herbs of the north, written in an uneven hand. She couldn't concentrate. Myril had said that she wasn't fated to die this year, but what if she was wrong? Myril's predictions were good but not perfect, not perfect enough to justify leaving Anamat on her weak leg. To be sure, this was where any assassin would look for her, but it was also the biggest city in Theranis. Its back passages had hidden her before and could hide her again. It was home, more so than Tiadun had ever been.

She briefly considered the prospect of going back to Tiadun, to see for herself the grave of the dragon they'd killed, to take vengeance however she could. She would get herself killed faster than anything that way, but at least she wouldn't be sitting around waiting for an arrow in her back. Still, the walk was long. She'd done it when she'd first come to the city, but she couldn't see walking so far again, not alone.

After some time, there was a knock at the door, but whoever it was went away. A heavier footstep came and went. Darna edged over to the window and peeked out. A prince rode by on his high horse with mounted guardsmen all around him and pages blowing horns and shouting, "Make way! Make way!"

The princes had horses. She might be able to go to some prince's keep, some rival of her uncle's, and hide there. It was a good thought, but how could she accomplish it? She could hardly hire herself out as a cook or a seasonal servant. Contracts had to be arranged before Midsummer dawn, when the princes returned to their home realms with their hirelings in tow. Most of those contracts would be settled by now; it was only a day and a half before Midsummer night.

Tevan. He would go looking for her in her room, but not today. Tomorrow she would go back to her own place to say goodbye to him.

At length, Myril returned. Darna flew up to unbar the door and let her in. Thorat was right behind her.

"You were here all along?" Thorat asked before Myril had a chance to speak. "I was waiting at the bottom of the stair. I knocked."

"I would have let you in if I'd known," Darna said, wishing she *had* known. The time would have passed more pleasantly with company, if she hadn't been mulling on the unpleasant subject of princes, their horses, and their hirelings.

"Never mind that; we're all here now," Myril said. She set down a pot – temple tea, by the smell of it – and poured for all of them.

"The Aralel says she can't help."

Myril sounded put out, but Darna couldn't help but feel it was a relief.

"She says that the provincial temples are too much under the control of the princes," Myril went on. "With the network of spies and gossips between one keep and the next, not to mention the usual priestess chatter. The temples are no place for a woman who wants to hide, she says. She's worried about Gallia's safety – she's staying in the elders' court for now. If Gallia finds you, the others won't be far behind." Myril looked at Thorat. "The Aralel agrees that the hills would be the best place for a woman who wanted to hide. I didn't say who it was for, though. It's rough living in the hills, good enough for someone like me... I think she was worried that I was the one who had to hide."

"So much for the wisdom of the highest priestess in the land," Darna said. "Hills probably aren't much good for a cripple."

"You're stronger than you give yourself credit for," Myril said, "but in this case, I think you're right. She did say that there was one province which almost never gives rise to any gossip, so much so that even the Aralel's networks of rumors have dried up.

"Which province is that?" Thorat asked.

"Slaradun."

"Tevan's going to Slaradun," Darna said, and that beginning of an inkling of an idea began to take shape.

§

Chapter Two

Garlands of flowers hung the length of Myril's street, dangling from every window, bright against gray stone and whitewashed walls. Above, the sky was clear and calm, a perfect Midsummer Eve. Darna had been in Myril's room for two full nights and a day, and its welcoming walls were beginning to close in, the drapes confining rather than comforting, the air stifling.

She couldn't stay there forever. At midday, Tevan would be coming to her room. If she weren't there to meet him, he might sound some kind of alarm, which would not do at all. Besides, she did want to say goodbye, regardless of whether or not she could convince him to go along with her plans. No matter what he said about her brilliance, he didn't like taking suggestions from her.

She was waiting for Eppie to arrive – Thorat had said that he was going to send his apprentice to guard her when she went back to her own room, so that she wouldn't be unguarded on the streets.

"Don't worry," he'd said. "Eppie's quick. She can skewer almost any guardsman in Theranis before he can draw a dagger. Besides, your friend won't mind her. No one ever seems to think she's much more than a scrappling. I could tell that he didn't like me coming there. He seemed to think I might be some sort of rival for your affections."

Darna blushed. She thought that Thorat hadn't noticed, but he was right, Tevan certainly wouldn't see Eppie as her potential rival. Then again, he might take an interest in Eppie.

He sometimes said that he liked boyish women, and she was never sure whether he meant that as a compliment or not.

Eppie arrived a little before gate closing, with her knives at the ready and a sword on her back. She looked different somehow, taller, older by more than a year, and less like a scrappling in every way. She drank Myril's tea until the bells sounded, then she and Darna set out, sticking to the back ways and alleys. For Midsummer Vigil, everyone past infancy was expected to stay awake through the night, so the midday rest would last longer than usual, almost until sundown. Darna would have enough time to convince Tevan - if he could be convinced at all.

They stopped at the mouth of an alley not far from Darna's place.

"Any guardsmen?" Darna asked. "Tiadun's livery is orange and blue - any of those?"

"Wait here," Eppie said. She slipped onto the street, as shadowy as the scrappling who begged beside the corner shrine. She returned within moments. "It's just the usual Midsummer crowds," she reported. "Not a sword in sight, except mine." She peeked out of the alley one more time. "Not much for pickpocketing, either. Used to be better."

"You're not going back to *that* today, are you?" Darna worried.

"Of course not," Eppie said. "I have other things to do now." She looked away as she spoke, discouraging further questions.

Darna handed her a short string of beads. "Buy yourself something to eat across the way, and watch for anyone coming to my door."

"I'll follow when your man comes, and wait on the stair. He won't know I'm there."

Darna handed her a few more beads. "How about you bring us a midday dinner?"

Eppie nodded. "I'd better go before they sell out of stew."

Darna used to hide all the time when she was living under the bridge and scavenging for scraps. Hiding in the alley felt like slipping back into old, well-worn clothes, but now she wished she could walk freely on the ordinary streets. She'd gotten accustomed to that freedom. At least here in Anamat, she knew the hidden ways. The provinces would give her no such cover.

Darna strode quickly across the street and up to her empty room. Everything was just as she'd left it – the disheveled bed, the empty cups on the table, the scrolls in disarray – but the place already felt abandoned.

She shook out the blankets and lit a bit of incense in a brazier, washed the cups in the bucket, and ran a damp cloth over the table. She hoped that Tevan wouldn't notice the air of loss and decay, the sense that what had lived there was gone already.

Darna looked out. Eppie sat at a table in the makeshift café across the street, head resting on her arms as if she were napping, but she wouldn't be asleep. She would be noticing everything, listening if not looking. Darna lay down on her bed beneath the window and closed her eyes.

The knock on the door startled her awake. She jumped to her feet and stumbled across, remembering just in time to be careful. A look through a hidden crack beside the door revealed that it was only Tevan, as expected. He was wearing a garland of small white roses around his neck.

"I came earlier," he said. He paused to kiss her. "You didn't have your garlands up, so I went back to the market to buy one for you." He took the garland of roses off his neck and looped it around hers.

Darna thanked him with a quick kiss. "I don't know how I forgot. We'd better hang them out." She took the garland to the window and Tevan helped her hang it.

"Shall we speed the ambassadress on her way?" he said, pulling Darna close.

It wasn't the rite, what they did together. It was only common sex. She'd told him before that it didn't make much difference, but even common sex fed the life of the land a little bit. It pleased the dragons, too. She'd never been able to make Tevan understand the difference between the rite and common sex, even though he was a native of Anamat. It was no wonder the foreigners couldn't grasp the difference between a temple and a brothel – they didn't know how to approach the temple; they only knew the customs of the brothel. Tevan's lack of understanding still annoyed her, but this wasn't the day to explain the difference. It was all in the attitude of the petitioners and whether or not the priestess could turn the men's lust to awe. Most couldn't. She certainly couldn't, not with Tevan.

He hiked up her tunic and stroked her thigh.

"Actually," Darna said, "I thought you might be hungry. I'm having a youngster bring up stew from the place across the street."

Tevan pouted, but before he could say anything, Eppie knocked at the door. Darna let her in and Eppie handed over the crock of stew. She raised her eyebrows as if to ask if everything was going all right. Darna nodded and glanced toward the stair. Eppie nodded too.

"I'll be back for the crock in a bit," Eppie said.

"There's no hurry," Tevan said, smiling at her speculatively.

Darna frowned. "No, there's no hurry," she said, "but do come back before the gates open again."

"Sure thing, ma'am," Eppie said, and made a sloppy, mocking bow, silly enough to make Darna chuckle, but too subtle in its mockery for Tevan to see it as anything other than clumsy. Darna thanked her and let her out.

§

Tevan was hungrier for sex than he was for stew, so Darna took the last of her scant pleasure with him before turning to the main reason she'd come back to meet him, not that he knew that she'd been away. He was well enough satisfied before they talked of the future.

"I'll miss you when I'm away in Slaradun," he said as he rolled off her. "My own personal priestess." He reached over to caress her hair, which, while still red, was less unruly than usual, thanks to Myril's attentions. "You smell nice. Is that a new hair oil?"

"It is." Darna reached for her lightest tunic, then remembered that she'd left it at Myril's place. She got up, put on the tunic she'd worn earlier, and checked the crock of stew. It was still warm, though no longer hot. She ladled it into the clean bowls Eppie had brought and poured a little ale for each of them.

"I could just stay in bed all day," Tevan said, lying down again.

Darna decided to eat anyway. She was hungry, whether or not Tevan was. "How are things going with your prince?" she asked.

That got him up. "The man is a pompous know-it-all," Tevan said, as if he weren't one himself. "He thinks that just because he's seen a few cities, he knows how to build a harbor, build a whole new city."

"A city? In Slaradun?"

"It's all very hush-hush," Tevan said. "I probably shouldn't be telling you, but who else can I tell? It's not as if there will be anyone worth talking to – or bedding – out in the province of the runt dragon."

Even if Salara was a runt, Tevan had no business insulting any dragon. "But there can't be enough people in Slaradun to make a city," Darna said.

"I don't think there are now, but this prince has plans, and I'd say he was dragon-touched, but he's too quick-witted for that. He did a preliminary drawing himself. He can write and read."

"A prince who can write and read, and admits it?" That was unusual. Writing was the domain of scribes and priestesses. Most princes preferred to concentrate on manly pursuits like hunting, foreign alliances, and having their rivals killed off. If they did read, they kept it to themselves and left official correspondence to their secretaries.

"He's arrogant, and he has a scrawny boy to do his bookkeeping who I don't like at all. There'll be precious little company out there, and I won't see you, or Anamat, until next Midsummer."

"If then," Darna said.

"What do you mean?"

"If he really wants to build a city, it's going to take a lot longer than a year."

"I'm only contracted for a year," Tevan said. "I can't go longer than that. My father's ailing and the family house will pass to me when he goes. If I'm not here, it'll be a mess."

He had mentioned his father's ill health before, but one thing Tevan had never done was to introduce her to his parents. She knew who they were, because they lived in the neighborhood near the guildhall, but she hadn't seen Tevan's father in a while. She hadn't given it much thought. Tevan didn't seem to either, or at least he hadn't mentioned it to her until then.

"Maybe you'd better stay in Anamat, then," Darna said. "Surely your family house is worth more to you than a year in Slaradun."

Tevan finally got out of the bed and came to sit at the table.

"It certainly is," he said once he'd swallowed his first bite of stew. "I wouldn't want to lose it for the world, but what can I do?"

"You could find another planner to replace you for the contract."

Tevan shook his head. "No one wants to go to Slaradun."

"True enough," Darna said, thinking of the long road through the mountains and her probably-not-prophetic dream of riding a horse.

"It's quite a project, to build a city. I'd love to do something like that."

Tevan shook his head. "You're hardly qualified."

"I had my master project," Darna said. "Technically, I'm as qualified as you are."

"You don't have the experience."

"Neither does anyone else," Darna countered. "No one in the guild has built a city or even laid the foundations for one. This prince can't be serious."

They ate without speaking for a little while, soaking up the last bits of stew with their rounds of bread.

"I don't want you to sacrifice yourself for me," Tevan said firmly. "You belong in Anamat."

Darna would have agreed if there weren't a death threat hanging over her head, but she did have to leave, and working in Slaradun would be better than attempting banditry in the hills.

"I think maybe it's time for me to see other places," she said, though it sounded like a lie to her own ears. "I haven't left the valley since I came here as a scrappling."

"A dozen years ago," Tevan said, nodding. "For my part, I've never left the valley at all. I don't like leaving the city. I could be quite happy staying in Anamat for the rest of my life."

"So, let me take your place in the contract," Darna said. "You can teach the apprentices to read – that's what I'm supposed to be doing with the coming season – and then after Midwinter, if you like, we can trade places."

Tevan set his bowl down and went to the window. "I don't think the prince will like that. He has some odd ideas about priestesses."

"There's no call for him to know that I'm a priestess. I'm really not anymore. I'm a guildswoman, same as any."

"Not the same as any to me." Tevan knelt down and kissed her hand. "I don't like the thought of you out there all alone."

Darna stood up and jerked her hand away from him. "You don't like the thought of me being here with company, either. You're jealous and possessive, and it's absurd. Look at me!" She jerked up the hem of her tunic to show the long scar along her hip and leg. It had grown pale over the years, but it was still there, still disfiguring.

"You're beautiful, even so," Tevan said. He stood up and scowled. "But if you feel that way, then maybe you should go out to the bleakest place in all Theranis and be alone. Maybe you'll like that better." He picked up his belt and pouch then stomped to the door, where he knelt to strap on his sandals. He didn't look at her. He was on his way out the door when Darna spoke again.

"The guild master will need to approve it," she said, "and the prince."

"You're the master's favorite."

Darna would have protested, but Tevan was already on the landing outside.

"Leave the prince to me," he said, his back still turned to her. "Good riddance to you."

He didn't look back. Darna gaped after him. The well-worn staircase shook in his wake. As he clattered down to the street, the bells sounded, signaling the end of the midday rest. It was the end, at last, of their all-too-long affair. She had nothing to say to him. He had nothing to say to her. It was right to end it, the empty shell of it, but she'd bungled it. She should have done it better. She was no priestess.

Well, there was nothing to be gained from mourning *that,* and at least she was a guildswoman, and she would stay alive, and maybe she would build a city, or at least map its foundations. That was something worth leaving Anamat for.

Besides, Tevan would get to look after his ancestral house, and that would please him in ways she never could.

She took a moment to stare out the window after her now-former lover as he stomped away down the sun-baked street, the waves of heat rising up around him as if the city would swallow him, as if Anamat would keep him for its own. That was the worst of it. *He* would never have to flee the city. He would have a home here always, whereas for herself, maybe the city had only pretended to welcome her into its secrets. It would never embrace her as it cradled Tevan, no matter what her virtues or skills.

She couldn't see his face as he rounded the corner, but by the set of his shoulders, he was probably scowling. He was going toward his family's house, not toward the palace at all. Well, he had all night to talk to the prince. She certainly wasn't going to brave the palace, not with her uncle and his armsmen waiting for her there. Out on the landing, Eppie cleared her throat.

"You might as well come in," Darna said.

"I have to go soon," Eppie said. "They're expecting me back at the training hall."

Darna sighed. "Maybe Myril or Thorat can come bundle up what I leave behind. There isn't much I need to take with me." Her tools were already at Myril's. She would need some more winter clothes. She stared at it all blankly.

"What do you need?" Eppie asked.

"A sack, I suppose." Darna stirred herself to action. She piled her possessions into bags as the first of the afternoon delivery carts rolled up to the shops and taverns to unload their wares.

By the time they left, the street outside was crowded again, but she did need to go speak with the guild master to get his blessing, at the very least. Eppie shadowed Darna as she walked the short distance around the corner to her guildhall, hood up. The pinch in her side always felt a little better after Tevan's visits. She would miss that, though not the feeling of obligation to him. Beneath her winter hood, sweat trickled down the back of her neck. Every person in Anamat seemed to be on the streets, and many greeted her as she passed, despite her slouch and averted gaze.

"You might as well say hello to folks," Eppie said. "It is Midsummer –"

Three guardsmen in Tiadun livery rounded the corner. Darna stepped in to the shade of a tea shop across from the guildhall as quickly and inconspicuously as she could.

"Two cups," she said, fumbling at her belt for the beads.

The guardsmen walked on. She couldn't get the beads off their string.

"Never mind," she said.

"They're already poured, guild-lady."

Darna finally got the knot untied and looked over her shoulder. Everyone on the street looked just like ordinary revelers except for the hooded woman sitting on the bench just outside the guildhall door, but Darna judged her to be no threat.

"I'll take the tea," Eppie said. "You go on."

The tea vendor grumbled but didn't seem to mind having Eppie there in Darna's place. She watched the street while Darna attempted to saunter across to the guildhall as if it were the most ordinary thing in the world, which it was, it was just that it didn't feel that way.

She stubbed her toe and cursed. "Tia's tits."

The old woman on the bench looked up abruptly. She was a handsome woman of middle years, vigorous and sharp-eyed. She squinted at Darna, who turned her face away as she hurried inside. The old woman looked familiar, but Darna couldn't place her. She wasn't from the neighborhood, that much she was sure of, but she wasn't dressed in priestess robes, either.

The old woman could be no threat, Darna told herself. What would an old woman want with a land grant and her pick between priestesses or Cerean slave girls? Besides, she had the whiff of someone who had as much wealth as she needed already.

Darna stumbled straight into the guild chief's study, not bothering to pause at the door.

The guild master was not alone. Tevan's stool fell over as he stood.

"I wanted to see if you would come," he said, sounding affronted. Then he stormed out, again without a backward glance.

The guild master waved to the stool. "You might as well sit. Your guild-fellow has told me that you requested to take his place in the Slaradun project. I don't know if I can condone this. I was counting on you to teach the young ones their letters."

"Tevan can do that," Darna said, sitting down.

"It won't suit him any better than it suits you. I confess I did not realize the depth of his greed for the family house, and how much he thought he needed to be on hand to claim it. It's a noble sacrifice on your part?"

"Hardly," Darna said. "The project does interest me. It's more ambitious than anything I'd be able to take on here."

The guild master chuckled. "And you are ambitious, and accomplished enough, too. I thought it would be good to broaden Tevan's horizons. You, at least, have seen the provinces."

"Not since I was a child," Darna said. "Not since I had any sort of education or understanding."

"And you want to leave the city now because..."

Darna shifted uneasily and looked to the open door behind her. "I'd rather not say. It's just that – it's that some people have turned against me through no fault of my own. I don't want to make trouble for you."

"If it's a matter of debts, surely the guild can settle that for you." The guild master looked concerned but not overly so. He was as close to a father as she'd ever had, not that that was saying much, but she did not want to be any more beholden to him than she already was.

"It's more complicated than that. I may be able to explain in a year or two."

"If any of us are here in a year or two," the guild master said, so quietly that Darna almost didn't hear him.

"Why do you say that?"

The guild master frowned at the fioor. "It's nothing, just a rumor from Cerea. It will probably come to nothing." He looked up and made a little bemused shrug. "Very well. We may alienate the prince of Slaradun – Tevan suggested that he might not approve of a change, or of a guildswoman rather than a man – but if it doesn't work on his terms, then at least you'll have seen Slaradun and have a chance to make your mark on what appears to be a very ambitious project. The prince of the poorest province is the least of our worries, though I think that Tevan's a fool to stay in the city, and... Well, he's no concern of yours now. Go have a rest – you'll have a long night and an early start."

"Thank you, Lord Planner," Darna said.

Several apprentices appeared in the doorway just then, so Darna took her leave, wishing everyone a happy night as if this were just like any other Midsummer. Relieved that the matter had been settled so easily, she forgot to look for danger as she stepped out onto the street.

"You are she; I'm sure of it."

The old woman – not so old, really – grabbed her arm. Darna would have spun away, but she was off-balance and the old woman's grip was firm. Darna yanked her hood up with her free hand. Eppie trotted over with one hand on the hilt of her sword. She stopped a few paces away, close enough to hear and threaten but not so close as to interfere.

"You are his daughter," the old woman whispered fiercely. "I was his mistress. You cannot let Calar rule. We must contest it. Come with me to the palace."

Darna looked at the old woman with new eyes. This was the woman that her father had spoken of so lovingly, the one he would not put aside. She was the reason – in part – that he had not looked for her when she was young, that she had not known him when it might have mattered to her, before she'd learned to hate him as a servant in his dank keep. His old mistress was still a handsome woman, her eyes clear and determined. Darna didn't like much of what she'd seen of her father, but she liked Calar less, much less.

"How could you contest it?" Darna asked.

"I cannot, but you can."

"I have nothing to contest it with," Darna said.

"I see him in you. I won't be the only one who sees it."

"That's what I'm afraid of. They have a price on my head. Maybe on yours, too. If you want to walk into a deathtrap, that's fine, but I'm leaving. I won't play their game."

"Coward," Gallia said. Now Darna remembered her name. The prince's mistress had not been cruel, only absent, hidden away back at Tiadun Keep, doing nothing to make life there better or worse. She released Darna's arm.

"We have until next Midsummer, if we live that long," Gallia said. "Remember me, and come to the tribunal."

Darna shook her head, a mute refusal. Behind her, she could hear the sound of guardsmen clanking along the street. So could Gallia. She hurried away in the direction of the temple while Darna ducked back inside the guildhall until the guardsmen passed. They were only Onarun guardsmen this time. Still, they might have heard of the price on her head. Nowhere would be safe, but Myril and Thorat were right: Anamat, the crossroads of Theranis, was least safe of all.

§

Darna tried to rest in the slow-falling twilight of Midsummer at the back of Myril's room. As night descended at last, she and Myril set out for the temple, where they would join in the chants to speed the ambassadress's journey. Darna wore her hood up and Myril listened for any sound of threat as they wove through the streets. As they stepped onto the bridge across the canal, Myril gripped her arm.

"Hurry," she whispered.

"What is it?"

Myril shook her head, only answering when they reached the far side of the canal. "They're at the top of the street, three guardsmen. They asked a scrappling up there about a red-haired woman with a limp. She...she'd probably seen you. You'd better not come back this way."

Darna felt sick, but she nodded. Then she spotted guardsmen coming their way from the other direction and ducked into a side alley.

"They're not looking for you, not those ones," Myril assured her.

"But they might see me and tell the ones who *are* looking," Darna said.

Myril nodded and led the way on, leaving Darna to keep glancing back over her shoulder. They didn't have much farther to go. Soon, they entered the temple through the side house, a half-secret way for priestesses to come and go unobserved and to change into their priestess robes for ceremonies.

In the red robes, Darna looked just like what the men from Tiadun were seeking, but Myril seemed unworried. With so many women crowded together in the sanctuary, surely it was safe enough for one night. The younger ones were robed all alike in red, the youngest in novice white, their features obscured by clouds of incense and flickering lamplight. Darna kept to the shadows. The sanctuary's dome reached up to the sky. Incense and colored silks, drumbeats and chanting filled the air. Darna had hated being stuck in the temple, but she loved the space of the sanctuary. Its stones came together in a perfect chorus, evoking deep histories. It awed her every time, its majesty, the artistry of its vaulted structure.

None of her fellow priestesses were paying her any particular attention. She and Myril took up their parts of the chant again and again as the hours stretched on through the year's shortest night. Although they were deep within the temple, Darna sometimes thought that she heard the sound of revelers on the streets outside. She hoped that Iola would live to see Midsummer again, to come back to this place at the next turning of the year, and that she would too.

It was getting close to dawn when Myril touched her elbow, breaking the spell.

"I think we should go see Iola," she whispered.

"Will they let us in?" Darna wondered. After all, they were no longer full priestesses, and the ambassadress was closely guarded, especially at crossing times.

"She'll want to see you, I think. I heard Sunna outside a little while ago. She'll let us in."

Darna took one long last look at the sanctuary, breathing in the cedar and myrrh, wondering if she would ever see it again. She hurried to catch up with Myril before she reached the peresi's courtyard.

The courtyard was the heart of the temple, even more so than the sanctuary. It was late in the night, but some petitioners lingered while the priestesses who'd given them audience were preparing to lead the ambassadress's procession down to the harbor. A slender priestess gave her petitioner his benediction at the door of her chamber. A treasurer sat behind a small round table, counting out the night's tribute into sorted bags. Others strolled toward the sanctuary to join in the night's final songs.

Myril strode through the busy garden, straight across to the gate of the ambassadress's quarters. Sunna was waiting for them at the gate of Iola's realm as if she expected them. She ushered them in and shut the gate quickly behind.

"Iola wants to see you, and then Thorat says I'm to take you to the northeast gate," she told Darna. "The cart with your things will meet us there." Sunna took a deep breath and let it out in a grumble. "I don't know if Iola will come back. I saw it, and it's not safe."

"Nowhere is," Myril said, her voice far away, her eyes gazing on what no one else could see. "She'll be safer there than here."

"Wake up!" Darna said.

Myril's shoulders jerked up and she shivered. Her eyes cleared.

"Was that about me, or Iola?" Darna asked.

"Iola, I think, but it could be you," Myril said. Her eyes were downcast now, counting her fingers, one of the tricks she used to bring herself back to the present.

"Come on," Sunna said, pulling Darna forward. "What's the danger to you, anyway?" she asked.

Darna wished she could take a moment to just enjoy the moonlit garden, but between Sunna's impatience and the coming dawn, there was no chance of that. "Calar wants me dead."

"That is worrying," Sunna said. They paused at the foot of the stairs up to Iola's doorway. She didn't ask *why* Calar wanted her dead. Maybe she knew, or guessed, already. After all, she'd been the one to chaperon her to the awkward meetings with her father when he'd come to look in on her during her novice years, to see that she was there before he delivered his tuition payments to the treasurers.

Sunna gestured to where Iola was waiting for them. "I told her not to go. I was there when Tiada was killed," she whispered. "The dragons would be right to take one of ours, to take her. I know it's her calling, and she'll go no matter what I say, but I'm not at all sure she'll come back alive, or whole."

Geta, one of the temple elders, appeared at the top of the steps. For the occasion, she was wearing ceremonial robes rather than her usual faded and flour-covered tunic. "Don't trouble yourself," Geta said to Sunna. "She knows the danger."

"And she's not a novice under my care anymore." Sunna sighed. "Still ..." Darna finally noticed that Sunna wasn't wearing priestess robes at all. Instead, she was dressed in something like a guardsman's tunic. Before she could ask why, and why she'd been at Tiada's death, Geta had a question for her.

"What brings you here on this night?"

"Myril said that Iola wanted to see me," Darna said.

Geta gave Myril a nod. "If that's so, you might as well come in," she said, but she beckoned only to Darna, leaving Myril alone outside. Sunna had already slipped away.

Iola's quarters were impossibly sumptuous. They made the red-and-gold-draped peresi's chambers look plain by comparison. The ambassadress's offering chamber was covered in ornament, each piece in perfect harmony with the next. No one made such fine temples anymore. The temple on the palace hill looked merely garish in comparison.

Iola stood in front of her offering place, naked. She frowned at the ceremonial robe in front of her and glanced over her shoulder to see who had come in. Her skin was as luminous as the moonlit dome above her, her hair darker than the night sky.

"I hear that you're leaving Anamat."

Darna couldn't think what to say.

"Sunna told me," Iola continued. "I haven't seen Thorat since days ago. I'd like to say goodbye."

To me or to him? Darna wondered. "Myril just said that you'll be safer there, under the earth." At least, that was what she thought that Myril had meant.

Iola nodded. "That's good to hear. I don't know if it's enough, but it's good to hear." Her voice creaked a little. "They said I could choose not to fly, but I *can't* not go, not when we've already betrayed them so much." She meant the dragons.

"*You* haven't," Darna said. "It's not your fault."

Iola turned to face her then, leaning against the edge of the offering platform. She looked past Darna as she spoke, as if she were already halfway to the dragons' realm. "I carry their faults with me, all of the princes, and the other, ordinary men who come sometimes. I carry them for the other peresi too, for all of us," she said. "I even let that... The new one, from Tiadun, he came, but I couldn't make him see. The one from Slaradun didn't bother to send one of his chieftains this year - that's what he's done before, since the old one died. He sent a gift, a bangle of some sort, as if that was what the dragons wanted, as if a gilded token could replace his seed. They're all slipping away, even Getedun. It's like I'm a thread that's going to snap, but I think I can hold the realms together for another season."

"You might not be able to," Darna said. "I hope that you'll return. I'll do whatever I can to help you come back." Though she was jealous of Iola sometimes, especially where Thorat was concerned, Iola was a true priestess, pure in her purpose as no one else ever seemed to be. There would be no more like her. Darna could see the truth in what Iola had said about being a stretched cord, just barely holding the worlds together. She commanded loyalty for what she was, not only as a friend.

Iola bit her lip and turned back to frown at the robe. "Help me get into this," she said. She was beautiful even when she frowned.

Darna lifted the robe onto Iola's back. "You wear nothing underneath it?"

"Nothing," Iola said. "I change into a different one before Anara comes to me, if there's time. It's very warm in their realm."

Darna admired the embroidery, the golden-threaded dragons and purple flowers, the border of mountains and forested hills on thick red silk.

Abruptly, Iola turned to her. "You have some of Tiada's essence in you, more than that man had. Send it with me."

They had not belted the robe shut yet, and it fell open. Iola pressed her body against Darna and kissed her, forcing her mouth open so suddenly that Darna couldn't think to resist until Iola pulled away.

Iola had the contented look of a sleepy cat in a puddle of sunlight as she released Darna. Darna was shaken. Iola had taken something. She had taken something right out of her, as if...but Darna didn't have any claim on the power the dragon had lent her so long ago. It was borrowed, but the dragon was gone, and it had done its work. Iola could take it back to them. It was only right.

Iola looked at Darna then reached toward her again. Darna edged away, but the offering place was behind her now, blocking her escape. "Here, let me help," Iola said.

Darna felt too weak to flee, and curiosity made her hesitate, too. She wished Iola would not touch her, not like that. Unlike everyone else in Theranis, she'd never dreamed of bedding the ambassadress. Apparently, Iola still thought it her duty to carry everyone she could into the rite. She drew close again, but instead of that dizzying, unexpected, disorienting kiss, she took Darna's hands in hers and closed her eyes. Darna closed her own eyes to try to sense what Iola was doing, and when she did, she felt the power of the earth surge through their joined hands.

"Take the blessing of the great ones with you," Iola said. Now her voice was resonant again, calm, the voice of the ambassadress in all her dignity, no longer a common thief of the power of sex, acting in the dragons' names. She dropped

Darna's hands and became almost ordinary again. "You'd better go now," she said. "Where is it that you're going?"

"To Slaradun."

"Tell me about it when I return. It would be very helpful if that prince could make his offering properly on Midwinter night. If I had that, then I think perhaps that I might be able to return."

To return, and to keep the world from breaking, Darna thought, but she would not promise what was out of her reach.

Outside, a bell chimed.

"Now go!" Iola ordered, and Darna went.

§

While dawn spread out across the sky and Anara flew high with Iola on her back, Sunna escorted Darna through the nearly deserted streets to the Northeast Gate. By the time the dragon was plunging into the earth again, Darna was sitting in an oxcart outside the city walls.

"I feel like I'm being hauled off to the dumping grounds," she complained as soon as Sunna was gone. Her muscles ached from lack of sleep. She handed her stick to Tevan, who had been waiting there to see her off, and he tucked it in among the bundles. He tried to explain to her again how he'd packed all of the plans and tools and how she should follow his direction, because after all, he was the more experienced of the two of them. She barely heard a word he said.

Everyone else in the city would be down on the harbor. She should be chanting with the priestesses as the dragon and Iola flew across the valley for all to see, but instead she was sitting in a cart feeling like a bit of junk no one would buy, going back out to the dust piles. She looked up out of old habit, even though she was in the wrong place to see anything, and there was Anara, wings red-golden in the sun, looking as strong as ever, in answer to the prayers she should have said. She thought that she glimpsed Iola, her silken robes fluttering between Anara's wings, but they flew toward the sun, and by the time she'd blinked its blinding light away, they were gone, gone into the chambered earth for another season, or forever.

Even in that nearly deserted market, horns, chimes, bells, and drums sounded as they plunged.

"Why so glum?" Tevan said as the din went on, oblivious to the weight of the moment. Iola might die. He didn't wait for an answer. "It's a project to suit your ambitions, and you're getting rid of me, too."

"I'm sorry," Darna said. "I didn't mean to hurt you; it's just that I have to leave the city."

"I don't understand that," he said. "No one *needs* to leave Anamat. We have everything here."

"It did come up very suddenly, but it's quite important," Darna said. She looked into Tevan's sad, droopy, lost-puppy eyes. Everyone worth mentioning was down at the harbor, but the northeast market wasn't entirely deserted, and she didn't want to be overheard. "Maybe I'll be able to tell you next year, if I return."

"Of course you'll return; don't be ridiculous."

"I don't know that," Darna said. If the assassins didn't find her, she would come back. She felt a little bit like the ambassadress must feel, going down to the earth. She imagined Iola and the dragon, plunging into the other realm. "Listen: I don't really want people to know where I've gone, if people come asking. There's someone –"

"Is it a bad debt?" Tevan said. "I would have thought more of you than that."

Darna shook her head. "Something like that. Let's say it's something like that."

"Well, in that case, you can raid the prince's coffers for enough to settle it, even a poor prince like they have out in Slaradun."

The cart's driver returned, carrying fresh-baked bread and two jars of tea.

Darna gave Tevan a quick parting hug, but they did not kiss. She didn't feel like kissing anyone, not after that moment with Iola. Tevan's kiss would be nothing compared to that, but she didn't want to feel its echo.

"I'll still miss you," he said.

"No, you won't," Darna said. "You'll have all of those apprentices to keep you busy."

Tevan groaned.

"Better you than me," Darna said, managing a smile as she climbed back into the cart. The driver slapped the ox on its haunches and they lurched into motion.

"I'll see you next Midsummer!" Tevan said, waving cheerily as she rode off over the dusty hills.

§

Chapter Three

With Myril's amulet tucked under her tunic and the city streets behind her, Darna let out a deep breath. She'd been on alert constantly since Thorat had brought her the news, even when she was safe in Myril's room. Outside of the city, she felt safer, so much so that she almost enjoyed the ride in the cart. Its bumping, unsteady progress kept her awake but only just barely. She felt jumbled up and put back together in haste after the days of hiding, like the lone pack of her own belongings somewhere in there among the sacks of tools and boxes of scrolls. The gates were behind her; she was exiled from the city for the half-year ahead, maybe longer. Well, at least she would be alive when Midwinter came and the gates opened to her again.

She'd seen the prince of Slaradun at a distance the previous Midsummer, but all she really knew of him was what Tevan had reported and what Iola had told her. None of it was good, but it was intriguing. She would have liked to see Tevan weasel his excuses to the prince. He'd said nothing about it that morning, or if he had, she hadn't been listening.

The cart rolled past the turn-off to the dumping grounds. During her first season in Anamat, she'd scoured those hillocks for scrap to sell. It hadn't been an easy time, but it had been vastly better than her life in Tiadun Keep. Despite the struggle to find her footing while Nira, the established scavenger gang leader, undercut her every move, she had fond memories of that short, sometimes hungry season. She'd camped with Myril, Thorat, and Iola under the bridge, when they were all just ordinary scrapplings. The time together had been an idyll, and she hoped that somehow, someday, they could all be together again, though with Iola as ambassadress, it didn't seem possible, even if she lived through her coming time with the dragons.

The orchards to the north of the city were fragrant with apricots and apples ripening in the summer sun. The driver was silent, occasionally dozing. The ox trundled along the road, keeping to the route he knew, flowing along with all the other traffic leaving the city in the wake of Midsummer dawn. After the orchards, their track joined the road out from the palace gate, the one the princes would be traveling on. The driver woke and called the ox to halt while a prince's train passed. Not the Tiadun prince's train, nor Slaradun's. Darna kept her face turned toward the orchards so the people walking by wouldn't see her, and so she could see Anamat as long as possible.

"It's not a day to be looking behind," the driver said after a while. "It's the beginning of new things, time to look ahead."

"So it is," Darna said, but she kept looking back at the city. They were on a little rise, and she could see the layout of the streets around the palace by looking at the ridgelines of buildings. It wasn't a part of the city she knew especially well. She wondered if the prince of Slaradun had seen much of Anamat, and if he wanted Slaradun to become like her city, which was a ridiculous proposition if she'd ever heard one. Slaradun was a nothing of a province, less than Tiadun, but it would serve her purposes, take her away from her would-be assassins. It was too fine and sunny a morning to imagine that anyone would try to stalk her with a drawn blade. She shivered at the thought, despite the growing heat of the morning.

"So, look ahead," the driver said.

Darna grunted in reply as they moved back onto the main road, but when she saw the orange-and-blue pennant over the rise in the road behind them, she did turn to look ahead. She also mumbled a furtive prayer to Anara that the oxcart would travel faster than the usurping, murdering would-be prince of Tiadun, at least until the next crossroads. She rested her hand over the amulet Myril had given her, trying not to clutch at it too obviously. Her heart thudded.

Oxcarts are not fast, but neither are processions of provincial rulers and their entourages with their many servants, laden-down donkeys, and still-tipsy armsmen. They ambled away from the city on sleepy feet, stumbling into each other as they finished their last jars of Anamat ale, looking to the sky as if any of them could see the dragon when she was flying, let alone now that she'd gone under the earth.

A man on horseback trotted up the road behind them. Darna glanced back just long enough to see that he had ridden out from the Tiadun entourage and that he would pass her cart in a few short moments. She wished for some hiding place, but there was none, so instead she tried to find some way to be less conspicuous. She yawned, stretched, lay down, and threw a blanket over her head. The horse slowed to a walk, a much faster walk than the ox's lumbering gait. The horse slowed further.

"What do you have in there, farmer?" the man on horseback asked.

"I'm not a farmer; I'm a carter."

"What do you have, then?"

"Guildsman on the way to a contract in the provinces, catching a bit of sleep now, I'd say."

"Long hair, and skinny for a man."

Darna fought to keep her breathing low and even, grateful for the creaking noise of the cart and a loud fart from the ox.

"That's the fashion these days, in the guilds," the carter said.

"Humph." The man on horseback snorted like his mount. "No wonder the Cereans think we're all women, for young men to wear their hair long like that."

The carter said nothing and the man on horseback rode back to his party. Darna heard the hooves retreat into the mass of travelers behind them.

"Are you asleep?" the carter asked after a while.

"Not really."

"Do you know what that man was after?"

Darna collected her thoughts. "I can't say. Thank you for saying I was a man. The priestesses say these roads have gotten more dangerous since the last trading season, what with all the foreigners."

"So they have," the carter said. "If you put your hair up like the Enomaeans, you'll be able to ride their horses, and those foreigners might not ask if you're a youth or a woman."

"That would suit me," Darna said. She still didn't like the thought of getting up on one of those dragon-shy beasts, and wondered what the headdress had to do with it. Did it mark the Enomaeans as allies, to the horses? If so, why hadn't the princes of Theranis taken up the custom? She felt a bit uneasy at the thought of talking to her new employer. If he were as much infiuenced by foreign ideas as Tevan had implied, he might not take kindly to working with a female planner. She should have asked Tevan what the prince had said to his bowing out of the contract. She resolved to delay speaking with the prince as long as she could, at least until they were out of the valley.

"Another one of them's coming up," the carter said. Darna burrowed back under her cloak and closed her eyes.

It was a different man this time, on a horse with a lighter step. The man's voice was a higher-pitched, too, as if to match his mount.

"My master, crown prince of Tiadun, is looking for a particular priestess, one with red hair." He paused. "If you see such a priestess, leave word with the captain of the palace guard. There's a fine reward in it."

Darna bristled at the thought of Calar being called crown prince. Perhaps Gallia was right; perhaps they should challenge him. She heard the clink of metal as the horseman tossed a coin – a foreign coin, not an Anamat bead – to the carter. There was a long, still silence, then the carter grunted and tossed it back.

"Those are bad luck," he said.

"It's a generous reward he's offering," the horseman said as he rode off.

The carter didn't try to speak to her again until they had passed through the next village. On its far side, he pulled the ox to a halt in a patch of shade away from the road. Darna sat up and looked around. They were in a small grove of pines surrounding a paved watering place, where a spring flowed out through a carved spout, splashing onto the smooth gray stones below. Darna thought she glimpsed a dragonlet in the deeper part of the shade, but she wasn't sure. It might be the last dragonlet she would see for a long time, if Salara were as shy as people said.

"What do you say about that man from Tiadun?" the carter asked at last.

"I don't know," Darna said, "but I'm not a priestess; I'm a guildswoman."

"It's all the same to me; we're Anamat people, I don't like this meddling from the provinces," the carter said with a shrug. "I suppose you'll be wanting to move on away from them in any case. I'll get you that headdress. The Slaradun train will set up camp in the field just there." He pointed out past the shady grove to a bit of pasture. "I'll see you settled in with the Enomaeans, but I stop here at the grove. The old ox needs a drink and we won't reach home before nightfall if I don't turn back here."

"That's all right with me," Darna said.

"The Tiadun folk usually turn off to the south at the crossroads before this village. Even if some of them did come this way, I don't think they'll look for a priestess among the horses."

"No, that's not where any kind of priestess would be found," Darna said. No priestess worth her offerings would consort with those invading creatures and their masters. Fortunately, she wasn't a priestess anymore. There'd been that dream, too. In any case, she could hardly limp all the way to Slaradun. Short walks along the city streets were as much as she could manage comfortably.

She thanked the carter for his help.

"It's no trouble," he said. "I'm a man of the valley, and you're an Anamat woman through and through, whatever else you are."

That was the most reassuring thing Darna had heard all day. "Yes, I am," she said with a smile. "Even if I am going to Slaradun for a season."

§

The Enomaean horse handlers greeted Darna with indifference. They were all yawning from lack of sleep, unaccustomed as they were to the long night's vigil. The carter carried her tools and Tevan's scrolls to be packed onto donkeys at the middle of the train. She would not see them again until they reached Slaradun Keep. For the journey, she had nothing to do but to watch for knives in her back and to learn to ride a horse, if the beasts would let her near them.

Well, they would have to. She shouldered her pack and looked for a place to rest, wondering where her stick had gone.

The Enomaeans, oblivious to her worries, showed her where to roll out her blankets under their makeshift shelter. That night, she bedded down under their lean-to of canvas and long sticks. Before sleep eased over her eyes, her mind skipped back over the last few days. She ought to have shaken Tevan off long before, but he would not have taken kindly to it, and she would have had to see him at the guildhall every day. This way was easier. She would not send him letters; there was no need. She realized, belatedly, that she'd always trusted the guild master more than Tevan.

The heavy hooves of the horses thudded against the ground nearby, far too close for comfort, but Darna slept despite her worries. She woke at dawn to the sound of the Enomaeans leading the horses back to the spring for water. The camp was beginning to stir, but it was a long way from being ready to go. She stretched and crawled out from her sleeping place, then walked back to the shaded waterspout where she splashed off her face and said a quick prayer to the dragonlet of the grove. She saw a bright flicker in the falling water, then nothing. That would have to do as blessing for the journey.

By the time she got back to the camp, one of the Enomaeans had set a saddle on a horse. He pointed at her, then at the horse. Darna cringed. She'd just prayed to the dragons, now she was going up on this thing, this thing which shied at them as if they were fire...which they were. Surely, this beast would be easier to face down than a dragon, or even a dragonlet. It was tamed, and it could get her over the mountains, away from Anamat.

The horse handler gestured for her to put her right foot in his hand. "I lift you up," he said. He was a slight man who moved with graceful ease, his eyes dark in the shadow of the cloth wrapped around his head.

Darna shook her head. "This foot is weak. I'll use the other foot."

"Horse don't like that, or red hair."

Darna put her hand on her head. Her headdress had come loose and a few strands of bright hair dangled loose.

"Good to wear that," the Enomaean said. "We fix later. Now try the horse."

"But..." Darna patted her head.

"Close. Try now."

And so she did, and though the horse tried to get out from under her when she was halfway up and the horse handler laughed at her fiailing, she did not fall.

"Good," the Enomaean said. "You sit straight, young man. Good sitting."

Darna nodded. She'd worn her loosest, coarsest tunic for the journey, and its shapelessness had disguised what little she had of womanly curves. No need to correct him.

"Also, not too heavy. Horse will like that. Not fat like princes." The Enomaean laughed, and Darna joined him. From what she'd seen, the prince of Slaradun was not at all fat but rather thin and tall. Still, it reassured her to know that these foreign servants didn't always revere their Theranian masters, that they were people with thoughts of their own. The Enomaean helped her down from the horse and went with her to get the morning meal, then they returned to their bedrolls, wrapped up their possessions, and mounted again.

Just before the column set off, a very young man bustled down its length, carrying a thick piece of parchment and a bit of writing charcoal.

"Enomaeans," he said as he came up. Then he counted them aloud. "One, three, six. Seven? All right, then, seven," he said to himself, shaking his head. "Now the only one we're missing is that planner."

"Here," Darna said.

The young man looked at her in surprise. "You're not the one we met, the one we contracted with." Apparently, the young man had not been informed of the substitution. She wondered if the prince had.

"No, I'm his guild-fellow," Darna said. "I've taken his place in the contract. He was supposed to have told you on Midsummer night."

The young man looked up at her, then down at his list. He rubbed out one charcoal mark and made another farther up the page. "You're hardly older than I am," he said. "I thought it took a long time to become a master planner."

Darna shrugged. "It takes a few years," she said.

"The prince won't like this. Are you sure it's according to the contract?"

"Quite sure," Darna said. "My colleague had family matters which required that he stay in Anamat.

The young man looked at her narrowly. He scarcely had a hair on his chin, and he didn't shave, either. "It's good, though," he said after a thoughtful pause. "The prince likes to have younger people. Not too set in our ways. My name's Kinner. I'm his secretary, in training, in any case."

"Darna," she introduced herself. "I may have seen you at the palace feast last year."

Kinner went pale, paler than he already was with his little stringy chin hairs. "You're a woman. He might not like that. I didn't know they had women planners."

Darna lurched, then straightened in her saddle as her horse began to move with the others. One of the Enomaeans had her on a lead line, which she didn't mind in the slightest. She didn't feel ready to command this beast underneath her.

Kinner walked alongside her, making no remark on her clumsiness.

"Most in the planners' guild are men, but not all, and I am a master planner, the only one that your prince is going to get this year," Darna explained. "Arrangements have been made, the ambassadress has flown, and the course of the year is set."

Kinner looked so queasy that she could almost hear his stomach churn. "I'll tell him," he said.

"I'm sure he'll understand," Darna said, feigning confidence. "Meanwhile, I can help you with your letters, if you need it. That was what I was supposed to be doing before I changed places with - with my guild-fellow. He'll be teaching the new apprentices."

Kinner blushed. "The prince says that I'm quite good already; no need to call for priestesses."

"I'm glad to hear it," Darna said, feeling rather priestessly despite herself.

Sensing her change of mood, the horse sidestepped, almost unseating her and nearly knocking poor Kinner over. The Enomaean at the other end of the lead line urged the horse to go back into its place in the procession. By the time Darna recovered, Kinner had run off to report back to the prince, hurrying to catch up with the long-legged mounts of the prince's guard.

There were no more disturbances that day, only the slow, irking chafe of the saddle beneath her. The sun beat down, they rested in the heat of the day, and they stopped at nightfall just within sight of the border shrine. In the morning, they would leave the Anamat valley. She would not return until spring, if then, but now her alleged uncle and his people were halfway to the edge of the valley on a different road, so she felt some hope that she would live through the coming season. Perhaps Myril was right that it wasn't her year to die.

She would miss Myril, fussing and all. She would even miss Iola, not to mention Thorat, but they would be gone on their own paths away from Anamat.

Yes, she would live. She would leave an offering at the shrine in the morning, to give thanks to Anara.

§

The next morning, Darna woke when the dew was still wet and the sun had not yet risen over the eastern hills. She lay still for a moment, looking up at the paling blue sky, listening. She heard the voices of the Enomaeans, not far away. There were six of them in all to care for the twelve horses. At first, she thought that they were discussing the day's work, but then they began to chant. Furtively.

Darna closed her eyes again and rolled, as if still asleep, to face the sound. She opened her eyes just enough to see through her mostly closed lashes. The Enomaeans were facing the sunrise, all six of them in a line, murmuring their prayer. Every now and again, the one on the end would glance over his shoulder as if to assure himself that the rest of the camp still slept, or maybe out of fear of the dragon lurking in the peaks above. Foreigners were usually terrified of dragons; they never seemed to be able to see their beauty but only their sharp teeth and talons, their piercing eyes.

After their prayers, the Enomaeans began to round up the horses. Darna feigned sleep a little longer, then rose and limped slowly away from the camp to find some secluded spot for her own morning ablutions. Her stick was nowhere to be found, and she felt that she needed it more than she had in years.

Everything hurt, from her shoulders down to her knees. The day on horseback had felt tolerable enough apart from the chafing and unfamiliarity of it, but the morning after? That was as bad as the first days after dancing classes in the temple, maybe worse. She felt old and weak. Every bone and muscle of her ached. She looked back across the valley, smooth hills rolling down into pastures and fields, orchards and farmyards, and the city beyond it all, bright in the rising sun. She wouldn't be able to walk back if she tried. She wondered where her stick had gone.

"Walk today?" said the Enomaean who'd led her horse the day before. He was not the leader of their group – that was the taller man, the one who tended the prince's own horse – but Darna thought that he had been the one to begin the prayer.

Darna shook her head. "I can't, bad leg."

"You have stick?"

"I can't find it. Maybe it's in the packs."

The man shook his head. "No walking stick."

That was bad. "What's your name?" Darna asked him.

"Nolerin." He stuck out his hand in the Cerean style of greeting, then realized his mistake and let it drop.

Darna smiled and introduced herself. "Darna, Master Planner. Lady Planner, if you like."

Nolerin blinked and seemed to be fumbling for a correct response when the leader of the horse handlers shouted out some command and he hurried away.

Why did these men come to Theranis with their wretched but useful beasts? Darna limped over to the horse she'd ridden the day before and attempted to stroke its chestnut flank, but it skittered away, bashing its hooves on the ground. She backed off and went looking for a stick in the nearby grove, but limping as she was, she couldn't find one that was both stout enough to lean on and easy enough to carry. She returned just in time for the morning meal. The donkeys carried several days' worth of bread from the city. It was not stale yet but would be soon. The servants prepared weak tea with a little honey and no milk. It was a poor meal.

Perhaps it was better at the other fire, where the prince sat with a half-dozen armsmen, the young secretary-in-training, and a scowling man in odd robes. He looked younger than any of the Cerean scholars Darna had seen in the city, and appeared none too pleased to be there.

The rest of the train gathered around the second fire, including herself, the Enomaeans, and about a dozen servants and donkey-drivers. The female servants held themselves apart and Darna didn't feel any desire to keep company with them. They would only remind her of her miserable years as a servant at Tiadun. The Enomaeans didn't speak the Theranian language well, but at least they seemed friendly. No one in the rest of the party had greeted her, apart from Kinner, the secretary-in-training. She resolved to learn as little as possible about the servants at Slaradun, and hoped that they would return the favor by asking no questions about her.

Darna took half of her second piece of bread and molded it into the shape of a flower to leave as an offering at the border shrine. Anara was away from the surface of the earth, off in the dragons' realm with Iola, so she would not take the offering herself, but her dragonlets remained, and they appreciated beauty too. Darna put the sculpted bread into the folded pouch at her belt and went back to the horses.

"No, you walk," Nolerin said.

"I couldn't find a stick," Darna said. It had taken her a little too long to get back from the fireside, and she didn't know where to begin looking among the packs for her own.

Nolerin frowned. "I find one," he said. He hurried off and soon returned with a clumsily trimmed branch, about half the girth of Darna's wrist and heavy. At least it would be strong.

"Anara's grace –" She cut herself short. "My thanks to you."

Nolerin merely nodded and went to his horses. She'd said the wrong thing. She took a deep breath and prepared for the hard walk ahead, the path running straight uphill to the border shrine without a single friend to complain or confide to in the whole weary line of prince's servants and hoofed beasts.

She lagged. She usually walked fast enough when she had a stick to lean on, but the sore muscles from her day of riding horseback ensured that nothing worked the way she wanted it to, not even her good leg. She told herself that she would catch up with them when they paused to make their offerings at the shrine. With so many, it would take some time, or so she thought.

Instead, they did not stop at all. By the time Darna reached the shrine, the tail of the last horse was whisking away flies at the next turn in the road, leaving only stirred dust in its wake.

Well, they would have to stop at midday, and she had the shrine to herself. It was a small, intricately carved wooden structure made from the cedar that grew on the nearby slopes. The statue of the dragon was carved from wood too, but with thin, shimmering metal scales tacked to her wings to catch the light of the sun or of offering lamps at night. The scales were only slightly tarnished. Darna wondered who kept them clean – she'd seen no priestess temple from the road below.

She looked back toward the city, but all she could see were the dark boughs of the pine forest and misty glimpses of the sea far away. The valley was gone already. She turned back to the shrine and laid her offering beneath the statue of Anara.

"Thanks be to my mentor, my protector, most bountiful of the winged ones. Blessings grace your journey to the chambered earth. Take care of Iola." Darna's voice caught in her throat. She should have just said one of the old crossing prayers, but she'd forgotten the ones for travelers on the road.

She'd never meant to leave Anamat at all, so why remember them?

A little cascade of gravel rolled down the road behind her. She looked up and saw the Enomaean, Nolerin, watching her at her prayers.

"The prince says no stop here," he said. "You lag too much."

"It's my leg," Darna said.

Nolerin nodded. "I say that. Get on the horse. Do not do that again, not where the prince can see."

Darna stepped away from the shrine, bowing to Anara, a farewell for the half-year, or maybe forever.

"I understand," she told Nolerin. "I will not let the prince see." She wondered why she had to hide this, an ordinary, public devotion. It reminded her that the prince hadn't gone to Iola. She wondered why.

"Like us," Nolerin said with a smile. He helped her up onto the horse. He did not seem to be angry with her at all, so at least there was that, but why in Na's realm would the prince forbid all prayers?

§

It took three tedious days to cross the mountains. Darna stayed on the horse most of the time. Riding made everything hurt, but she was simply too slow on her own feet, even slower than the reluctant donkeys at the middle of the train. Some of the guardsmen moved to the back to watch for bandits, but they saw no trace of them apart from one trampled campsite at the edge of the small lake halfway across the mountains.

Despite the rocky ground of the campsites, Darna slept well. She slowly got used to the ache of her body, and though the horse still shied when she mounted, he seemed less hostile each day. She was his unwelcome but inevitable burden, and, as Nolerin had pointed out, at least she was not too heavy for the beast. She listened to the Enomaeans as they talked amongst themselves, picking out the patterns in their speech, what they said at greeting and parting, the words for *horse*, some for food. It was a distraction for when her neck grew tired of craning up to see the rocky peaks scattered with scraggly pines and low-growing herbs. She recognized some of the herbs from the temple gardens but didn't stop to pick them until she saw one of the kitchen servants hurry aside to take a bit of one that the priestesses sometimes used to cast out an unwanted pregnancy.

If the kitchen servants could take herbs like that, then so could she. When they camped that night, she took her heavy makeshift walking stick and explored the hillside until the men converged around the cooking fires. She found the club-footed herb that could ease some of her pains and also took a little of the one to make her womb bleed itself empty, just in case. She hadn't needed it yet, but it would be good to have on hand, just in case. She suspected that she was barren, but one could never be sure, and even if the baby might inherit Tevan's family's house, she did not want to be so closely tied to her now-former lover. It was a great relief to be free of him, to have only her own life to concern her. It would be lonely, but she'd endured loneliness before and could manage it again.

On the fifth morning out of the city, the road wound sharply down. At midmorning, the vista opened up: Slaradun. Darna could see the outlines of it, the living shape of what she'd seen only as rendered on a map, the long stretch of poor farmland between the timber-covered mountains and the rocky coast, with the keep town halfway along its shore.

The horse ambled forward under her, carrying her away from the sudden vista and back behind another ridge of stone, just the sort of place bandits might attack from if they were foolish enough to ambush such a well-guarded procession. Up ahead, Kinner, the secretary-in-training, was standing at a narrow place in the road, marking his sheet of parchment as each person, animal, and load of goods passed. Darna nodded to him as he marked her on the list. He looked up at her and down at his list again.

"Oh," he said. "The prince wants to speak with you, Lady Planner."

The horse stumbled on a rock and Darna scrambled to stay on. She slid to one side, only just managing to right herself. Nolerin looked back and nodded his approval. Apparently, she wasn't a completely hopeless rider, even if the horse resented having a priestess on his back. She was fairly sure that the horse sensed the dragons' touch on her, although the men around her seemed to be blind to it.

Kinner was still looking at her, waiting for a response.

"I haven't had a chance to study the plans my colleague sent along with me," Darna said.

"He wants to see you at the border," Kinner said, wearing all the borrowed authority of his master but still looking like a weedy youth. "He said that you must go to the front of the line and dismount there to speak with him."

"If that's what he wishes," Darna said. She wondered if Kinner had told the prince about the substitution, or if she would have to explain it all over again.

Kinner moved on. Nolerin swung down from his own horse and tied it to the next horse in front of him, then led Darna's horse past the long line of donkeys and servants, right up to the brightly liveried guardsmen surrounding the prince and his Cerean companion. The road turned under another sharp, high outcropping of dark granite.

The view opened up before them, broader than before. Darna saw the shrine there, not destroyed but neglected, its crude clay sculpture of the small yet elegant dragon laden down with dust from the road, growing moss on its wings. A single faded flower lay in the offering place, limp, dry, and brown.

§

Chapter Four

The shrine looked all wrong. The lines of it were in the right places, but the dust and neglect seemed to blur them. Darna wanted to sweep it clean, to lay fresh flowers in place of the dead one. Then it would regain its balance. She frowned at it, but from her perch on the horse's back she could do nothing. When she looked to Nolerin, he shook his head ever so slightly, discouraging her. He led her to the far side of the track, tied the horse to a bush, and helped her down.

"Go walking to the prince," he said. "Bow."

Darna thanked him and leaned on the heavy stick while her legs adjusted to the ground. She was standing on a small patch of grass. It was a miniature meadow, perched on the mountainside. The prince had stopped at the far end of the meadowed ledge, with three of his guardsmen and the Cerean man flanking him. Kinner stood to one side, twisting his hands together and biting his lip. The whole procession juddered to a halt along the trail.

Darna made her way forward, standing as tall and steady as she was able, trying to ignore the streak of pain in her thigh until it subsided as she knew it would. She was almost at the prince's feet, or rather, the feet of his horse, when she finally looked up.

She had seen him at a distance, so she knew that he was tall, with dark hair still untouched by the pale threads of age, but she hadn't looked into his face until that moment. It was long, thin, and perfectly symmetrical. He had blue eyes, as blue as the ambassadress's eyes. He had that same kind of beauty, favored of the dragons, but here in masculine form and veiled with scorn. She wondered what he would have thought of Iola, if he'd gone to her. They would have been near mirrors of each other.

"What is this?" he demanded as she approached.

"You commanded me to see you, Your Highness," Darna said.

"I asked for the planner. It cannot be you. I thought you were a woman of Enomae, and wondered where the planner I contracted had gone."

Darna reached up with her left hand, remembering too late that she was still wearing the headdress of the Enomaeans. It seemed that Kinner had not told him about the substitution. No wonder the boy looked so nervous.

"Pardon me," she said. "I had forgotten about this. I'm told that the women of Enomae do not wear them, but it covers my hair. The horse doesn't like it."

The prince squinted at her. "Red hair," he mumbled. "Superstition, even in their beasts." He scowled. "Why did the man I contracted think that you were an adequate replacement for him? We had discussed these plans of mine. I dislike this flaunting of contracts. It makes me wish that I'd been able to stay in Cerea, and not for the first time. Things are clearer there, simpler, more logical. This land has much to learn."

Darna bowed. The movement gave her a moment to collect her thoughts. When she straightened up, she looked directly at the prince while the Cerean beside him scowled at her. Although the prince had striking features, she could see the shadows under his eyes, telltale signs that he had not slept well in some time.

"Tevan, my colleague of the planners' guild, is a native-born son of an Anamat house," Darna explained. "He was called to stay, a matter of family inheritance more important to him than this project, which he told me of before he asked me to take his place in the contract. I understood that he was to speak with you, to tell that I was coming in his place. It seems that he didn't."

"No, he did not. It does not speak well for the guilds of Anamat to send an unqualified woman and a cripple."

Darna's fingers clutched her stick until the pinch in her fingers steadied her anger enough that she could speak. "I am not unqualified. I am a master planner. I am three years Tevan's junior, but I'm as good as he is, or better. He's said so himself." He'd said it only to flatter her, but he *had* said it. "As for the cane, it's true that I need one at times, but apart from this small limp, I'm no sicklier than most." She gave him a pointed look, impertinent, compared to the obsequious postures of the guardsmen around him.

The Cerean's nose twitched, probably only because his liege was forced to converse with a lowly woman. She didn't understand the Cereans' scorn for women, but she'd seen it often enough to recognize that it was real and apparently universal among them.

"The guildsmen of Anamat have no honor, to fiaunt contracts," the prince grumbled. "You would not find that scorn in Ganat or Cerea."

"Perhaps their contracts are different," Darna said. "Yours were drawn up with a master planner. Tevan himself was not named, and so, as I am also a master planner, I am fully qualified to step into his place. You may examine the contract again when we reach our destination and can find it among the boxes of scrolls."

Darna locked eyes with the prince. She did not look away. He had a strong gaze. His eyes were maybe even bluer than Iola's. The memory of Iola's dragon-summoning kiss came at her without warning. She shuddered and blinked it away, but either he hadn't noticed her discomfiture or he'd chosen to ignore it. When she looked again, he had turned away from her.

"Well argued," he said, "but do not think that I am pleased." He nudged his horse to face the open expanse before them and looked out at it as he spoke. "I called you here to see the place we are to remake, though perhaps in your haste to take your colleague's place, you have not seen the plans." He paused but did not look back at her, then took a deep breath and went on.

"Here you see the road up to the principal quarry," he said, pointing off to a spot along the northern ledge, not too far from where they stood. "We have black granite there, and gray, with a few veins of pink." He waved his arm in the other direction. "To the south we have a smaller quarry, some marble there, not as white as the marble in Anamat, more of a yellow sort. It will do for finishing the finer buildings, but we will not open that quarry for work until after the foundations have been laid." He looked back at Darna.

"I had planned to begin that work this year, but then I thought that I was to have a master planner to direct the laying of the foundation stones."

"I am here to fulfill that contract and I will not be blamed if you fail to carry it out," Darna said. At least, the guildsmen back it Anamat would not blame her. She supposed she could live with the prince's displeasure. It would not be pleasant to endure his scowls for a season or two, but it was a kind of unpleasantness she could weather, especially if he was too practical to send her away, too eager to build his city to delay its progress by a year.

The keep was perched on a wide bay halfway along the province's long shore, with a protective headland jutting out beyond it.

"If that bay is deep, it will make a fine harbor," she said.

The prince nodded. "It is. For now, we have only a few small fishing boats there, but in time, in not very much time, I believe we can build a harbor to rival Anamat's, maybe surpass it." He looked out across his lands as he spoke, but the Cerean touched his sleeve and said something that Darna did not quite catch, something like, "That woman should not be here; you should not listen to her," if Darna understood him at all.

The prince waved his Cerean advisor away and looked back at her. "Enough for now," he said. "I will call you again after you've had some time to review the plans sent with you, and to see the area around the keep for yourself. Return to your place with the horses." He smiled then, only for a moment, but in that moment she saw his unlikely optimism, his eagerness to build in this dreary landscape. "We will try to work together."

"Yes. Thank you, Your Highness." Darna bowed. He did not seem to want more answer than that. He turned his horse back to the trail and kicked it into motion, his retainers following behind, and the Cerean scowling at her as he rode away.

The path wound again below the shrine, taking the prince out of sight before she could think of what else she might have said. She turned to find Nolerin and her horse waiting for her.

"Let all go by," Nolerin said, indicating the donkeys and servants on the trail, kicking up dust as they passed. "Wait."

Darna nodded. Her encounter with the prince had left her discomfited. She still felt the sting of his first words, even though he had warmed a little at the end. A woman and a cripple, he'd said. She was those things, but that was not what she'd come here to be. She'd come here to help him build a city. He had not been shortchanged, and she would prove it, would show him that she was more able than he assumed. He had stood down to her argument, so she might yet have a hope that she could make the prince see that at least she was a planner, if not an able-bodied man.

As the last of the donkeys ambled wearily past, she let Nolerin help her up onto the horse. Judging by what she could see of the land, the prince's schemes to build a city - or at least a larger trading post - were not ill founded. The bay was good, bigger than Anamat's harbor and as well protected from the weather as Anamat's outer bay. A straight and even road ribboned past the keep, going north to Naramun over a long, low ridge - all sheep pastures, no place for bandits to hide - and south to Helanum through gently sloping but rocky hills. If the roads continued well beyond that and were as good as these, then Slaradun was well positioned to be a trading center for the western half of Theranis, if such a thing were necessary, which it was not.

The horses at the rear of the procession came around the bend, keeping to the side of the trail away from the shrine. Nolerin led Darna's horse back to its place in the line. As they rejoined the march, Darna bowed to the shrine of Salara. She might be the least of the dragons, but she was still a dragon. They were entering her realm, and not everyone in the prince's service had forgotten it. Some of the dust had been hastily swept from the statue, and the withered flower on the offering place was gone, replaced by a round of stale Anamat bread and a fresh bunch of daisies from the slopes above.

The prince must have missed that. He seemed to miss a great deal of what was happening around him, but she didn't think that he was a fool. He was scornful, arrogant, and displeased at being surprised by Darna's presence, but he was not a fool. And now she was going to build a city for him.

§

They lumbered down out of the hills and made camp that night beside the first village along the road. The next day's ride carried them across the plain beside the bay, all the way to their destination. They arrived at dusk with the sunset still bright in the sky and Slaradun Keep looming over the land, dark against the clouds. It looked as dragon-repelling as Tiadun Keep had been. Four towers anchored its corners, with walls between them that had slit windows on the second story and larger windows higher up, mostly shuttered. The keep's thick granite walls would block out the rain and sun and repel whatever invasions might come over land or sea, but they did not invite the dragons in, not even in peace or fair weather.

Servants met their arriving prince at the gate. Darna could see the low roof of a feast hall on the opposite side of the yard. Most of the men drifted toward it as soon as they dismounted, but a young maid showed Darna to her rooms. She was to have two connected chambers, situated on a long, empty corridor high up in the eastern part of the keep, looking out over the village below and its harbor. In Darna's outer chamber, a broad table spanned half the width of the room under a window that had shutters lined with thin waxed skins behind the usual heavy wooden ones. Darna hadn't seen anything like them before.

"What are these for?" she asked the serving girl.

"Don't know," the girl said. "He had them put in." She carried Darna's pack into the second room, which had no such set of second shutters.

"If I wanted to write, I would just open the window," Darna thought aloud.

"You haven't seen the wind and rain here, in the winter," the girl said. "You won't want the shutters open much." She dropped Darna's bag onto the floor. "They'll have dinner in the hall, or I can bring it here to you."

Darna looked around, taking in her new situation. These were good rooms, far better than most of the chambers in Tiadun Keep had been. She thought of the long walk back down to the hall, the inevitable small talk and bickering around the board, rehashing the tedious journey, then the trudge back through dark corridors. She found that she had no desire to rejoin the company, not for this meal, and probably not the next day, either.

§

In the morning, Darna found a tray with bread and tepid tea sitting just outside her doorway. Her rooms were warm and bright in the morning sun, and she had them to herself. She was glad enough not to have to go searching for breakfast. As she ate, she began to unpack the baggage that had been left in her room in the night, sorting through the scrolls and surveying tools that Tevan had sent along. There, among the tools and plans, she found her trusty old walking stick. She picked it up and felt the familiar heft of it, light enough to wield with ease but strong enough to hold her weight. She paced, getting the feel of her chamber, then set out to explore the town, or rather, the village.

From her vantage in the keep, she could see that the place was nothing like a city, and her walk did nothing to dispel that first impression. There were two long streets running parallel to the shore with houses ranged along them and a few more shacks along the water's edge, reeking of fish. The village had a small market square at its center, between the two streets, with two taverns and a new building rising up on its northern, uphill side, a timber structure that looked like it would be a large house or possibly another tavern.

Darna stopped at the center of the square. Apart from the two-story tavern and the new building, the square was bounded by a solid line of heavy, low cottages with a mix of thatched and tiled roofs. She had slept late and had been a long time poking around in the boxes and parcels, so it was getting close to the right time for the midday rest, but still the village seemed eerily quiet. Something was missing.

When Darna realized what it was, she hit her cane on the paving stones in frustration. "Na's balls," she said to herself. "He's razed the village temple." She paced over to the construction site. Tools had been left where they lay, and sure enough, she saw pieces of marble in the rubble, that creamy, yellow marble the prince had mentioned. It was almost golden, beautiful stuff. She'd never seen anything like it in Anamat.

The workers would be back soon, knocking their temporary tavern into shape where the temple had stood. They wouldn't stop on her orders, not if the prince's welcome had been any indication. She wouldn't, if she were in their position. She wondered if the prince had sent word of her arrival to them. He'd been so annoyed that she wasn't Tevan that she suspected he hadn't. Regardless of whether or not they knew who she was, the rough framing of the new building was ample evidence that the workers here weren't skilled enough to rebuild what they'd so recently destroyed.

Any change of direction would have to wait until after her next meeting with the prince and until she was introduced to whoever was currently overseeing the works. In the meantime, she had to come up with some sort of a plan to at least mitigate the damage he'd done by razing the temple, which was a foolish, possibly suicidal thing to do. Surely, the prince would see that he couldn't have a city without at least one temple. Then again, his aversion to stopping at border shrines and the fact that he'd neglected his offering to Iola might just go further than that. The Enomaeans hid their prayers, prayers that didn't even address the dragons.

Still, the destruction of the temple didn't make sense; it seemed too extreme. The princes resented the priestesses' power – she'd seen that much – but none of them had been so foolish as to destroy a temple outright. Letting them fall through neglect was less work and seemed effective enough at undermining the priestesses' authority, from what she'd heard. She had her doubts about Calar's piety, but he wasn't a legitimate prince, and besides, he was far away in Tiadun. She'd come to this bleak place so that she wouldn't have to worry about him. Could the prince of Slaradun hate the dragons more than Calar did? It wasn't a comforting thought.

She paused to check that she was still alone before bending down to pick up a piece of the yellow marble, this one lightly carved along one edge. She held it in one hand while she rested her other hand on the cobbles, trying to feel the pulse of the land. She closed her eyes and waited. At first she felt nothing, then it came as a faint echo, more of a flutter than a pulse. The dragon hadn't passed this way in a long time.

She heard a clatter from inside one of the cottages and startled up. It was time to get back to the keep and whatever midday meal she was going to be offered. She was so distracted as she walked that she almost tripped over Kinner as he emerged from of one of the cottages.

"Darna, Lady Planner," he said, giving her a bow. He looked just as startled as she felt.

"Kinner," she answered. "Secretary-in-training."

He looked nervously up and down the street. "What brings you here?"

"I need to get my bearings," Darna said. "I'll look over the scrolls and then I'll revise the maps. When I'm done with that, I'll take those to the prince to discuss alterations to his preliminary plans."

Kinner swallowed. "I see. I thought you might have left, after he... You know, he would have preferred to have that man come."

"It makes no difference now; he can't have Tevan and I'm here. I've only just arrived, and it's not the traveling season, so I won't be leaving, at least not before Midwinter."

Kinner gave a nervous glance back at the cottage he'd just come out of. "I see. I'll tell His Highness."

"Thank you for relaying my message," Darna said. The curtain in the window moved. "What is it that brings you here?"

"It's my mother's house," Kinner said. "I came to bring her some things I got for her in Anamat, and to join her for the midday meal. It's better, her cooking, than what the prince gets."

Inside the window, someone made a scoffing sound.

"I'd like to meet her," Darna said.

"Well, I – I suppose." Kinner went to the window and whispered to whoever was inside, then looked anxiously up and down the street again. He beckoned Darna over. "She has a visitor already," he said. "You can't come in, but come another day. You can say hello through the window now, so you'll know her if you see her."

A woman of middle years, gray-haired but strong-looking, pushed the curtain aside. She was picking through a basket of berries, and from what Darna could smell, Kinner's assessment of his mother's cooking was only fair. The soup by the fire smelled heavenly, nearly as good as Myril's. Kinner's mother set her basket down and stood to greet Darna.

"So, you're the new planner the prince wanted so badly," she said.

"Well, perhaps not exactly what he wanted," Darna said. "And you're Kinner's mother. I'm pleased to meet you. Your son seems like a bright young man."

Kinner's mother blushed at the compliment. "As clever as any in the village, but with no stomach for the sea, so he wasn't much use to the men here."

Darna tried to see past her, to see what the interior of the cottage was like, but Kinner's mother moved to block her view.

"So, the prince is already not satisfied with your services?"

Darna chuckled. "Well, Kinner says that he would have preferred a guilds*man* to a guilds*woman*, but I can't change what I am, and he'll have to judge me by my works."

"The dragons' blessing on you." Kinner's mother looked nervously over her shoulder, just as her son sometimes did, and closed the curtain.

"And on you, too," Darna said, but instead of looking nervously over her shoulder, she looked up to the sky, just in case Salara was there. She was not. Out of the corner of her eye, Darna caught a glimpse of another fragment of creamy yellow marble, moving like a dragonlet, but when she turned to look directly at it, it was only a fallen, inert piece of stone.

She'd something else, too. In the dim light of the cottage, just before Kinner's mother had closed the curtain, she'd seen that other guest. It was a priestess wearing threadbare robes and rocking on a stool by the fireside, covering her face with her hands.

§

For the next half moon, Darna studied the plans that Tevan had drawn. They were sketchy and incomplete, so she spent her days re-mapping the site of the future town to her own satisfaction. Kinner brought ink and parchment for her work and the servants brought her meals. She walked all over the surrounding farmlands and village, getting the lay of the land, but she stayed to her own quarters when she was in the keep. She rarely saw the Enomaeans anymore, having no reason to go to the stables. She wondered if they still said their prayers at dawn, and hoped that the servants wouldn't mind the small altar she'd set up in her sleeping chamber. She might not be a priestess anymore, but she hoped to see Salara some day, so she made what offerings she could.

She had seen two dragons in her life: Tiada, life force of her home province, and Anara, the red-and-gold dragon of Anamat. Many people saw Anara, or at least they were less shy about saying that they did. Of all the dragons, she was closest to humanity, but Darna had only seen her a few times outside of the festivals. Mostly, she only felt the dragon's presence in the land and in some of the buildings of the city. She sometimes saw dragonlets too, the little reflections of Anara that lived in the quiet corners of the city and visited its shrines.

Tiada she had seen more often, despite living in the blinding keep all those years. Maybe it was because she'd been a child then, and children often saw better than adults when it came to dragons. Or maybe it was because Tiada had healed her – mostly – and had brought her back from near death after she'd been run down by that boar. It was hard to believe that the dragon who'd saved her was gone, that her orange-and-blue wings would never break through the clouds again to stir up the seas, to repel the foreigners who had stolen her lifeblood.

Darna knew next to nothing of Salara, the dragon of this province. The novice priestesses of Ara's Landing studied the features of every dragon in the realm, but Salara was shy and small. Her realm's colors were brown and a green so dark that it was almost black. She blended with her landscape, and it was said that she would only reach to a man's shoulder in height. Darna had never heard of anyone seeing Salara, not that she spent much time with any provincial priestesses, let alone ones from Slaradun.

She thought of the dragons sometimes as she sat at her table, looking out over the poor little town below, but mostly she studied and sketched, waiting for the prince to summon her. The prince would be replacing the keep eventually, but according to the notes Tevan had left her, he planned to leave that project until after the harbor was well established as a trading post, which would take many years, maybe a lifetime. In the meantime, Tevan's plans were going to need a lot of changes, starting with the eastern breakwater. He'd set it at just the wrong place, but he could hardly be blamed for that, given the sorry state of the maps he'd had to work with and the fact that he'd never set foot in the place itself. She hoped he was enjoying Anamat. Maybe he'd gotten the better end of the bargain, as far as work was concerned. If the prince dismissed her without accepting any of her work, then her time here would be wasted apart from the fact that it was keeping her alive, if this solitary exile could be called living.

She fussed with the drawings until she could do no more, and still the prince had not summoned her. She waited another day. She sorted through what she'd done. A half-moon had passed since their arrival. Had he forgotten her? Finally, on a long, languid afternoon when the sun wilted the green gardens of the little village below, she closed her shutters, rolled a few drawings together, and went to find Kinner.

She followed the long, dark hall outside her rooms down to the stairwell at the end. It was dry and well swept but eerily quiet. It took her down to the central courtyard, empty except for the pair of guards standing at loose attendance by the gatehouse. There wasn't even a servant sweeping. She tucked her drawings under one arm and went up to the gate.

"Excuse me," she said. "Do you know where I might find the boy Kinner? The young secretary?"

The guard barely looked at her. "Might be down in the village, or in His Highness's library. I wouldn't know."

"The library," Darna echoed. "And where is that?"

The guard pointed toward the keep's southwest tower and turned away.

Darna considered thanking him, but he'd begun intently picking the dirt out from under his fingernails. The second guard had wandered off in the general direction of the kitchens. She crossed the courtyard to the squat, brooding tower with wide but shuttered windows near the top.

The afternoon sun streamed through the tower's slit windows in bright beams. A strip of carpet lined the center of the stair, cushioning her footfalls. Doors led off to the southern rooms, the ones over the great hall, but not to the west wing where the stables and guardsmen's quarters were. The only stair to that side was on the third landing, and that was barred. The windows grew bigger as the tower went up. She arrived at the top of the stair and caught her breath. The door there was no bigger than the entrance to her own rooms and was closed, as the doors below had been. She leaned her ear against it to listen. There was someone within, maybe more than one person. She heard a mumble of voices. Definitely more than one.

Darna cleared her throat. She knocked at the door. When there was no response, she pushed it open.

After the shadowed landing, the light was blinding. Three figures stood silhouetted against the windows, against the bright sky and sea beyond. They were looking at something far out across the waves.

The Cerean was there, and he said something in his own language that Darna couldn't quite catch.

"We must close them," the prince replied in the same tongue. It was then that he turned and saw her.

Darna's eyes had adjusted well enough by then that she could see his frown, but she couldn't focus on his expression when she was so distracted by the library itself. The room was marvelous, not only for its bright natural light and stunning location but for its contents. There were rows of shelves, racks of scrolls, maps laid out on tables. The carpet was deep, so soft-looking that she wanted to kick off her sandals and feel it under her toes, but her eyes turned back to the scrolls, tablets, and bound collections.

Kinner and the Cerean tutor closed the shutters, which were translucent like the ones in her rooms.

"I did not summon you," the prince said.

Darna bowed. "I am aware of that, Your Highness."

"Then why did you come? Why, for that matter, are you not back in Anamat?"

Kinner was looking down at his feet as if perhaps he hadn't told his master of Darna's comings and goings in the village. She wondered if anyone else would have. The prince must have known that she was beginning her work, but he hadn't asked.

Darna took the rolled maps and drawings from under her arm and held them out to the prince. He made no move to take them.

"I've been working on these," she said. "I have an improved map of the existing site, and a different design for the breakwater. You should set it into the shore another hundred paces further to the east, where there's an existing outcropping of rock and the tides move less swiftly. It also expands the size of the future harbor somewhat."

"As it would, if you don't try to move the western edge," the prince said. After an agonizing pause, he reached for

Darna's proffered documents, then went back to the window, turning his back to her as he laid them on the table.

Kinner hung back. The Cerean frowned. Darna had not mentioned that the new arrangement also took advantage of the pattern of energy in the land. She'd placed the breakwater at a quiet place, where it would not cut off the almost imperceptible flow of Salara's power. She glanced at the Cerean. He would not like that explanation, nor would the prince. She decided not to mention it yet.

The prince studied the drawings. When he was done, he turned to face the room again. With the bright glare behind him, Darna could barely see his face. She took a step to the side, to see him better.

"I'm sorry to have troubled you," she said.

Out of the corner of her eye, she saw the Cerean smile, a tight, triumphant little smile.

"Not at all," the prince said. "These are as good as you said they would be, much better than I expected after the ridiculous replacement your guild thought it could make without my authorization. I do want to begin work with you. Expanding this village into a town will be a great boon to my people, I believe, but I have guests arriving soon and cannot attend to this today. Tomorrow morning, return here with your drawing implements and small tools. We will discuss the breakwater and the placement of the outer walls."

"Yes, Your Highness." Darna bowed again. The Cerean's usual scowl had returned. He glared at her.

"Kinner," the prince said. "Escort the Lady Planner back to her quarters."

With that, she was dismissed. She backed out onto the landing and Kinner scampered after her, closing the door behind him.

"This way, Lady Planner," he said as he began to run down the stairs.

Darna limped after. He waited for her on the next landing.

"Sorry," he said, looking over his shoulder. "I forgot. We should take the short way." He glanced up the stair again, then beckoned for her to follow him back up the way they'd come. From the second-to-top landing, he led her through a low doorway into the slope-roofed top story of the south part of the keep. "It only connects up here," he whispered, "but if you're going to be using the library, I think it will be all right. Just most of the servants aren't allowed in this part of the keep."

"I see," Darna said, though she didn't really. "I'm not a servant."

Kinner shrugged. "Everyone here is, to the prince, except his Cerean friend."

"Friend?" Darna said. She wondered if they were lovers, if the prince hadn't gone to Iola because he had no interest in women, but she hadn't gotten that feeling from him, not at all.

"They studied together in Ganat," Kinner said. "Harzet came here to help with the negotiations, and they're preparing contracts for the Ganateans. He'll stay on to be a tutor if the prince has children, and meanwhile, he's teaching me his language."

"If the prince has children?" Darna said. "But there's no keep mistress."

"He's not planning to have one. The governor's mistress, in Anamat, and I think some other people were trying to arrange one for him. They were saying that he has a cousin in Helanum who would do well, but he won't look at her. She's a priestess, and besides, he's going to marry a Ganatean princess, by their rites, and she can never try to rule in his place. Women don't, in Ganat. That's what this trade delegation is about."

"They don't much here, either," Darna said, but the tradition was that priestesses ruled in between the death of one prince and the coronation of the next. Priestess training wasn't fashionable anymore for the daughters of princes and chieftains, even though it had been only a decade ago when she'd been trained as a priestess. He could find a mistress without it and make alliances with his fellow Theranians, if he wanted an uneducated woman.

"What is this trade delegation?" she asked Kinner.

"That's the guests; they'll be arriving any time now. We saw their ship from the tower, just coming over the horizon. That's what we were looking at as you came in. I'll have to go make sure that the cook knows that we're expecting them to dine in the main hall. All the guardsmen must be there too, not in the servants' hall. You should be there too."

Darna hesitated.

"You can sit at the builders' table, I think. The chief carpenter and stonemason will be there, along with the foreman. If you're going to stay..."

Darna nodded. "I should meet them, if I'm going to stay and help set the beginnings of this project in motion. But tell me, why are there Ganateans coming now? It's not trading season."

Kinner nodded. "And that's exactly why the prince thinks he can build this village – I know it's not as big as other keep towns – into a city. We can trade all year round here, and so long as Anamat harbor is closed half the year, we can bring the foreigners' ships here."

Darna gasped. "But the ambassadress is under the earth. Trade and travel on the surface of Theranis, especially with foreigners, endangers her."

"I don't know about that," Kinner said. "His Highness doesn't believe that the ambassadress goes under the earth, anyway. You can't tell him that she does." He stopped then and looked at her. It was a warning, a friendly warning. "Don't say anything about it, not where the prince can hear you. He says we must cast off all of that, cast out the priestesses and their meddling - that's what he calls it. He's very firm about it. I won't tell him about your altar. Lots of people have them, but as long as he doesn't see them, it's all right. You see?"

Darna felt a chill run over her skin despite the heat beating down on the roof just above them. "What about Salara?"

"I don't know," Kinner whispered. Then he shook himself and opened a door. "I'll leave this unbarred for you," he said. "Don't tell anyone, all right?"

"Of course not," Darna said. She had no one to tell anything to.

The prince had Ganatean guests and it wasn't trading season, not even close. It seemed that he'd done more than just turn away from the worship of the dragons; he was eradicating all their customs. No wonder Salara was nowhere to be seen.

§

Chapter Five

Darna's first glimpse of the keep's great hall made her want to turn right around and go back to her rooms. There were too many men. The smell of their sweat almost overwhelmed the slightly more appetizing aromas of the hastily prepared meats on the sideboard, but the smell of fresh-baked bread drew her in. Serving women moved about with pitchers of ale, refilling cups. The prince presided over it all from his high table on a dais at one long side of the room. Harzet sat to his right, and a heavily ornamented man of Ganat sat on his other side. The Enomaean horse handlers – those who'd come on the journey to Anamat, plus a few more – sat at the far end of the hall along with a few local boys. The next table seemed to be comprised of fishermen, only two of whom had brought their wives. At another table were farmers from the lands closest to the keep. At the middle of the hall, a handful of village chieftains shared a long table. Next came a table of what appeared to be local craftsmen, intent on their jars of ale. Darna recognized a few of them from her walks through the village.

Kinner appeared at her elbow. "Lady Planner! You're late."

Darna bowed to him. "I apologize. I needed to bathe, and I had to make do with a pot from the kitchens."

"Doesn't everyone?" Kinner asked, as if he didn't know that most other keeps had proper baths, and that she, like most guild members, was accustomed to Anamat's public baths. "But come. You're to sit at the workmen's table. His Highness told me to introduce you."

He led her to the head of the workmen's board. There wasn't a single woman among them, no wives or priestesses. She wondered why they hadn't brought any, but the table *was* crowded already. She couldn't see a single priestess anywhere in the room, and she wondered why. Even if the prince didn't like them or the cult of the dragons, surely he must see that it was imprudent to keep them out so thoroughly. Perhaps this prince, like her father, bowed to foreign gods. There was a strange fervor about him.

Kinner cleared his throat to get her attention and introduced her to the foreman, a man with callused hands and a grizzled beard who looked none too pleased to meet her.

"They sent a girl to replace me," he said, shaking his head. "I'd heard rumors from the stableboys, and I said it couldn't be, but here you are."

Darna looked around. Kinner had disappeared as abruptly as he'd come. The prince nodded to her from the high table, so she bowed. He indicated that she should sit, and a man slid down the bench to make space for her. He was a stonemason, to judge by the thickness of his wrists and the dust still clinging to his tunic.

She thanked him for making a place for her, then turned to the foreman. "I'm not here to replace you at all," she said. "I'm a planner of Anamat, not likely to be here for more than a season. I'm only here to make drawings of what the prince wants to have built, for the record, and for after I return to the city."

The foreman frowned. "Don't have much use for drawings myself, but I know my trades. He's having us build a new tavern."

Darna nodded. "I saw that. On the site of the temple, isn't it?"

The stonemason sitting beside her froze with his ale halfway to his lips. He set the fiagon down again and spoke, slowly. "Now, we didn't like that bit of work, but it's done now. No undoing it."

"It would be difficult to rebuild, but perhaps –" Darna glanced up at the high table. The prince was deep in conversation with the emissary and another Ganatean, who was nearly as heavily dressed. They both looked like hearty men, darker-skinned than most Theranians but not so dark as the Enomaeans. "Perhaps when all of this is done, we'll see a new temple of some sort go up," Darna suggested. "Maybe better than the one you had." She thought she saw one of the workmen further down the table shaking his head, but it was only a glimpse out of the corner of her eye.

The man beside the foreman appeared to be the chief carpenter. He leaned across to speak to her. "It wasn't a big place," he said, "but it was fine enough. I think if we had plans, if we knew what to do, we could equal it." That was an absurd boast, but Darna nodded politely for him to go on. "But there's nothing going to happen until those traders come in and make this place rich, if anyone can. That'll take years, more if we're lucky," said one of the other men, giving a nod to the top table. Mumbles of assent went down the board.

"And when it does, it won't be like the old place."

"Should have left it as it was."

"She's got to be better than that foreigner," someone mumbled. The carpenter shushed him.

Harzet. Darna glanced up at the high table to see the Cerean glaring down at her. It was as if the prince trusted foreigners more than his own people. She wondered why.

A serving maid arrived with Darna's fiagon and trencher. As she ate and drank with the men, they seemed to warm a little to her presence among them. By the end of the meal, she was beginning to feel as if she might, given a year or so's time, be able to make something with those men. They were not the most skilled – if they had been, they'd have been in Anamat – but they were more than able to lay the foundations. The foreman even smiled at her once, then he remembered himself and scowled again. But he *had* smiled, and she could tell well enough that none of them liked Harzet. In any case, by the time they finished building the breakwater, it would be spring and she would be gone.

Looking around the crowded hall, she wished that she was back home in Anamat and among friends, but she reminded herself that it was better to be alive in the wilds of Slaradun than dead in the city she loved.

§

In the morning, Darna followed the route Kinner had shown her the day before. She waited outside the library door to catch her breath. Inside, she could hear the prince arguing with someone – probably Harzet – in Cerean. Her ears took a moment to adjust to the language. They were arguing about the Ganateans and their contracts.

As Darna pushed the door open, they stopped talking.

"The lady planner," Harzet said, not bothering to veil his distaste.

The prince chided him in Cerean, saying something to the effect of not wasting digging time when the tide was low.

"Your Highness," Darna said. "You requested my presence."

"Yes. Come here. I have made a small alteration to the plan for the breakwater, as you see here." He paced over to the table by the window and pointed to a parchment there, a copy of the one she'd brought him the day before. It was a good copy. The change he'd made was minor, and it would bring the breakwater a little closer, pulling away from the dragon's energy, but not too much. "I will be busy entertaining my foreign guests," the prince said, "but I believe you can direct the men to follow this plan. You met the foreman last night?"

"I did, Your Highness," Darna said. He was standing so close to her that she could almost feel the hairs on the back of his hand. Then he took a few steps away and spoke to Harzet again, saying something like:

"*Direct the boys to pack the carts. We leave tomorrow. Both quarries and the timberlands.*"

"*Certainly, Ivanat,*" the Cerean said. He left without bowing. He seemed not to defer to the prince at all.

"We will need more granite from the quarries, if you can order that to be brought in," Darna said. "Just the plain gray stuff for the breakwater."

"There's enough here to start with already. It's stored over at the far side of the village." The prince stopped suddenly and turned to her. "Do you speak Cerean?"

Darna shook her head. "Hardly, but I understand a little and can read it well enough."

"Really?" The prince – Ivanat, that was his name – walked back and stood over her. She had to crane her neck up to look him in the eye. "How intriguing. How did you come to learn that language?"

Darna shrugged. "There are many Cereans in Anamat these days, and I thought it might be useful to know."

He seemed satisfied with that answer. "So it will, and it's very similar to the language of Ganat." He picked out a scroll from one of the racks and laid it on the table, next to the plan for the breakwater. "You might want to read this, then. It's a Cerean treatise on city planning. I expect you to have read it by the time I return from this journey. You may come here to study it in this room; I don't want it getting lost. Harzet will remain here to make sure that all is going according to plan, but you will supervise the beginnings of the construction in his stead. He may inspect your progress from time to time, but he has other work to do. You will take half of the crew working on the new building to begin work on the breakwater. Is that understood?"

"Yes, Your Highness."

"Good," he said. "You may go tell the men of their new assignments now."

Darna nodded and bowed. She felt the prince's gaze lingering on her as if he had some question he would have asked her but had decided to hold back. For her part, she would have liked to ask him why he was trading with Ganat at all, let alone marrying a princess of that land, but she didn't think he would be pleased by the question, and as a planner, she had no reason to ask it. She hurried away to begin her work in earnest. Escaping the prince's gaze would calm her racing heart. He made her nervous, but she half-wished he'd asked her to stay, and not just for the scrolls in the library. The prince himself intrigued her, blasphemous banishing of the priestesses and all.

§

Darna joined the workmen for the midday meal that day and asked the foreman to divide the laborers into two groups. After that, she spent most mornings in the village, working on preparations for building the breakwater. In the afternoons, she would go to the library to read the Cerean scroll, but Harzet was always there, staring at her with open hostility. As far as she could tell, he was doing nothing in the library except glaring at her. He acted affronted anytime she asked him a question, interrupting his scowling. She soon gave up on trying to make conversation with him and read the treatise as quickly as she could, which was not quickly enough for Harzet.

When she was done, she doubled back and read it again, because she knew it would annoy him, and he annoyed her so she could only return the favor. Harzet glared at her one last time as she opened the first page again, then he retreated. She had the library to herself after that, but it felt like a hollow victory. The treatise *was* interesting, but it mostly had to do with the alignment of canals, which Slaradun might never need, and only barely touched on the arrangement of streets around the city's sacred precincts. She learned that the Cereans worshiped a man-shaped god of the sun and a goddess of the earth, and that the priests were esteemed for their skill in debate and learning. As far as she could tell, the Cereans had no priestesses. Their temples were usually nested within the palace complex, as the princes' Cerean tutors and alleged friends had insinuated themselves into the keep towers of Theranis. Outside of the palace, there were only street-corner shrines, and very few of those.

Darna and the village workers built sledges and rafts to move the stones for the breakwater. They sharpened picks and shovels to shape both stone and earth. Darna used her plumb line to measure the depth of the water, borrowing the fishermen's idle boats when she could. Nearly all of the workmen were or had been fishermen. It was the village's principal trade, and the waters of the bay were rich, while the land around the little town was not. Once she had sounded the depths, she came back to shore and tallied what volume of stones they would need. Kinner had gone with the prince, but every few days, one of the men rode out from the keep to carry messages to the prince and his visitors in their tour around the province.

One day, about three quarter-moons after the Ganateans had come, Darna was walking past Kinner's mother's house when she heard a muffled sob. She glanced up and down the road to confirm that she was alone. Everyone in the village seemed to be constantly glancing over their shoulder to see what was coming up from behind. She did the same, whether because she'd caught the habit from them or because she was still worried about assassins, she wasn't sure.

She walked around the side of the house as quietly as she was able. There, sitting on the back step, was the ragged-robed priestess, still crying as she'd been when Darna had spotted her inside the cottage on that first day. The priestess looked up, saw Darna, and scrambled to her feet. Her face was long and pale, young-looking except for the worry lines on her forehead.

"Wait!" Darna called as the priestess turned and began to hurry away. "Wait!" Darna scrambled after her.

The priestess turned then, set a finger to her frowning lips, and shook her head so that her limp hair flopped around her shoulders like seaweed too long out of water. Darna hurried to her. The priestess backed away, but then she stumbled. Darna caught up to her. Leaning on her stick, she reached one arm down to help the young woman to her feet. The priestess did not take her hand, but Darna stayed where she was.

"Don't tell him I'm here," the priestess hissed. "No one tells him I'm here, or I'll call the wrath of Salara down on you whether you believe in their power or not."

"Believe in whose power," Darna asked, "the princes' or the dragons'?"

"The dragons', you dolt. Can't you see what I am?" Finally, the priestess took Darna's hand and yanked herself up, nearly toppling Darna in the process. Darna staggered back to regain her footing. The two women stood facing each other as they steadied themselves.

"I can see," Darna said. "You're the same as me. Priestess with no temple."

The priestess spat on the ground. "You're no -" She stopped before she said the word and looked at Darna. "I've heard about you. You're the planner from Anamat and you're working for him. You're no priestess."

Darna shrugged. "I haven't heard about you. You are a priestess, and this village keeps its secrets, doesn't it?"

The priestess glanced up and down the street. "Not as well as it should. Maybe you'd better come inside."

She took a few steps down the street to the next cottage's back door, where she pulled the curtain aside to invite Darna in.

The room was small and dark. It smelled like an old storeroom, as if onions and damp turnips still hung from its rafters. The priestess let the curtain fall, plunging the room into full darkness. Only a thin shimmer of light shone around the edge of the curtain, which glowed red where the light touched it. She did not light a lamp or invite Darna to sit. She moved silently in the darkness so that Darna was never quite sure where the priestess stood.

"Who, and what, are you?" the priestess demanded.

Darna took a deep breath. "I am a full member of the planners' guild of Anamat, but before that, I was a priestess of Ara's Landing. I completed my novitiate, and for most of the next year, I served in the peresi's courtyard. I left there to take the apprenticeship with the planners' guild, which is what I had wanted to do before they took me as a novice."

"You left as soon as you could but call yourself a priestess?"

Darna shook her head, but then realized that the other woman couldn't see her in the dark. "I could have left earlier," she said. "They might have let me go before initiation."

"Really? And not pay your apprentice fee?"

The young priestess edged behind her, apparently better able to navigate the pitch-dark room than Darna was. Here, she was pushing too close to a part of the past that Darna wasn't ready to reveal – her connection to the now-dead prince of Tiadun.

"I could have found another way to pay."

The priestess snorted. "It's very expensive, they say, like the priestesses of Ara's Landing."

"Well, I'm not one anymore. I'm just a guildswoman." The priestess said nothing to that. "What of you? Where did you train?"

"Here, in this village, when we had a temple. I had a priestess mother and was born in the hills. I couldn't have done anything else, but it was a good enough life until He came back and banished us all."

"You didn't leave, though," Darna said. The prince had clearly intended to banish all priestesses from his sight, but this one stayed close, yet invisible. Priestesses kept secrets, but she'd never heard of one keeping herself a secret. "What's your name?" Darna asked.

The priestess hesitated before answering. "Ciffolga," she said. "I guess it doesn't matter if you know. You're Darna. I heard that too."

Having introduced herself at last, the priestess lifted the lid from a hidden brazier and lit a small clay lamp. After the darkness, the lamplight was more than enough to see by. Darna noticed the hooks in the rafters, from which the onions must have hung, but the rest of the storeroom had been transformed. Tapestries covered its walls. An altar stood against one tapestry-covered side wall, with a tiny nook at the other end for washing and changing. There was no place to sleep, only the offering place.

"You have to sleep there, too? I'm sorry," Darna said.

Ciffolga chuckled. "All right, so maybe you are a priestess. I used to try to, but I can't really, not when I've just summoned the dragon-currents into it. Now, sometimes I go sleep next door, with the herbalist, since her son..."

"Kinner. He's mostly up at the keep now."

"Exactly. He doesn't tell the prince I'm here, but he's just a boy. I worry that he might let something slip."

Darna wondered if the prince would notice such a slip of the lip, or if he suspected that she was there, anyway. Surely, he must have some idea of what was happening in the village, or perhaps he didn't, closeted as he was with his friends from Ganat and Cerea.

"What happened to the temple?" Darna asked.

"As you can see, it isn't there anymore," Ciffolga said. "He ordered it destroyed as soon as his father died, but even his father hadn't given us our due. He'd shut down the chapel in the keep and had it turned into part of the stables."

Darna felt her stomach turn. "That's terrible. I suppose that's where the baths were, too?"

"No, the keep never had its own baths. They always came to the ones under the temple. The... Some of the men say that they might still be there, under that new tavern they're building," Ciffolga said. "People got used to the shrine being gone from the keep, and the prince says we'll get used to this, too, but I don't believe him. He said that the temple was falling apart, which it was, but only because they neglected it. The roof was leaking, the chambers were damp, but the men still came, and so did Salara, at least when I was young. No one has seen the dragon for years now."

"Not even children?" Darna asked.

Ciffolga shrugged. "A dragonlet every now and again, but never Salara herself, not since a year or two before the prince came back and had the temple torn down last year."

"Before the temple was destroyed?"

"Even then. I think it was about five years ago that she went away. The old priestess said that she'd gone under the earth. I used to have dreams of her, but not anymore. Not until lately." Ciffolga frowned. Perhaps her dreams had not been pleasant. "I imagine it's nothing. I don't have prophetic dreams."

"I don't either," Darna said. The one about the horse didn't count. "I wonder if the prince thinks that Salara is gone."

"He wouldn't care. How could he? He never asked. They're all dragon-blind in the keep, down to the guardsmen and the serving girls. I won't have any of the men from the keep, only from the village here."

"Are the villagers not dragon-blind too?" Darna asked.

"They still come," Ciffolga said. "They believe that the dragon lives, and they know I'm still here. More priestesses will return when we have a new temple. Can you tell me when it will be built? Where it will be?"

"I'd tell you if –" Darna hesitated. "I'd tell you if I thought that the prince was going to build one, but I don't know what he has planned. I'm only working on the breakwater so far, and mapping out where the walls will go. Then he thinks that foreign traders will come outside of the season, in the falling year, when the ambassadress is under the earth. After that, he'll work on the keep, but he's said nothing about a temple." She was fairly certain that he wasn't planning to build a new one, but not sure enough to tell Ciffolga to abandon her hopes.

"You're the master planner here. You tell him where to build one." Ciffolga pursed her lips. It was a challenge, a dare, maybe even a command.

"I can't force him to do anything. He might consider my advice, or he might not. I'm only a hired advisor, and I doubt that I'll last much past Midwinter, but I won't leave before then. I do care for the ambassadress's fate," Darna said. She wondered what the ambassadress meant to Ciffolga, if anything, if the poor, hidden provincial priestess could imagine the worry that went with Iola every year.

Ciffolga drew herself up to her full height, her head almost touching the makeshift offering room's rafters. "Consider this a decree of the dragons," she said.

Decree of the dragons or not, it was going to be a challenge to convince the prince to do any such thing. "I hear you, Priestess of Salara," Darna said.

Ciffolga smiled a wry smile. "Good." Then she looked uneasy again, as if unsure that she was, in fact, Salara's priestess. How could she be sure, if Salara was nowhere to be seen, except possibly in dreams?

"You'd better leave now," Ciffolga said. "I have a petitioner coming."

Darna bowed on her way out as Ciffolga shook out the cover on the offering place, but neglected to light the ritual incense.

§

Back at the keep, Darna decided to go look at the Cerean treatise again. It included drawings and maps of the cities of Cerea. Three of them were nearly as large as Anamat, and a fourth, far from the coast, was larger. No spine of mountains divided that land, but there were many harbors. She'd looked them all over, but she still didn't understand why their principal city was so far from the coast. Perhaps they were not so much of a trading nation as she'd thought.

She found the library blessedly empty, and bright in the midday sun. She took the scroll out and laid it out on the table under the window. It gave her no new answers. She turned to look around at the other scrolls and folios. There were so many – nearly as many as there were in the guildhall.

Were there any about the cities of Enomae or Ganat? She wouldn't be able to read those, but if there were diagrams...

She was just reaching for one of the larger folios when she heard a step on the stair. She darted back to her table and set her gaze on the assigned text.

Harzet cleared his throat. "I'm sure you've read that through by now."

"What if I want to read it again?" Darna asked. She scowled at the empty sea beyond the windows and resisted the urge to turn around and tell Harzet to leave her in peace.

"You cannot possibly glean anything useful from it, ignorant as you are of the customs of my country. I don't know why Ivanat thinks that you can."

Darna turned to face him, leaning back with her hands on the table behind her to steady herself, or at least her temper. "I am a planner. I find this very interesting – all those harbors, but no major city on the coast. Why is that?"

"The seat of the god was in the middle of the plain," Harzet said.

"And yet that city has no temple, not one of any size."

"We do not house...such base pursuits in our temples."

"And what do they do in Ganat or Enomae? Does His Highness have any maps for those places, or scrolls like this one?"

"I don't know. You were only told to read that one, and you have, so leave this place and go chip at your stones or whatever it is you're doing down in the village." Harzet's lip curled.

Darna stayed where she was. She looked over the shelves and racks. "You haven't read all of these?" she asked Harzet.

"Only the ones which interest me. I concern myself mostly with the trade arrangements."

"Trade arrangements. I have heard that Cerea is a great trading nation."

"It certainly is; we have five times as many trading ships as this land, and more than Ganat and Enomae put together. We rule the seas."

Darna nodded, thinking of the gilded Cerean ship that had come to Anamat in her scrappling season. She'd seen it a few times since, and there were others, but no more than there were of ships from Ganat or Enomae. They might rule the seas, but they most certainly didn't rule Anamat harbor.

"And where do they go? Are all of those harbors trading ports?" Darna asked.

"Some of them," Harzet said. "Most trade of any importance comes to the city at the center."

"Overland," Darna mused. It seemed impractical.

"You have finished with this, then?" he asked, gesturing at the scroll behind her.

"I suppose so. I might know more about your Cerean cities than you do now."

He scoffed at that. "You haven't seen them. With the possible exception of Ivanat, your people are hopelessly provincial." He took the scroll and stuffed it back into its place on the shelf. Darna thought that she heard the sound of a rip.

"Why are you here, then, if you hate us so much?"

"It's not hatred. I simply do not respect your backwards religion, and I find many of your customs offensive."

"Oh?"

"I cannot approve of Ivanat's decision to bring an Anamat guildsman here, let alone a woman who cannot possibly understand what he is trying to do here."

"Which is what?"

"It's not something you need to know."

"If I'm not told anything about it, of course I can't understand it!"

Harzet sighed. "It's of no importance. The trouble is that building this city will tie him to this place, whether or not the traders come."

"Why do you think they won't?"

"I didn't say that. You should be gone. You may return here if Ivanat grants you permission, when he returns, which I will advise him not to do."

"If I am not permitted to come here, then I ask you not to interfere with my work in the village."

Harzet tipped his head, squinting at her. "Very well, then. I bid you farewell until my friend returns." He turned his back to her, shutting out further conversation.

Darna left the library, with its sweeping views out over the bay, and retreated to her own, much cooler chambers. Autumn was coming. The days were still bright, but they were growing shorter. The cool seeping up from the stones no longer felt like welcome relief from the heat of the sun. Out in the meadows beyond the village, the grasses were drying into a pale mist over the fields. The villagers said that the winter rains would come in another moon or so, and half of the craftsmen had abandoned the construction sites to help bring in the harvest. They'd gotten the roof and walls onto the new tavern, which looked temporary, just timber and dirt, no stonework to stand the test of time and Slaradun's winter winds. Darna hoped to have the breakwater finished by Midwinter, so that she would leave at least something behind, but if the rains were as bad as the villagers said, things might go more slowly.

Because Harzet had sent her back to work from her own rooms, she saw the prince's caravan returning before the Cerean did. They'd been gone a full moon-round. She rolled up her work and went down to meet the prince on the road, but the village workers reached him first. Ivanat and three of his armsmen were looking at the beginnings of the breakwater while the Ganateans and the rest of the guardsmen went ahead to the keep.

The prince turned at the tap-tap sound of Darna's approach. "You've done good work here," he said. "Walk beside me and tell me what more you'll need from the quarries. I'll have the orders sent up in the morning."

Darna bowed as the prince kicked his horse back onto the lower of the two village roads.

"I have a list back at the keep," she said, breathless from trying to keep up with the horse's long stride. The prince looked impatiently back at her, but then he pulled the horse to a halt and handed his reins to one of the guardsmen.

"Go on ahead," he told them. He turned and looked out at the harbor. The fishing boats were all pulled up on the rocky shore, out of reach of the high tide. The Ganatean vessel lay at anchor farther out but inside the proposed curve of the breakwater.

"Our guests will have to leave soon if they're to reach their homeland before the winter storms," the prince said. "Once they've gone, I will be able to devote my attention fully to this project. Tell me, after reading that treatise, what do you have in mind?"

"I don't know that my thoughts on the matter will make much difference, if I'm to leave after Midwinter."

"That remains to be seen. I'll need someone to direct the works until early spring, when Harzet and the Ganateans return. I'm hoping to have the town walls mapped out and marked by then, so that the men can work on them through next summer."

"Harzet is going, too?" Darna was so surprised that she didn't even think to hide her happiness at the news. Slaradun keep might be glum, but if Harzet were gone from the library, there would be at least one place there she could fully enjoy... except that the prince would be there too.

Ivanat's eyes crinkled. "You haven't come to like each other, then? I thought you might, as scholars."

Darna shook her head. "I don't consider myself a scholar, and neither does he."

"It's irrelevant what you consider yourself, but in any case, yes, he will be leaving to look after my interests in Ganat, to ensure that the terms of the contract are carried out. So, you see I will need someone to record the works, to requisition the needed materials, and to begin hiring more skilled craftsmen. In that, Harzet would not do, as he is unfamiliar with the guilds of Theranis. So, you see, you must stay until I can replace you this coming Midsummer."

"I see," Darna said.

The prince did not reply, and it suddenly occurred to her that she hadn't answered his question. "I found the treatise interesting but incompatible with my sense of what a city should be."

"How so?" Ivanat asked.

"The city of Anamat has three principal centers: the governor's palace, the harbor, and the temple. This, according to our tradition, is what makes a city, the balance of trade, governance, and the temples."

Ivanat snorted. "Go on."

Darna took a deep breath. "The cities of Cerea have only their palace, with a temple of some sort inside it, and the harbor. The one at the center has only the palace, which is surrounded by its markets. That one center must grow very crowded, chaotic."

Ivanat hesitated before answering. "I suppose it is. I was only there when I was young. I didn't consider what might happen to the palace if there were a riot in the marketplace, but I can see now that it might be a cause for concern. However, we have no need for temples here."

"You don't even have one inside the keep. Even the Cereans have that."

"That is irrelevant. The worship of the dragons is abhorrent to our foreign allies, and I would not wish to offend them."

"But you do not mind offending your own people?"

The prince slowed his step. "The Cereans and Ganateans have a way of life which is superior to ours, even if their arts are not quite so fine. Their customs are clear and logical, always orderly, none of this courting of chaos your priestesses insist our peasants pay tribute to." He did not mention that he had been supposed to pay his own tribute to the dragons, and that he neglected it. "When the villagers become accustomed to these changes, they will be glad to be free of the temples. There are advantages to having only a single ruler of the land which will benefit them all."

Darna nodded as she thought, but the prince seemed to take it for agreement, though she didn't mean it that way. They lapsed into silence the rest of the way back to the keep. Darna observed the prince closely as they passed Kinner's mother's house, and the one where the priestess had her makeshift offering place. His expression did not change. It seemed that he didn't know that the priestess was there. As they made the next turn, she sensed a flicker of movement out of the corner of her eye, a bit of dark green. It might have been nothing, but when she looked back to the prince, he was shaking his head slightly and blinking as if to clear a speck of dust from his eyes.

She wasn't sure whether or not that movement had been a dragonlet – she hadn't seen one since arriving in Slaradun – but she *was* sure that the prince was trying to convince himself that the dark green flash couldn't be a sign of Salara. That meant he'd seen it too.

§

Chapter Six

The Ganateans set sail as the harvest was gathered in, and soon the winter rains began, clouding the province of Slaradun in ink-dark clouds that blotted out the moon. The stretch between harvest and Midwinter was a monotony of identical gray days. Darna scarcely noticed the time passing. Ivanat had invited her back to his library, where she spent her days perusing texts and making notes. From time to time, she ventured out to pace the dimensions of various structures on the muddy land. She wondered how she might persuade the prince to place some building like a temple in the town, but she could find no better site than the old temple's spot on the village square. Even there, she could scarcely feel the dragon-currents, almost as if the dragon was gone and the land was dead, but not quite.

She walked the bounds of the future town and set stakes in the fields to mark possible avenues. Sometimes, the prince went with her. At first, he complained of her slow pace, but then he seemed to grow accustomed to it. They spent several long days debating the merits of one arrangement over another, or just talking. He would tell her about his studies in foreign lands, and she told him something of Anamat. She never mentioned the temple, or the dragons, sticking to what she'd seen of foreigners there, and the guilds.

Some days, she almost forgot about Slaradun's missing dragon until she went back to her rooms at night and found the small altar sitting neglected in the corner. Then she would light a lamp and a bit of incense, murmur a prayer or two, and look out at the cloudy, starless sky before closing the shutters against the never-ending rain.

One morning, she woke earlier than usual and set out alone, thinking to move a marker on the far side of the village where there was a little hill. She hadn't been up it, but that morning, she wondered if the dragon-currents might be easier to feel there. She'd taken to carrying a dowsing rod to look for them because they were too faint for her to detect without it. She tucked it into her cloak along with her other tools and set out into the gray mist of morning. The stiffness of her hip worked itself slowly out as she walked past the village.

She walked around the outskirts, but she glimpsed movement at Ciffolga's doorway. She hadn't seen the priestess since the first and only time they'd spoken, but she thought of her often, doing what she could of the rite in that dingy storeroom with its borrowed drapes. Surely, there had to be a better way, but she hadn't broached the subject of the temple with the prince again. He seemed to be quite firm in his belief that he could build a Theranian city without a temple. It would be something if she could see these foreign cities for herself and feel their pulse, rather than just relying on Ivanat's tales and dry treatises. He did admit to her that apart from Cerea, all of them had temples to rival their palaces.

The hill was a low one, with a smooth slope rising up to a perfectly round summit, like a giant's knee pushing up a blanket. Darna climbed to the top and stopped to gather her breath. It was a splendid spot. She could feel the life of the land pulsing in it without taking out her dowsing rod. A current ran down one side of the hill to the almost-completed foundations of the breakwater, another to the keep, and several toward the hills. The pulse of the land was so strong there that she almost laughed with relief. Salara was not dead. There, she could feel the dragon.

A glance down at the village confirmed that no one was approaching. The villagers probably hadn't seen her. She lay down on her back and felt for the rhythm of the landscape, the places where it crested and flowed. She felt the whole province spread out around her, from the mountains of Na down to the point of the land in the west. One thread, stronger than the rest, ran up along the road to Anamat until it diverged to a hidden place in the hills.

What was it? She sat up and looked but couldn't see where or what that thread of energy led to. It was important, an artery of the land. She wondered if there were priestesses in those hills, or if that current led to the gate of the dragon, Salara's way into the chambered earth.

A movement in the town caught her eye. The foreman was walking along the street behind Kinner's mother's house, headed toward the keep. He was supposed be coming to meet with her and the prince to discuss the last of the work to be done before the Midwinter rest. With the weather so bad, the prince said that it was only practical to let the men rest as they were accustomed to doing. Darna did not point out that it was also a custom dictated by the dragons, for fear that the reminder would make him change his mind. Besides, he would be going to the tournaments with the prince of his neighboring province, just as he went to Anamat at Midsummer.

Although he'd gone to the Midsummer Council, he'd snubbed the ambassadress. Going to her was really the most important part of a prince's responsibilities in that season. Darna shook her head at the thought. She tried to imagine him in Iola's chamber, bowing down to her. Maybe that was the trouble. Maybe he just didn't like to bow down to anyone, not even to bed Iola. It was hard to imagine him letting her lead him to the altar. He was too stiff for that, too scornful, but there was heat in him, too. She'd felt it, just as she'd felt the flicker of life in the land, suppressed but essential.

Darna hurried back to the keep, walking along the streets to save time. She slowed when she passed Ciffolga's door. She heard voices from inside and wondered who might be there, but she had no time to pause. Back at the keep, she went straight to the prince's tower, where the foreman was waiting for her in a plain room at the tower's base, sitting at a long table and looking too tired for conversation. A servant ran to fetch the prince. While they waited, Darna watched the tired foreman out of the corner of her eye. Did he guess that she'd seen him near the priestess's room? Perhaps he could be the one to plant the seeds of a new temple in the prince's mind or find a way to build one despite his prince's intentions. No, she'd pledged to do it herself, and she could escape the province if she failed.

The prince arrived shortly. They sat around the table and agreed that the workmen would move another few stones out to cap the breakwater at its outer end that day and the next, then they would stop for a half-moon's rest. They would have to work from first light to dusk, but the days were short. The prince and Darna would spend the next few moon-rounds mapping the city walls and some of the principal thoroughfares while the workmen rebuilt whichever of the fishermen's houses would have to be taken down to accommodate the new design. They would resume work on the breakwater in the spring.

"I hope not many houses will have to be moved," the foreman said, stroking his grizzled beard. He'd let it grow long in the cooler weather.

Darna wondered whether the new streets would leave Kinner's mother's house and its neighbor where they were. If she couldn't convince the prince to build a new temple, at least she could adjust the plans to leave Ciffolga's converted storeroom intact.

"You'll need both crews on the breakwater until the rest, I think," the prince said as he rose from the table.

"We do, Your Highness," Darna said.

She and the foreman rose to leave, but the prince stopped her. "I have one more matter to discuss with you, Lady Planner."

The foreman bowed and left, leaving Darna alone with the prince.

"We will depart for the border tournament two mornings before the full moon," he said. "The tournament fields are a long day's ride from here. If we set off before first light, we can reach the border by dusk."

"So, you will only be gone a few days?" Darna said.

"I would like you to come with me," he said. He looked down at her. He was a tall man, and he was standing too close, looking too intently into her eyes. For a moment, Darna thought that he was going to kiss her. Her lips began to open, but then he turned away and went to the door.

"I can show you the marble quarry on the return journey, though it is longer," he said, his tone purely pragmatic. "We will let the bulk of the men ride back here after. I do not think there will be a better time to go to the quarries."

"Yes, Your Highness," Darna said. He had looked away, but she did not think she'd mistaken the heat in his eyes, the flutter of the pulse on his neck that mirrored the racing of her heart. She bowed and backed out of the room, not looking up to see whether or not his gaze followed her as she left.

§

On the morning of their departure, Darna rose in the dark of night. She wrapped the tools of her trade in oiled cloth for the Midwinter rest and packed them away with her scrolls. She carried with her only her best tunic and her stick. It would be a short journey, even including the detour after the tournament, and the servants had packed all the bedding and provisions they would need. In Anamat, Midwinter had meant a much quieter version of the Midsummer festival, and in Tiadun, it had been celebrated with muted, anticipatory feasting. Only the priestesses and the men who fought at the tournaments kept vigil. Darna had never been to a provincial tournament before. They were generally attended only by the princes, their keep mistresses, a few chosen servants, and their champion guardsmen.

The journey was supposed to be made on foot, out of respect for the dragons and for the journey which the ambassadress was making, but the prince of Slaradun preferred to travel on horseback. He said that it would be faster, but in deference to his neighboring ruler's sensibilities, they could leave the horses at a nearby village and walk the final stretch to the tournament grounds on Helanum's border. Helanum, the neighboring province to the south, was known as one of the more beautiful and prosperous provinces. It was full of orchards and vineyards that produced some of Theranis's best wines, while Slaradun had only timber, smoked fish, and cold rain.

On the dark morning when they set out, the light of the almost-full moon scarcely penetrated the clouds. Darna was to ride at the back of the train again, with the two Enomaeans. Some servants had gone ahead the day before to set up tents at the tournament grounds and to start the cooking fires.

"I have not seen you much," Nolerin said to Darna as he showed her to her horse. His speech had become smoother and easier in the half-year since their last journey together.

"I didn't mean to stay away, but I had a great deal to do," Darna said.

"And Slaradun Keep is not the friendliest of places," Nolerin added quietly.

No one else seemed to have heard him. "Were you here before?" Darna asked.

"No, never. If I were, I don't think I'd have come back. I only arrived in Anamat at the beginning of your spring trading season," Nolerin said. He handed her a long piece of cloth. "In the darkness, the horse might not see your hair, but it will be easier for her to know you if you wear this again."

Darna wrapped the headdress on as she had every morning of her journey from Anamat to the keep. She thanked Nolerin and let him help her up onto the horse. The horses disliked the smoking, flickering torches, so they waited in the courtyard until the beginnings of dawn brought enough light to make out the road before them. They didn't speak again until they were outside the gates, on their way through the village. Darna's horse's leg sank abruptly into the mud. She threw her arms around the horse's neck, which it did not like. Nolerin managed to steady the horse while she regained her seat.

"Your riding has not improved," Nolerin observed.

Darna knew that. Sitting on horseback felt new all over again. "You've seen that we don't have horses here; ordinary people don't, at least," she said. The train of horses had stretched out long enough that they could speak privately.

"What other impressions do you have of this place?" she asked.

Nolerin chuckled. "Now that I'm seeing your winters, I'll be going back home to Enomae as soon as I'm able."

"You might like the city better; the winters in Anamat aren't so rainy. The southern provinces are a bit warmer, too, but most winter days are cloudy there, too."

"Have you been there?" Nolerin asked.

"No," Darna answered, too quickly. "I don't know much more about them. Tell me about Enomae."

And so Nolerin did, regaling her with tales of his homeland and the city of Calandria stretching as far as the eye could see, brilliant in the never-dimming sun. He said that Calandria made Anamat look like a mere village, which Darna supposed was an exaggeration. The rain dripped on down as they rode. Late in the morning, they paused at the house of a village chieftain for bread and tea.

The chieftain came out to greet the prince and invited them all to sit on his porch. It was a small village, too small to support a tavern, so the chieftain's porch was the central meeting place, and it was big enough to shelter everyone in the prince's small party. There weren't many of them, only those who would fight in the tournament and their seconds, the two Enomaeans, Darna, and the prince. Darna scarcely knew the names of the men from the barracks, though she'd seen them practicing their swordwork in the courtyard. They were all tall, surly fellows who never so much as greeted her. The Enomaeans stayed with the horses, and so Darna found herself sitting on a bench alone.

The prince finished speaking to the chieftain and returned to join them. Rather than sit with the fighting men, as Darna had expected he would, Prince Ivanat of Slaradun sat down beside her, almost as if she were his mistress, not merely a guildswoman.

"It will be good for you to see the province," he said.

Darna looked around at the poor village. Its thatched roofs were in good repair, but the soil looked thin to her eye, though she was no farmer. "It's no rainier than it is at the keep, at least," she said. That was the best she could say for it.

"The villages may not be much to look at, but you... I would like someone with me at the tournaments who can record the proceedings if I have any negotiations with the prince of Helanum."

Darna hadn't expected that. She should have known that he would have some practical reason for bringing her along. "I'm no secretary, but as you know, I can write well enough," she said. "Why not bring Kinner or wait to make agreements until Harzet has returned?"

"I've given Kinner your traditional half-moon's rest, along with the other villagers. Besides, I had rather that Harzet not be privy to *all* my dealings." The prince squinted out at the rain.

"I'm sure I can record what's needed," Darna said.

"Besides, I have nothing in particular to discuss with Helanum, not yet, and...well, I don't need to explain my reasons." The prince got up then and went to talk with the fiercest of the fighting men, leaving Darna alone to stare out at the falling rain.

§

Through the afternoon, the rain slowed to a light, drifting mist. Late in the day, the skies cleared, and they reached a small village in the hills. They left the horses there, and Darna left her turban with Nolerin before she walked on with the prince and his party. It felt good to have her feet on the ground again, and the walking might ease the stiff muscles she'd gotten from riding on the horse. She lagged behind. For a while, no one noticed, and she had a bit of space to herself. The prince walked with the armsmen. As evening began to streak the sky with bright colors – including the deep blue of sky she'd seen so rarely since coming to Slaradun – the prince stopped to wait for her.

A string of rocks along the ridge of the hills marked the boundary between the realms, but Darna could have seen it without those markers – the vegetation was noticeably different on either side. Near the tournament grounds, the seam between the realms split so that two lines of white rocks stretched out in a circle around a smooth, grassy valley. The valley was touched by both realms but belonged to neither. It had a flat patch at the center marked by flags, its grasses trimmed short and even. The tents of the two princes stood on either side, their dragons' colors hanging limp from their flagpoles in the still evening air. Each side had a tent for the prince, a larger but simpler one for his fighting men, and a third small shelter for the servants.

"Where am I to sleep?" Darna wondered aloud, not considering the fact that Ivanat was walking beside her. She hadn't meant it as a question to him.

"I hadn't thought of that," the prince said. "You could –" He stopped, smiled, and shrugged. "Perhaps you could sleep on the shrine porch, if you don't mind the company of priestesses?"

"Why would I mind?"

"Never mind," the prince said. "Sometimes, I forget that you're a woman of Anamat, and all that means." He sneered a little.

"Which is what?" Darna asked.

The prince ignored her question and her annoyance. A liveried messenger was approaching from the Helanum prince's camp. The prince walked up to meet him and took the message, then returned to Darna's side.

"We will go to dine with the Helanum prince and his mistress," he told her. "You will come with me. If they ask your role, say that you are my secretary, and that my usual man is occupied with other matters, and so you are taking his place."

He was avoiding looking at her. Darna watched the messenger cross the campsite. "Why do you worry about that?" she asked.

He shrugged. "It's nothing that should concern you."

It annoyed her, though. "When you brought Harzet to Anamat, who did you say he was?" she asked quietly. "You'd rather the Helanum prince not know that your secretary is a foreigner?" Or perhaps he was worried that they'd mistake her for a mistress despite her plain clothes and her common manners.

"Some of the princes here have their superstitions," Ivanat said. Then he turned and smiled at her. "But let's not worry about that, shall we?"

After a brief pause at the prince's tent to make sure all was in order there, they walked across to the Helanum prince's tent, where the dinner was spread. The table's long boards were thick and weathered, as if it had waited in the valley all year for this Midwinter celebration. Roasted lamb, honeyed breads, and ewers of Helanum's finest wines stood on a side board, and the servants from Helanum filled their trenchers and bowls. Darna stayed quiet, watching. She drank slowly, not wanting to miss anything, but the servants kept refilling her glass and she kept sipping. Slowly, the warm hum of the wine filled her belly. There were no negotiations, only idle talk of hunting and the relaying of gossip that minstrels had brought to Helanum. No minstrels had come to Slaradun as far as Darna knew. No one mentioned Tiadun or its usurping would-be ruler. She wondered if anyone was keeping watch over her uncle and his Cereans.

After the servants finally stopped refilling their glasses, she and the prince crossed back to the Slaradun side of the valley together. He walked very close beside her.

"They knew your guild from your robes," the prince said. "Wouldn't you?"

The prince sighed. "No, I suppose there were some things I missed, being away for so long." Suddenly, he reached across and caught her hand in his. She looked over at him, but he had tipped his head back and was looking at the stars sprayed across the sky with the moon just rising over the mountains, washing them away. The last of the clouds had cleared, and the stars were bright all the way down to the western horizon.

Ivanat changed course abruptly, tugging her toward the grove that surrounded the border shrine. The priestesses would be sleeping there, one from each province, waiting to bring the champion of the tournament into the rite the following night, to send his energy to the dragons for the safe crossing of the ambassadress along with the prince's devotions. Darna remembered what Iola had asked of her, but tried to put it out of her mind. Maybe she would persuade Ivanat to go to a priestess the next night, but for now, he was holding her hand, drawing her toward the shade of the grove. She wanted to touch him, to draw him close, to have him for a little while, but only as herself, not as a priestess.

He dropped her hand as quickly as he'd picked it up. "I'll walk you to the shrine," he said.

"You don't have to." That wasn't what she wanted, not now. The glow of the wine rose to her head, wiping out the worries that might have stopped her, just as the moon swept the lesser stars out of sight with its dizzy brightness. "I'll go with you to your tent," she said.

"You shouldn't," he said. As they reached the stand of trees, he stopped and looked down at her. They were still some distance away from the shrine. The ground beneath the trees was blanketed with fragrant needles, smooth yet prickly. Darna stood in front of him and looked up, feeling really rather woolly-headed.

"I don't care," she said. "I want to." She'd wanted to since she first met him, only she hadn't quite admitted it to herself. It had been impossible; it had been complicated.

Here, under the trees, it seemed less so. Still not simple, but simple enough.

"In other lands, a man may bed his servants," Ivanat said.

"Some do, even here in Theranis, but I'm not your servant."

"No?" he said, raising his eyebrows.

She moved into the shadows, and for a moment, she thought that he was going to walk away, but then he followed. In two long strides, he caught her again. He took her face in his hands – warm, smooth hands – and brought his lips down on hers. He kissed her gently, but only for a moment. Then he kissed her more deeply and pulled her deeper into the grove.

He spread out a cloak – Darna couldn't remember whose – and pushed her down onto it. She wriggled out of her tunic and he cast his off, too, until he glowed naked in the spotted moonlight filtering down through the frost-covered branches above. She did not feel the cold of the night. The heat between them eclipsed it. He hesitated.

"It's all right," she said.

He looked up to the moon. "I suppose Midwinter is tomorrow," he said.

"You should lie with a priestess then."

"I won't. No, I can't."

Darna frowned. She thought about getting up and leaving, but he was so close, so warm. She drew him closer. Tonight, they could join as themselves. She didn't have to worry about Iola in her flight; she didn't have to be a priestess, or his mistress. Ivanat caressed her and she shivered with a pleasure that she hadn't felt in a long time, not like this.

After, they lay on their sides. He ran his hand over the curve of her body, down to the unscarred side of her hips, then nested it in the bushy hair between her thighs. Then he half sat up, leaned over, and kissed her one last time as he withdrew.

"Come to me tomorrow night?" he said.

Darna rolled over to be underneath him again, but he was already gathering his clothes. The cold of the ground seeped up through the cloak. "I will," she said. "I certainly will."

She sat naked as he clothed himself. He strode away with all the arrogance of his kind, their disregard for the life of the land. She had his seed in her, his life force, but she hadn't sent it down to the dragons at all; she would keep it for herself. She wanted to rock him inside her again and again, but tomorrow night was the crossing, and that would be different. It would have to be, if she wanted Iola to live.

§

The next morning, Darna woke to the sound of chattering voices, women's voices.

"I don't see why we should have a guildswoman in the temple," one of the priestesses said.

"It's only a shrine, and travelers stay here all the time," the other one said. "Where else will we put her?"

"She could stay with the women from your keep."

"It's not *my* keep, and she's from your side."

Darna yawned loudly. "I'm awake," she announced, sitting up. She'd slept well, better than she had the night before, back at the keep. Her life at Slaradun Keep felt like it belonged a long time in the past, even though she'd woken up there the morning before. It was the night in between that felt like the crossing into another world. After Ivanat had disappeared into the darkness, she'd gotten dressed and followed the glimmer of lamplight to the shrine porch, where she'd found a box of old furs, musty but warm, ready for any traveler passing through. She'd nestled under them through the rest of the long night. She probably should have spoken with the priestesses when she'd arrived, but she hadn't. If she had, they'd have known what she'd been doing, and they might have gossiped.

The prince of Slaradun had no keep mistress, and over dinner, the mistress of Helanum Keep had told him that he should get one soon. She'd said it quite pointedly, looking at Darna even though she was only a simple guildswoman and therefore not suitable. The moment had passed and it seemed as if Ivanat hadn't noticed the suggestion.

As a priestess, she would be suitable to be keep mistress, and if she were the daughter of the prince of Tiadun, even more so. There was no one better suited to be a keep mistress than the offspring of a prince, temple-trained. Until now, the only advantage she'd seen from her alleged parentage had been that the prince of Tiadun had paid her fees at the temple, which had allowed her to leave it sooner than she might have otherwise, though not to where her father would have liked. Now it might mean that she could have Ivanat, Prince of Slaradun, in her bed every night if she wanted him, and if he wanted her. That was the question: did he want her? He hadn't brought her back to his tent, but he *had* told her to come the next night. He had his marriage contract from Ganat, but surely even there, princes sometimes had both a mistress and a wife.

The two priestesses were looking at her disapprovingly. One was young and very beautiful, with brown hair and rosy cheeks. She wore Helana's colors. The other was older than Darna by a decade or more, with a little gray streaking her black hair and the stiff smile of a priestess whose temple is not at the height of its powers. Her robes were dark green, almost black, Salara's colors.

Darna sat up to face them. "I do have rights to sleep here, just as any traveler does. I'm a guildswoman, and what's a guildsman but an overgrown scrappling?"

"It's a festival time. We priestesses need the whole of our shrine," said the one from Helanum.

Darna sighed. "I could go sleep with the armsmen, or the servants tomorrow night, if you object to my being here."

"You already did, with one of them. I can smell it on you," The older one sniffed. "Would you like to use our baths?"

"You have baths?" Darna asked eagerly. The shrine was a small wooden building, but it ran up against the hill. In the night, Darna hadn't seen all of it. Water ran out from under the side wall of the shrine, steaming briefly before it cooled in its open streambed. A bath would be wonderful.

"It's not much," the Helanum priestess said.

"They don't have any baths at all in Slaradun Keep," Darna said. "It's got to be better than a bucket of cold water."

"Then why don't you go to the temple?" the Helanum priestess asked.

The older priestess gave Darna a warning look.

"It hadn't occurred to me," Darna said. The older priestess relaxed visibly. Of course, it hadn't occurred to her because there was no temple. The fact that its springs had been buried under it was yet another crime to lay at the long, white feet of her new lover, but not now. Later, after she'd enjoyed another night with him. She didn't need to think beyond that.

§

Chapter Seven

The two priestesses wreathed the champions in garlands of evergreen. Servants laid out tables on the tournament field and piled them with roasted boar, apples, bread, and wine. As the stars came out, they lit torches all around, their bright-dancing flames ringing the circle. Darna drank her fill as the feast rolled on past midnight and the moon rode high on the dome of the sky.

Eventually, the champions staggered off to take their blessings from the priestesses. The groaning boards lightened and the celebrants staggered away. Ivanat had spent the evening with the prince of Helanum and his court, but Darna had kept to the fringes and the shadows, watching the noblemen. Their world was strange to her. What would it be like to be part of it? As the Helanum prince walked back to his tent, Ivanat glanced up at Darna. She nodded to him, then made a show of retiring, walking off in the general direction of the shrine. When she got there, she realized that she couldn't have entered it if she'd wanted to. The older of the two priestesses stopped her on the shrine porch.

"I know about you," she said quietly. "You claim to be a priestess, and you made a promise that you would have him rebuild our temple."

"I didn't promise to make him do anything. I'm only an advisor. Did Ciffolga tell you about me?"

"I have my ways of knowing," the priestess said. "We want that temple rebuilt."

Darna shook her head. "I only said that I would try to convince him. It would take more than a few words to change his intentions, and I'm only here for a season." She turned at the sound of a man approaching, and the priestess grabbed her roughly by the arm.

"It's Midwinter night," she hissed into Darna's ear. "No priestess should lie alone. Go and do your part."

Darna shook herself free. "Why wouldn't I?" she said, although she'd been yearning for something different from the rite itself, and her would-be lover was no petitioner. It would be a feast of desire alone, not the ritual meeting of priestess and devotee. She wouldn't be able to accomplish what a priestess should, but perhaps the dragons could make do with only the heat between them.

The man approaching the shrine bowed to the priestess and Darna strode away.

Whatever desire Ivanat might feel for her, she was not a priestess in his eyes, and it would have to stay that way if she was to keep him as a lover. They hadn't summoned the dragons the night before any more than her affair with Tevan had. No, this was just between a man and a woman, leaving the disappearing dragons out of it, but she did want to help Iola along the way, if she could. She would try to accomplish that small part of the rite, to assure her friend's survival. Ivanat might not notice, and if he did, well, he'd drunk at least as much wine as she had. Maybe he would forget by morning.

Darna crept through the shadows to the prince's tent. She wasn't sure whether anyone saw her go in or not. The tent was empty when she arrived, warmed by a brazier. She took off her sandals and let her feet sink into the soft carpet, then dropped her cloak on a low stool. It was rich for a tent, though not so rich as the chamber of a peresi at Ara's Landing. She wished that she had the red robes she'd worn as a peresi, the thin ones that caught the light, the ones she'd danced in years before. She looked around for a little incense to throw into the brazier but found nothing, so she just took a moment to feel the pulse of the earth beneath her feet, weak as it was in the borderlands, far from the dragon's gate, drunk as she was, her vision cloudy.

She heard a sound outside and backed into the shadows beside the bed. Ivanat stumbled in, saw her, and stopped in his tracks.

"Go on back to the feast," he said, waving the guardsman behind him away. "I'll fall into bed on my own." He stood where he was while the guardsman clattered off, making no move to approach her.

"Perhaps you should leave," he said. "I apologize for last night. You're right to say you're not a servant, you don't belong to my domain."

"Oh. I thought you wanted to," Darna said. So much for her fantasies of luminous silk, of dancing into her lover's arms.

Ivanat sighed. "I did, I do; it's only that it's...it's complicated."

"It doesn't have to be. It's Midwinter night."

He looked over his shoulder and tied the tent flaps closed, then took one step toward her to just enter the room. She sat down on the bed. He shook his head.

"The fact that it's Midwinter night means nothing to me."

"But the fact that I don't belong to your domain is a problem?" Darna asked. That statement made no sense to her.

"I suppose not. It's only that it seems unnatural to me."

"How?" He wasn't making much sense. She wished she'd drunk a little less wine.

He sighed again and came over to sit beside her on the bed. He picked up her hand and held it, stroked it while he seemed to gather his thoughts. He didn't look at her when he spoke.

"I have been a long time in Ganat and Cerea. There, men of my station have sometimes been known to go to whorehouses, but in general, it is seen as better to consort with the females under one's own roof, the ones you care for and protect. It is a different way of life. I can't see how you could stay under my protection."

"No? I'll be here, in your domain, until spring."

"And then my bride will come, and they would have me cast you out if they knew, and besides, I know that you want to return to Anamat."

"I do want to, but –"

"Don't pretend that you don't. I've seen how you look that way, whenever you think I'm not noticing."

"It's not that; it's –" She wasn't sure which would be worse to him, the fact that she was sometimes looking for Salara bursting through her gate, or that she was sometimes looking down the road for signs of travelers, come out of season to seek the bounty on her life.

He let go of her hand and shifted away, as if to rise, but she got to her feet first and stood over him. "I want to stay," she said. "At least for tonight, at least for a little while."

Midwinter dawn was approaching. She could feel the faint currents quicken beneath her feet, even there on the borders.

"Please?" she said.

"You really want to?"

"Do you think I'd still be standing here if I didn't?"

Ivanat took her hands in his and brought her down to kiss him. Heat burned through her, not just the heat of the earth but his heat too.

"I would own you for tonight, then," he whispered. "Take off your clothes."

It was a far cry from a ritual bowing-down to the forces of the earth, and the prince had nothing of Tevan's obsequious attentiveness. Ivanat stood, pushing her back, and looked down on her.

"Do it," he said.

Her desire coiled into a flame, longing to consume him. She let her cloak and robes drop, leaving only her light linen tunic.

"Take it all off," he said.

"No, you must, too," Darna said.

"I will, when I'm ready."

"You're ready now."

He gave her an odd look, but he unbuckled his sword belt and let it fall where he stood. He kicked off his sandals and peeled off his layers of tunics in one swift movement. Then he reached forward, took the neck of her tunic, and ripped it down the middle.

§

The night flew by, the moon again reeling above, washing out the thousand stars in its wake. Darna drew the prince in, but instead of feeling the currents of the earth take her in, she felt them pushing back against her, like another man had entered her mind. She shook off the feeling.

"What was that?" he asked.

"I don't know," she said, but the feeling was still there. She tried to draw him into the earth, but he seemed not to notice. Just before dawn, she felt the black-green wings of Salara beating through the rocky hills under her back. Ivanat said nothing of it, then or later, and she did not ask him. Then she took him one more time and slept in his arms until the rainy morning grew bright and the camp woke around them.

§

Late that morning, they walked back into the realm of Salara, with the servants and armsmen following behind. Darna walked beside the prince as they left the meadow, but then she fell back until she was by herself at the end of the small procession, behind the servants with the bundled tents. She had a good stretch of the road to herself. She wanted to think, to let her thoughts fly ahead of her across the land, but her mind stayed stuck in her body, playing over and over again the memory of the two nights just past, and the time leading up to them.

Midwinter night had left her feeling warm and alive, if a little sore. She hadn't thought that he'd wanted her, and she still wasn't sure. Maybe it was better that way. He'd shied away from the scar on her leg, doing his best to ignore it, as Tevan usually had. Unlike Tevan, Ivanat had the power to chain her to his keep, or at least make her want to stay, rather than letting her go back to Anamat. She'd never wanted to be a keep mistress, and he didn't seem to want her for one, either. He didn't know who she was, and it was safer that way for many reasons, but if he did know, she could be his mistress. That would mean staying with him. Still, it had only been two nights, and not much in the way of courtship even for that.

Late in what should have been the midday rest, they reached the village where they'd left the horses. Nolerin smiled to her in greeting, and she was about to smile back when his expression went flat and he looked down at the ground. She turned to see what had startled the Enomaean, and found Ivanat smiling down at her, newly possessive.

"You will ride with me," he said, "at least for this journey. We should reach the marble quarry tomorrow afternoon, and we can spend some days there, if you like." He looked over to where the horses were being saddled. "And please, don't wear that ridiculous cloth on your head."

"You don't think that the horse will balk at my hair?" Darna asked.

"I can control it if it does," Ivanat said.

"Very well." Darna took a deep breath and let the prince help her up onto the horse while Nolerin looked on, his expression blank.

Nolerin and two of the armsmen stayed with them as they traveled to the quarry of yellow marble and down through the timbered hills. They wandered longer than they needed to, visiting several villages on the way. Every night of their journey, all through the waning moon, Darna shared Ivanat's bed as if she were his mistress. He smiled a little sometimes, though still rarely, and only when they were alone together. They talked very little most days, and when they did, it was mostly of the practicalities of travel. Darna wasn't sure that she wanted to learn more of Ivanat than she already knew, or to tell him any more of herself. They met physically, and that was something, that was real. They learned the patterns of each other's bodies, feeling their way closer and closer with every night together.

Darna thought she could have gone on like that forever except that she felt so alone during the day, even by Ivanat's side. Nolerin no longer spoke to her as a friend. He barely greeted her. He was no warmer to the prince. In fact, he had started treating her as if she were the prince's consort, and as if he did not like it, not that his opinion should have mattered.

On the last night of their journey, Ivanat hesitated before joining her in bed.

"We cannot continue this at the keep; the Ganateans will hear of it," he said as he stripped off his clothes.

"The Ganateans?" Darna rolled over and sat up. "But why would it matter to them?"

They were in a borrowed room of the village chief's house, not as grand as the prince's own quarters but comfortable enough. Ivanat paced across the room and picked up a small stone box. He turned it over in his hands, then came to sit beside her.

"What would normally be kept in this?" he asked.

"Incense cedar, or other incense. I suppose you could keep other things in it if you wanted," Darna said. Was he trying to change the subject? "Why would the Ganateans care?"

Ivanat sighed and came over to sit beside her, resting one hand on her thigh while holding the box in his other hand. "I thought you'd heard that I was to be married to a young woman from a prominent family there."

Darna nodded. "I had heard that, but my understanding was that it was more of a trade alliance than anything else. Are you..." She wasn't sure how to put it.

"I've only barely met the girl, last year, and have no particular feelings for her, if that's what you're asking, but I would be expected to keep other women away until she bears an heir." Ivanat looked down, opening the empty box and staring into it as if something might have appeared there while he'd held it. "It's not that I want to stop; it's just that if it was known that we'd been together like this, they would demand that you leave, and I don't want to be parted from you yet."

Now Darna got up, taking a blanket with her and draping it around her shoulders as she paced. "I knew that you wanted me to leave at the end of my contract, but why go any sooner? Why now, when we have this?"

"I think it would be best if you leave before she arrives. I'd be tempted, and I don't think... I thought you would be happier in Anamat."

Darna considered that. Apart from the nights by Ivanat's side and the death threats, she probably would be. She had friends there, she felt at home in the city, but that wasn't enough to make her want to go back already. She didn't relish the thought of being supplanted in Ivanat's bed, but she disliked being set aside preemptively even more. "I might be happier back in Anamat," she said at last, "but just now, I don't want to go away."

She stood in front of him and looked down. He was tall enough that he didn't need to tip his head back much to look at her, even while seated on the bed. "Why are you marrying her?" she asked. "Why not take a Theranian mistress?"

"I can't expect you to understand."

"Do you think I'm so dull-witted as all that?"

"No, not at all. I didn't know a woman could be so intelligent until I met you."

Darna stiffened. It was a bit like a thing Tevan might have said, flattery mixed with insult.

"I'll try," he said with a sigh. "If I were to marry according to Theranian tradition, then I would have to take a priestess or a temple-trained nobleman's daughter. Implicit in the arrangement is that I would share my realm with the priestesses and their so-called temples. I will not do that."

"Why not?" Darna didn't need to point out that the practice was going out of fashion, that he could easily find a woman of suitable station who wasn't a priestess. It wasn't her duty to tell him so.

"Why not?" he echoed. "That should be clear. They bleed the wealth from the land and play into the peasants' superstitions. They usurp those who have been trained from birth to rule in matters of law and judgment."

Darna turned her back to him as she spoke. "You think that the priestesses are less able to judge than these village chieftains, half of them dullards, almost all of them illiterate?"

"There is a clear hierarchy of rule between village chiefs and their prince. The priestesses confuse all that."

"I cannot agree with you," Darna said. "The priestesses I have known are more fit to rule than what I've seen of village chieftains." *Or of princes*, she added to herself.

"Really? And how many priestesses have you known? Have they taught you any of their tricks?" He got up from the bed and embraced her from behind, trying to pull the blanket from her shoulders. He seemed angry at the mere mention of priestesses.

Darna pulled away. "I've known plenty of priestesses, and their tricks, too," she said. "It seems to me that with this marriage you're so hasty to make, you'll be giving more power to Ganat than you would have had to share with the priestesses. Half the princes in the land ignore the priestesses most of the time, anyway."

"I suppose that might be true, but there's more to it." He wrested the blanket from her shoulders and ran his hand down her naked back. Her hairs tingled, rising to meet his touch. He placed his other hand on her shoulder, holding her in place.

"There was a prophecy when I was born. My grandmother made it – she was a priestess. She was in trance and she said that the dragon would destroy me. When she woke from the trance, it was decided to send me away. I wouldn't have returned to Theranis at all, I didn't expect to, but my father died without leaving another heir, and so I returned; I had no choice."

It was an odd prophecy but not unbelievable.

"Prophecies are unreliable, and when I returned, I learned that the dragon hadn't been seen in many years. I tore down the temples so as not to invite her back. Gods and demons. Neither will come unless they're invited in."

"You destroyed the temples, just because of one prophecy?"

"No," he said impatiently, more like his usual self. "I destroyed them because they are corrupt too, because they bleed the land."

"They also feed the land," Darna said.

He shook his head. "Superstitions. I thought you more intelligent than that."

"It's not a superstition unless you can't see the truth in it."

He frowned and turned away. "The trouble is, I don't think I've destroyed them all. I ought to be able to, but I can't. The people hide things. I know that they're hiding them, but I have to gain their trust somehow. Someday, they'll see that this way is better."

Darna nodded. He would never destroy all the temples, not when priestesses and villagers were willing to make new ones out of old storerooms.

He reached out and stroked her cheek. She didn't back away, but she didn't meet his eyes, either.

"What if the Ganateans hear of what's between us now?" she asked

Ivanat shrugged. "I can pay these men to be quiet, and none of them are spies for Ganat. Some of the other servants are. The Ganateans pay them well, and I can't fault them for taking the coin. I can't get rid of them, either, because they would only be replaced by other, more subtle spies. That is why I trust Harzet above any of them – I know that he will never take their bribes."

"Why not?"

Ivanat shrugged. "Simply because he has enough wealth of his own. We have been friends for a long time, and it's not the kind of thing that would amuse him. But let's not talk about him." He paused. "What about these priestess tricks you know?"

"You wouldn't like them," Darna said. He'd hardly noticed them on Midwinter night. "Besides, it might summon Salara."

"Only a priestess in a temple can do that," he said.

Darna knew as well as anyone that the temples themselves had power, but the dragons could reach anywhere in their realms, with any ardent offering. "I don't want to destroy you," she said. She imagined it, pulling the full force of the dragon into the rite as if she were Iola, or even Myril. It would destroy her, too, in all likelihood.

"I can't think of a better way to die." He was joking, as if he didn't understand that it was a real danger.

"I won't let you die tonight. I'll want you again." She could pretend lightness too.

"We'll find a way," he said, seriously.

They kissed and fell into bed. Darna reached her mind down into the earth, into the dragons' ways. She could feel something stirring, but it was so unlike Anara's power that she didn't think it was the dragon. She ran down the dragonways to meet it but could only feel just into the skin of the earth. The artery was sealed, the way to the chambered heart of the earth closed from where she lay, or nearly so.

The dragon was still absent, invisible, or at least unlike either of the other dragons she'd known. She felt something in the earth but couldn't name it.

"Come back to me," Ivanat said. "Don't..."

The echoes ceased. She was only in her body again, and it was just as well. Ivanat only wanted her for warming his bed this one last night. She felt into the earth one last time, but there was only the hard bed beneath her and the prince of Slaradun, caressing her like a common woman. She should have hated the silence of the dragon, but she reveled in it because it let her pull Ivanat in more tightly, willing him to stay alive, hoping that his grandmother's prophecy had been a false one.

§

They were glum and silent the next morning as they rode into Slaradun Keep. Darna took her place behind the guardsmen again. Nolerin rode slightly behind her and he cast his gaze down whenever she looked at him, hoping to speak as they had before. She hadn't wanted to lose his friendship, slight as it might have been.

Kinner met them at the gate and led Ivanat back to his library, away from her. She climbed the stair to her cold, empty rooms. The keep felt more desolate than ever. She'd had a lover, and now he was spurning her without even knowing the secrets she'd kept from him. She should have told him that she was a priestess, and she should have gone back to Anamat. Darna sprawled across her bed and cried into the unresponsive furs until she slept, alone again.

§

Chapter Eight

On her first full day back at the keep, Darna took a short walk into the village to check on the breakwater. On the way back, she stopped at Kinner's mother's cottage to ask after the priestess Ciffolga.

"She's not here," Kinner's mother said. "What is it you're wanting?" She was kneading dough for bread. She scarcely looked up, as if willing Darna to go away.

"I'd like some of the priestesses' tea," Darna said.

"Like the peresi use?" Kinner's mother kept working on her bread, but her movements slowed.

Darna nodded.

"Come back tomorrow. I'll have it on the window ledge. One large Anamat bead for two moon-rounds' worth."

The price was higher than Darna had expected, but she'd never had to pay for it before; she'd always just taken some from the temple or from Myril's stores. She left her bead on the windowsill. She didn't mind the price too much – the prince would pay her well enough for her planning services that she could afford it easily. She left, grateful for the lack of questioning. Then again, there probably wasn't much that Kinner's mother missed, and what she hadn't seen or heard of directly, she could probably guess. Herbalists always seemed to know what the people around them were doing, even if they didn't have Myril's preternatural hearing.

A few mornings later, Darna got a summons from the prince. She hadn't seen him since they'd returned. They'd agreed on staying apart most of the time. She didn't want him to guess that she was a priestess, and he'd said that it would be simpler, easier for him not to see her. Still, she missed his company and not only in bed. She washed her face and shook the wrinkles out of her clothes, then hurried to the library. She entered without pausing to announce herself, but Ivanat wasn't there.

Kinner jumped up from his seat by the window. "Lady Planner!" he said. "You should have knocked first. His Highness doesn't like to be surprised."

"Pardon me," Darna said. "I'd forgotten. Things were not so formal at Midwinter, when he took me to see the quarries and the timberlands." Kinner probably had no idea just how informal things had gotten, though his mother had probably guessed.

"He didn't summon you," Kinner said, looking nervously out of the door.

"He sent a note, asking me to come."

"Oh, I see. Well, he'll be here soon. I have tea. Would you like some?"

Darna nodded, and Kinner poured. It was weak stuff to Darna's taste, but at least it was warm and sweet. In the mornings, the library was cold. Kinner had been working beside a small fire in the brazier, and Darna wandered over to it to warm her hands. While there, she looked down at Kinner's work. He had been copying over a page in Cerean script. It was a letter from Harzet, she guessed, describing the winter festival in Ganat.

"How did this come here so soon?" Darna asked.

"Harzet brought it himself," Kinner said. "His Highness said that I should copy it, to learn what's in it."

"But how is Harzet here already?" Darna asked. Absence had not softened her dislike of the Cerean.

"I'm sorry, I wasn't clear. This is one that he brought last spring, almost a year ago," Kinner said. "He won't be back until halfway to Midsummer, or close to that."

Halfway to Midsummer meant at least three more moon-rounds without the Cerean's hostile presence. It was enough time to find her feet again, now that Ivanat had jilted her.

"He might be here sooner." Ivanat was standing in the doorway, looking at her. Darna hadn't heard him coming. Not sure what to do with herself, she bowed to him as she had when she'd first met him.

"No need to be so formal," he said. "Kinner, go down to the village and take whatever messages the Lady Planner has to the foreman there. Return here when you're done to report on their progress with the tavern."

"Yes, Your Highness," Kinner said. Darna gave him a note for the foreman, then the young secretary hurried out and away.

Ivanat remained standing just inside the doorway until Kinner was gone. Then he took the heavy wooden door of the library, swung it into place, and barred it from the inside.

"Your Highness?"

"Call me by my name when we are alone together, Darna."

He hadn't used her name much before that, not even on their tour of the province, and the sound of it in his voice startled her. "Ivanat?" she said.

"That's better." He tested to be sure that the bar was well in its place, then sat down on a stool by the brazier, facing Darna. "I am sorry. I didn't mean to cast you off, or rather, I did, but I see now that was a mistake. I'd like you back, as much as I can."

"You seemed sure," Darna said. Wariness tempered her desire, but she didn't back away as he stepped closer. She wanted to feel him on her again.

"I've thought of you every night. You can't be with me at night here, but there's still the day."

"There is," Darna said slowly. She went to the window and opened the oiled, translucent shutters to look out across the dark blue sea. "It would be a waste to be alone all this winter."

"Do you have a man back in Anamat?" he asked.

Darna shook her head. "I did, but our time together was over. My leaving ended it, but it had gone cold long before. It had always been a little cold." She shivered to think of it. Ivanat was nothing like Tevan, nor was he like the fantasies she'd had of Thorat. The men who'd come to her in the temple had been petitioners, not lovers, so she could hardly compare Ivanat with them. She wouldn't have thought that she could want to be with someone who scorned the dragons so much, but here she was, already yearning to recapture their nights together.

"What do you see out there?" Ivanat asked.

The waves were windswept, their whitecaps stretching out over bands of dark green and blue all the way to the horizon. Something shimmered in the clouds for a moment, as if the clouds could reflect the sea rather than the other way around. Could it be? She leaned out, ignoring the prince. Yes, it was something like a dragon wing but not like the ones she'd seen before. It was thinner, more translucent but sharper-edged. Besides, it was gone. Salara had no reason to appear to her, not when she was aligning herself with the prince, an avowed enemy of the dragons.

"I see nothing, only the sea and sky," Darna said after a while. "Cloudy, except for a little bit out near the horizon."

"As long as no ships come sailing in, will you be my lover?"

She kept looking out the window, hoping to catch that dark green trace of movement again, and then she saw another flash of blackish wing at the edge of her vision, gone before she could turn her gaze to it. When she was sure that she wouldn't see it again, she faced Ivanat. He crouched over the brazier, looking penitent. His normally stern face beseeched her as he sat rubbing his hands, clasped together almost like the Enomaeans in prayer.

"I would be your lover," she said. "I could be your keep mistress, if you would have me."

He shook his head. "I can't. I told you that. I'm promised elsewhere, and you're just a guildswoman. Still, we have this little bit of time."

"Just a guildswoman," Darna said. If only this story she told of herself were true. It was close enough to true most of the time. She wasn't ready to change it yet. "Very well, then, let's be lovers for a season." She didn't want to be stuck in this outpost keep forever. Besides, he only wanted what he knew of her, not all of her, not the truth of her. No, he would not want all of her, even if she did want to show it to him, which she was not yet ready to do, if she ever would be.

"Good," Ivanat said. He stood, took her cold hands in his now-warm ones, and kissed her. And more, but only in the library, and only when the door was barred and they knew that they were alone.

§

They continued in that manner through the winter as the rains beat down and the days grew slowly longer. She came to do her work in the library most days, and he met her there. He threw down a blanket on the rug in the filtered winter sunlight where they could feel the warm pulse of each other as the days slipped by, but never the nights, the lonely, rainy nights. Darna never saw the chamber where he slept and where he would bed his wife when she came.

Still, it was good, for what it was. When they were not alone behind that barred door, they drew up plans and laid out markers for the walls around the town. The workmen finished the new tavern and built a long dock for the Ganatean trading ships. When Darna came to get more tea from Kinner's mother, the priestess Ciffolga was there. She told Darna that the men were planning to rebuild the baths beneath the tavern, in secret if necessary, and that some of them were already digging through to parts of the temple that had been buried but not entirely destroyed. All through the village, Darna started to see more signs of the lingering faith in the dragons, a bit of an offering here or there and a gesture of supplication to the place where the temple had been or to where the priestess kept her makeshift offering chamber.

One day, Darna and Ivanat walked out to the low hill overlooking the village, the place where Darna had lain on her back before Midwinter, where she'd felt the dragon-currents converge. It was a rare sunny day, not warm but not bitterly cold, either. They walked side by side but did not touch, not where they could be seen so easily. The land was open for a long way around.

"My grandmother used to bring me here sometimes when I was a child," Ivanat said as they climbed the hill.

"The one who prophesied –"

"Don't speak of it."

"You say it was superstition, but sometimes I think..." He feared it, plain for anyone to see. He feared the priestesses and their dragons. He didn't fear Darna, but that was only because he didn't know so much about her. Tevan had only feared that she would supplant him in the guild, and he'd been a jealous lover. She wondered if Harzet had once been Ivanat's lover, if that was the root of his dislike of her. She wasn't sure about that, but sometimes the prince's wistfulness for his friend made her wonder.

"I've noticed that you wear a charm," he said. "What's it for?"

Darna felt Myril's charm under her tunic. "A friend gave it to me for protection on my journey."

"Your journey is over for now. You're here with me. I'd like to give you something else to wear."

"I don't –" Darna was going to protest that she didn't want anything else, but then she saw what Ivanat drew out of his pocket, and it took her breath away. It was dazzling, lit from within, shining under the cloudy skies, a heavy black-green stone set in gold. It was a dragon stone, one of Salara's, but one that had been given to the people, not stolen out of the belly of the land.

"It's a beautiful piece," she said. "I'd be honored, but it's..." It still belonged more to the dragon than to the prince, whatever he believed. Maybe he didn't know that.

"Wear it for me," he said. "Take that dirty thing off."

Darna pulled the charm off over her head. It *was* dirty, just a bag of old herbs, really, with a folded prayer inside. Still, she didn't want to let it go. "I could wear both," she said, but then she realized how ridiculous it would look, a country charm beside a princess's pendant. She put Myril's charm in her pocket.

Ivanat looped the golden chain over her neck, yoking her, but he did not kiss her. They were still in the open. "It belonged to my grandmother, the one whose prophecy made me leave this place. It might have been from the temples. She was a priestess before she became keep mistress, as the tradition was in those days."

"It's been the tradition until very recently," Darna said.

"Customs change slowly, and that one isn't gone yet. I suspect that even the young noblewomen who weren't sent to the temples have been trained in priestess ways. It takes so long. Some men of my father's generation questioned it, and though there are a few young noblewomen who might be suitable, none are from provinces that wish to ally with me.

For Slaradun, I need to seek alliances beyond these shores."
He looked down to the dock, then away, back to the hills.
Darna noticed that his gaze followed the line of dragon's
energy up to the gate to the dragons' realm, perhaps, or to a
temple near the border.

"What's up there?" she asked.

"There was an old temple, long abandoned. We came
across it when I was showing our resources to the delegation
from Ganat. I didn't know it was there; otherwise, I would
have led them further around it, and our local guide didn't
warn me, but he must have known that it was there. I left
instructions that it was to be destroyed, but I doubt that
they've been carried out. It doesn't matter. Time will take its
toll; the forest will pull it down eventually."

Time would destroy any temple if the priestesses and
dragons didn't keep building it up again.

"Why not leave the other temples alone?" Darna asked.
"Surely, they would fall too."

Ivanat shook his head. "They might have, but it would
have taken far too long, and in the meantime, they're a
constant reminder to the villagers and farmers, pulling them
back to practices they'd be better off without. In the forest, it
doesn't matter so much. Only a few hunters and woodsmen
would see it."

Darna looked away from him, back down to where the
future town was marked out. Tracing the line from stone to
stone, she could see it clearly now. It would be a fine town,
not as big as Anamat, but much more than a mere fishing
village.

"You could look out over the town from here," Darna
said. It would be the perfect place for a dragon to perch. "You
could build a pavilion here, something elegant, something
purely for beauty, to admire the view and take tea."

"It sounds very sedate," he said, looking down at her.

"Maybe a little enclosure, too," she said, smiling up at him.

He stopped halfway to reaching her. "It wouldn't be the same without you," he said, "but if you returned, we could meet here... No, you must never return. We should get back to the keep before the rain starts."

A dark cloud had rolled up over the horizon, and the swirl of whitecaps out on the sea was getting thicker, waves racing toward the new breakwater.

"You said that your grandmother was a priestess," Darna said as they hurried down the hill. "What about your mother?"

"Also a priestess, I'm told. I don't remember her. She went back to the hills, that's what they said, and it was then that my father brought the Cerean tutor. After a few years, when she still hadn't returned, he took a new mistress, the daughter of a village chieftain. She sent me away to Cerea and to Ganat. Maybe she hoped that I would drown on the journey, leaving her own child as heir to this keep, but the child died almost as soon as it was born, and her own death came only days later, I'm told. They were long gone by the time I returned. Across the water, out of reach of the prophecy of my destruction, I learned more than I ever would have here. Perhaps I've outlived my doom." After a brief silence, he asked her, "What of your mother?"

"Also a priestess. I have no memory of her either." Darna thought back to that small village in Tiadun. She'd been miserable there even before the boar had crippled her. "In the beginning, I was raised in a village as a foster child," she explained. "When the couple who were raising me had their own children, I knew that I would have to go to Anamat, but then..."

"Then what?"

"This." She gestured to her leg. "A boar ran me down, and after that, they had no more use for me in the village, so I was sent to the keep to be a servant there. I was glad to go."

"You had a debt to pay for your healing?"

Darna shrugged.

"And then did you run away to Anamat without filling your terms of indenture?" he asked.

"I did," Darna said. "Anyone would have."

"That's the trouble," Ivanat said. "These traditions take the best of our young people from their provinces, making us all far too dependent on Anamat and its governor."

"Even in Anamat, the governor's power is limited," Darna said. "Besides, the provinces aren't big enough to maintain guilds on their own, not the range of guilds we have in Anamat."

"I don't agree with that," Ivanat said. "We would do well to stem the tide of youth going away."

"I'll go back to the city, too." She reached out to squeeze Ivanat's hand.

"Or you could go back to your home province," he suggested, giving her hand an answering squeeze.

"Never. Not now." She jerked away from him.

Ivanat stopped and looked at her. "Why not?"

Darna took a deep breath. "I just can't, and I can't tell you why, either."

"Why not? Of course you can tell me."

"No, it's better this way. I'll be going back to Anamat."

"I suppose you will," Ivanat said, starting forward again. "Meanwhile, we still have a little time."

"Only a little," Darna said.

When they got back to the library, they kissed, which led to another afternoon of rolling across the floor in each other's arms and nearly burning themselves on the brazier, sweat mingling with parchment dust and desire. Kinner came and

knocked at the door once but went away when there was no
answer. After he had gone, they giggled together like truant
children, and Darna wished that the winter would go on
forever.

§

It did not. All winters, whether cold or cozy, must give
way to spring, and when the meadow grasses began to sprout
green beneath the pale, bent stalks of the year gone by, the
sails of a merchant ship appeared on the horizon. They saw it
first from the library, when they were naked and slick with
sweat, as the spring sunlight streamed through the window to
warm them better than the dark coals could.

"It's a Ganatean ship," Darna said. "Will it be bringing
your princess?"

"I don't know," Ivanat said. "There should be two ships.
Harzet said that he might return first, before her."

"I should leave," she said.

"Don't go yet. The mountain road will be too cold; there
might still be snow in the passes. We should send word to
your guild, though, that someone must come to replace you."
Ivanat sighed.

"It will be better that way. I can go, you can continue to
build this place into something new, and you'll have your
foreign bride." And his barren land. She'd come to appreciate
its sparse beauty, but it wasn't Anamat and never would be.
She didn't want to see the Ganateans. She wanted to be back
among people who knew her, who could see the dragons and
loved more than feared them.

"I have other messages to send to Anamat as well,"
Ivanat said. He went to the door and opened it. "Find Kinner
and have him come here to work on those letters. They should
reach the other provinces in time for their representatives to
visit me here before they go to Anamat for Midsummer. I'll

have some of them here for the final negotiations and for the wedding."

"What other provinces? I thought you were keeping this secret from Helanum."

"Not Helanum. Naramun, though, and Kiralun. Possibly Tiadun. Their new prince is allied with the Cereans, who are in turn allied with some of the cities in Ganat."

"He's not the prince," Darna said.

"Who else would be? I don't think the Governor's Council will hand the province to the Duke of the Southern Reaches outright, even if they tolerate his infiuence."

"Who's that?"

Ivanat's eyes narrowed and he closed the door again. "I thought you had no interest in provincial politics. It is your home province, though. The prince presumptive has contracted with a Cerean duke who has ambitions beyond his own shores."

"Surely, not even a Cerean would trust a usurper who killed his own brother," Darna muttered.

Ivanat dropped the bar back into place across the door and looked at her with new, different interest, like some specimen he was inspecting.

"What do you know of Tiadun?"

Darna took a deep breath. "Only rumors, but my sources are very good. You shouldn't trust Calar."

"I heard a rumor that there was a challenge to his rule, but all of the other princes seem to accept his rule as legitimate, except for his neighbors to the north. They said that his brother died in a hunting accident."

"The former prince was killed by Calar's own arrow, or one from his sons. I'm not sure exactly, I wasn't there, but you should know this."

"I'll keep that in mind," Ivanat said. "It's a pity you have to go. I'll miss you, and you would have been a fine keep mistress."

He kissed her quickly then opened the door again. "You'd better go write that letter to your guild. I'll send a courier to Anamat in the morning."

§

Darna's nerves had steadied some by the time the evening meal was spread in the great hall. She'd heard the cook shouting orders to the servants all afternoon. The feast was no more than an ordinary meal at the governor's palace in Anamat, but it was large enough for the provinces. Everyone in the keep had assembled to greet the small advance party of Ganateans, though the princess would not arrive for at least another moon-round. It was a reprieve. Ivanat was right: she didn't need to leave just yet; she could wait for the weather to settle.

Ivanat and the leaders of the Ganatean advance party had not yet appeared, but about two dozen sailors and oarsmen sat at a table next to the keep's guardsmen, waiting for their bread and broth. A few Enomaean sailors sat with their countrymen among the horse handlers and stable boys. Apart from the construction foreman, the men from the village were not invited to the feast. The foreman was standing by one of the braziers on the floor near the high table, so Darna joined him there to warm her own hands.

"It seems the trading season is open," Darna said after they greeted each other.

"They're here, in any case," the foreman said. "That boy told me the oarsmen are to lodge in our new tavern." He shook his head at the thought. "It's wasted on them."

"What, the tavern, or the fact that it's where the temple was?"

A look of fear crossed the foreman's face. "Quiet about that, now. We've covered what needs covering."

He said no more as Kinner, followed by Ivanat and Harzet, entered the room. Harzet looked wan and pale, as if he'd had a bad journey on the sea, but he was smiling, as was Ivanat. They looked happy to have each other's company. Seeing them together made Darna wish that she was back in Myril's rooms. She would send a letter to Myril with the courier in the morning, but it wasn't the same, and she couldn't bring herself to write of her affair with Ivanat. Some tales had to be told face-to-face.

"Darna," Ivanat called to her. "Lady Planner," he corrected himself. Harzet raised an eyebrow and whispered something to Ivanat, who brushed him aside.

Darna walked over to them while Ivanat pointed out the features of the great hall to the Ganatean emissary and his aide, speaking their language, which Darna did not understand enough to follow along. Ivanat introduced her to the Ganateans, still speaking only their language, and she bowed to them. The emissary said something to Ivanat, who made reassuring noises in response.

"Lady Planner," Ivanat said, "please pardon our use of this foreign tongue. I hope you will sit beside my secretary, to hear his tales of the cities of Ganat. The foreman may sit beside you, and you will both give him an update on the status of the work beyond my poor summary."

It sounded false, forced, everything he said sounded wrong, but she bowed and said, "Certainly, Your Highness," as if this were always the way with him.

Harzet had wandered away and was standing at the high table, frowning down on everyone. As Darna approached, he gave her a thin smile, teeth clenched behind it.

"I trust that your journey was smooth," Darna said, her smile no warmer than his.

"I'm ashore now," Harzet said. "Bear that in mind, woman."

Servants filled their goblets with Helanum wine. It smelled beautiful, like the sweetest of harvests.

"I'm well aware that you're here," Darna said. "We have proceeded well enough without you. I'm to give you a report."

"So I understand, but I could smell the reek of you in the library. You loose women are an offense to our gods."

"As you are an offense to ours," Darna said. She walked away from him then to tell the foreman that they were to sit at the high table. The foreman was delighted, and oblivious to Harzet's glares, which in any case were not directed at him. Ivanat seemed not to notice either. Harzet made desultory efforts to tell her about Ganat, complaining that he had to speak in the cursed tongue of Theranis again.

§

The Ganateans settled into the guest chambers below Ivanat's rooms. They met often with the prince, but Harzet remained their principal guide and host, and neither they nor Harzet could be everywhere at once. Whenever Darna and Ivanat found themselves alone and unobserved, they stole the moment, but it was always furtive and rushed, unsatisfactory.

Nearly a full moon-round later, they were hiding in a nook below a stair, groping each other behind a heavy curtain.

"I don't see the need for such secrecy," Darna said. "I don't think the Ganateans would be much bothered if they knew. These two here seem like they're only concerned with the strength of the harbor and what they can sell from the hills, the timber and yellow marble. I think it's Harzet you're trying not to offend."

"Harzet is my trusted friend," Ivanat said, drawing away. "I know that he does not approve, and I value his friendship."

"Above mine, I see."

It had been a long morning – one of the foundation stones for the wall had cracked on its journey, and there'd been a long argument about who was to blame.

"Would you poison me against my closest friend?"

"He'd like to poison you against me," Darna said. "After all, I'm a cursed whore of the dragons. I'm probably raining curses on you even now."

"That's ridiculous," Ivanat said, straightening out his clothes.

"Every Cerean I've known lives in terror of the dragons' curses, including those who should know better. Harzet makes those warding gestures whenever I pass."

"Maybe he does, but you have to leave soon, and he does not. I've asked him to be as civil to you as he would be to any man of your profession." Ivanat seemed to think that making the request was enough to make it so.

"He didn't like me from the first, and it's worse now that we're lovers."

Ivanat shrugged. "Were lovers. I told him it was over, but I should have known he'd already guessed and notices that it goes on. It seemed necessary to speak of it when I was apportioning the fee to be sent with you. It's rather larger than it would have been otherwise."

Someone passed by outside the alcove where they'd hidden, probably just a servant, but they held their breaths anyway.

"All the more reason for him to think that I'm cursing you," Darna whispered.

"Maybe you are," Ivanat said, cradling her head in his hands, "but right now I don't care." He kissed her again. "May I come to your rooms tonight?"

"To my rooms?" Darna said. "Please do." She thought of her little shrine, and the incense there. It would give her away, but it no longer mattered. She was leaving soon.

"Good," Ivanat said. "The other ship will come soon, and so will the princes from the other provinces. Then you really will have to go."

§

She lit a piece of incense and offered her prayers to Salara, then hid the shrine box in the corner. Evening lit the sky, the moon rose, and she waited, looking out at the clear night sky, basking in the light of the moon, feeling almost as if the dragons who were frozen in the stars above could speak to her. After a while, she drew the blanket over her shoulders. He did not come. She lay down and fell into a fitful sleep, waking at the first gray light of dawn when she heard the latch on her outer door rattle in its catch.

It was Ivanat. She led him in, taking him by the hand.

"I will miss you," he said.

"And I'll miss you too, more than you know."

She remembered what it had been like to lie in the rite, to reach into the earth as she had at Midwinter, even though she'd never been very good at it. This night felt different from their fumblings under the stair, their stolen moments in the library. The world was asleep; she did not need to be so much on guard. She let go, forgot her body as it writhed with joy and sent her heart swirling up among the stars, flying in his arms.

The sky outside was growing bright when she rose from the bed, leaving him lying in the yellow lamplight. She threw open the shutters.

There, flying out of the rising sun, she saw the dragon, plain as the day coming up at his back, wings strong and black-green, shining in the light. Salara was long and thin, more like a snake than any dragon she'd seen before, not plump and playful like a dragonlet, more like a viper with wings, the prince's doom.

She had thought that Ivanat was asleep, but he must have woken when she opened the shutters. He stood behind her, resting one hand on her shoulder, the other arm circling her waist. The heat of his naked body warmed her.

"What is that?" he whispered.

"Salara," she said. "The dragon."

"The dragon who will destroy me. She's not gone after all."

"No, he isn't," Darna said. There was something un-female about the dragon, something in the way Salara moved, and also in the pushing-up she'd felt in their Midwinter joining, before she'd known about the prophecy, not that anything she might have done could have summoned a dragon. Salara's colors were the same, but this did not look like the dragon she'd seen in statuary and painting back in Anamat's temples. Only Na, the wild dragon, had that long shape, though this dragon was more solid than Na was said to be, less misty.

Salara disappeared into the rising dawn. Darna turned to look at Ivanat and knew that he could see too, and that it was not the first time he'd seen the dragon after all.

§

Chapter Nine

He grabbed her arm and swung her around to face him. "What illusion is this? Have you wrought it?"

"It's not an illusion or a dream." Darna could smell the salt wind off the sea, but it carried the closer, sharper scent of old fish in the fishermen's nets.

He looked past her and his grip on her relaxed a little, but he did not let her turn to the window. "I suppose you're telling the truth, as far as you understand it, but this thing, whatever we just saw, it's not the dragon I thought I saw as a child," he said. "It's the same color, but it's different, and it can't be real, or..."

"Your grandmother might have prophesied that the dragon would destroy you, but not all prophecies come to pass," Darna said, reaching for some slender chance that he might be reconciled to the dragon, that he might not be destroyed.

He shook his head. "It's not only that. I couldn't believe in the reality of the prophecy if the dragon wasn't real. That's what I learned in Cerea, in Ganat, that all of our dragons were an illusion to keep us from seizing the power of the land. I didn't believe Salara existed, not like that, flying in the sky. I've told the Ganateans that it's not real; I've told them again and again. Harzet would think me a fool, or worse, if I proclaimed Salara real."

"I don't think he would dismiss you so quickly," Darna said. She pulled away and turned back to look out to the place where the dragon had been. "He's gone." She closed the shutters. "You saw her, or him."

Ivanat sat down on her bed and buried his face in his hands. "I don't know that I did. I'm addled from lack of sleep. It might have been a dream." He leaned back against the wall, staring at the ceiling.

After a little while, he went on. "You don't know how it is in other lands. They think we're fools, deluded by women. In other places, women have no place in ruling the land; they only rule their households, at most, and sometimes not even that. Everything they do is subject to men's rule. When men from other lands see that our priestesses have temples finer than our princes' castles, they think that we are ruled by them, hopelessly corrupted by the power of their sex, enslaved to their demon gods."

Darna nodded. It was nothing she hadn't heard before, more or less, but it was different hearing it from Ivanat, who seemed to have believed it. The artisans of Anamat had only thought the foreigners were fools, but Ivanat lived by the opinions of his foreign friends, foolish as they were.

"I was ashamed of this place," Ivanat said. "When I came back, I wanted them to see that we, or at least I, could be strong, that I wasn't hopelessly corrupt. Maybe I was corrupted from birth, from infancy, or maybe you corrupted me. I fear that I would let you do it again. I'll seem a fool if I admit now that I was wrong. The Ganateans wish they had the power of our dragons, and I can only bear giving it to them if it's nothing. I don't know now." He lapsed into silence.

"Will he come back?" Ivanat asked after a while. "And why do you call the dragon 'he'? I thought they were all females, and that was why they had priestesses, rather than priests."

Darna shook her head and sat down beside him. "Na, the dragon of the mountains, is male, and he's the oldest of his kind. I don't know what Salara is now, but she, or he, looks different from the other dragons I've seen. In priestess lore, it's said that a dragon can change its sex under the earth, and that that's what happened in other lands when the dragons were being starved out, just before they went away forever. Salara's been gone a long time."

"So, it seems I've brought this curse on myself, or my father did," Ivanat said. Then he snorted and seemed to be about to say something dismissive. Instead, he went to the window as if to open the shutters again. He stood there, hand on the latch, hesitating. "Go on," he said.

"The planners say that Na will not allow anything permanent to be built in his mountains, and that if a man tries to build so much as a cottage in the hills, the dragon will shake him off."

"Bandits live there, though perhaps they don't build," Ivanat said. "Would the dragon shake off civilized people and not those wild men?"

"I don't know, but it's possible."

"So, our dragon is a male. I wonder if he will want priests instead of priestesses now." Then he chuckled. "It doesn't matter; he won't have either."

"Would you rebuild the temple?"

He shook his head. "No. It's a tavern now. It will be a simple whorehouse for the sailors before long. It would be impossible to put it back as it was."

That much was true. The marble pieces Darna had unearthed reminded her a little of the older places in Anamat, buildings that were far finer than anything she'd seen being made. The old work included most of the city's temples and part of the palace, along with a few houses and guildhalls. Darna didn't know why those old arts had declined or been lost, but it was clear that the older pieces were better.

Ivanat opened the shutter a crack so that the red light of the rising sun came streaming in. Then he slammed it shut once more and turned to face Darna.

He sniffed. "You burn incense here?"

"I do," Darna said.

He took a deep breath and paced back over to stand before her.

"You need to leave. Every day that you stay here it becomes more complicated."

Darna embraced him. "I know."

They lay back down together on the bed, just touching, not moving much.

"I think that I can have your payment arranged today, and someone to guide you back to Anamat. You may stay here one more night."

Darna squeezed his hand. "I'll go down to the village to say my farewells today, then."

"Do whatever it is that you need to do," he said. "The servants will be awake soon. Maybe they're awake now. I should go."

"Go, then!" Darna got up and dragged him to his feet.

Their parting kiss was brief and hard. If a servant saw Ivanat as he stole away, she didn't care. He was only troubled by his own mind; he didn't really care for the opinion of others. It was only an excuse. As a fallen priestess, she could take satisfaction in the fact that he'd seen Salara again. It was a grim sort of satisfaction, though, knowing that she might have helped to summon his destruction. She certainly hadn't meant to. At least he wouldn't be able to forget the sight of the dragon now, and perhaps he would remember her, too, after she slouched home to Anamat.

She hoped that he would not forget her.

§

Even with Kinner's help, it took Darna most of the day to pack. After midday, she set out for the village.

First, she ventured down to the stables. That was where the keep's shrine had once stood. She could see where the line of stones had been broken up, where the still new-looking granite had been put in at the stable wall. She found Nolerin crouched on a stool in one of the stalls, cleaning a horse's hooves with a pick. It was the same horse she'd ridden from Anamat, a gentle-looking creature now, though she still felt uneasy around it.

"My lady!" Nolerin leapt to his feet when he saw her and swept an awkward bow. For the first time, she noticed that despite his slenderness and quick movements, he was not particularly young. He seemed nervous around her now, but she wanted to thank him for his kindness when they'd first met.

"I came to say goodbye," she said. "I leave for Anamat tomorrow morning."

"You?" he said. His eyes widened, then he smiled a smile that was quickly replaced by a frown. "But I thought you would stay. We were told to prepare two horses and a pack donkey. I am to accompany... Well, we thought it was that Cerean fellow going to Anamat on the prince's business."

Darna shook her head. "I'm afraid not."

"But this is good," Nolerin said gently. "I will go with you. No need to say goodbye now."

"You will?" Darna said. The news cheered her more than she'd thought possible. Though she'd seen little of Nolerin in the keep itself, he'd been friendlier than anyone else in Slaradun, at least until she fell into Ivanat's bed. "I'll be glad to have your company," she said. "Now you can tell me more about Calandria, and I can tell you more of Anamat."

"Your language is beginning to be not so difficult," Nolerin said. Then he gave his furtive glance to the door. "Lady," he said, more formally, "I must continue to prepare."

"So must I," Darna said. "I'll see you in the morning."

§

Darna left the keep by the main gates and headed out into the village feeling a little lighter on her feet. The men were working on the wall, laying out its foundations near where the breakwater hit the shore. The foreman saw her coming and walked out to meet her.

"Lady Planner," he greeted her. "What brings you here? We didn't expect you today."

Darna looked out at the breakwater. "I'm sorry to say there's been a change of plans. I'll be leaving in the morning."

"What?" The foreman's voice came out in a shout. Some of the men stopped their work to watch – the foreman was a level-headed man, not prone to such sudden outbursts. He waved the men back to work and lowered his voice. "Has our prince lost all sense? Why is he sending you away?"

Darna had been prepared for that question, so she didn't blush or stammer. The foreman seemed to have no notion of the extent of her affair with Ivanat. "As you know, I was a replacement for my colleague. I think that he should be ready to come and take my place now, and that will be preferable for the prince. He says, and I don't doubt him, that his foreign allies find female guild members odd, an offense to reason."

"Well, it might not be their custom, but they're not in their own land, so they can't tell us what to do." The foreman sighed. "But I suppose he can."

"He can," Darna agreed. "To tell the truth, I've missed Anamat and my friends there. This place isn't always so welcoming, and I'm eager to be going home again."

"I'm sorry if we haven't made you feel at home here," the foreman said, "but maybe it's for the best that you're going back to your own people."

Darna nodded. She looked around at the bleak, sodden earth, greening as it was. It would be beautiful in summer, but she would not be there to see the late spring flowers bloom. "The wall will take a long time," she said. "What do you think will be next?"

"Whatever he tells us, or whatever your colleague instructs."

Darna looked up at the hill, where they'd planned to build the pavilion. She'd included it in some of the drawings but not all of them.

"If anyone asks you, would you remind them that the prince and I discussed building a pavilion on that hill? It should be aligned with the breakwater and with that ruined temple in the hills."

"It's not all ruins." The foreman stopped himself. "I mean, it's not long abandoned, if it is. But how did you learn of it?"

Darna shrugged. "Someone must have mentioned it. I haven't seen it myself."

"I'll bear all that in mind if anyone asks me, not that I think they will. Come on, then. Let the fellows say their farewells," the foreman said, clapping her on the shoulder.

Darna gave a short speech, then bowed to each of the workmen in turn. She wasn't usually prone to emotion, but the leave-taking made her throat tighten. She blinked away the tears. It was lack of sleep, the fact that she'd seen the dragon at last. Taking her leave of all this and Ivanat. She would not succumb to tears.

She turned toward the sinking sun and the road back to the keep. It would take a long time to build the muddy village into any kind of town, let alone a known trading port. She wouldn't see it herself, not by staying another year. It might take a decade or more. Still, she would have liked to have seen what it would become. It would never be Anamat, but it would be something.

She passed the site of the old temple with the new tavern sitting awkwardly on top of its hidden baths. A common whorehouse. Had he really said that? But he had. She hoped that Iola was still alive. Surely, if she'd died, there would have been some news of it from Anamat, even in Slaradun. She would see Iola soon and maybe hear a bit of what she'd seen under the earth. Maybe she'd discovered that Tiada hadn't died, after all. Darna was still thinking of Iola and her passage back to the surface of the earth when she came to Kinner's mother's house.

She knocked. Inside, she heard a shuffling, then Kinner's mother opened the curtain.

"Lady Planner," she said. "Come in. I didn't know if you would come. Kinner was just here and he told me that you were leaving. I wondered why."

Darna shrugged and gave her more or less the same excuse she'd given the foreman. "But I do need to speak with Ciffolga. I thought it would be better to come here first rather than go to her place."

Kinner's mother's eyes narrowed. "Yes. I see the sense in that. I'll go find her."

For a moment, Kinner's mother was silhouetted by the sun coming through her back door. The light made her look less like a common villager and more like a priestess. Darna wished that she could ask how she'd learned her craft of cooking and healing, and if she'd been at the old temple, but she didn't want to ask for fear that she'd be asked questions she didn't want to answer herself.

Ciffolga came soon, dressed in another ragged robe, this one darker than the one she'd worn before. Darna bowed to her.

"I'm going back to Anamat," Darna said. "Do you have any messages that you'd like me to carry to the temple there?"

Ciffolga gave Kinner's mother a small signal, and Kinner's mother went outside to stand guard, carrying a basket of vegetables to peel.

"I have my own means of sending messages," Ciffolga said, "but if you stop at the border temple, tell them to be wary. The prince and the foreigners will be going that way again soon."

"They will?" Darna said. "What for?"

Ciffolga's nose wrinkled. "For the dragon stones, what else?"

"I'd hoped that he'd changed his mind."

"Why would he? We've all seen what he's done. He'll never change. You're a fool to do his work for him, betraying us all."

Darna took a deep breath. "I've done what I could. There is a piece of the plan he and I put into place that can serve Salara for a temple, though it won't be the same as the old one. Nothing we could build now would be. You know the hill outside the village, toward the mountain?"

"That little bump? It's a good vantage point, but what about it?"

"He's agreed to build a pavilion there. You can... We can hope that they will shape its summit like a dragon tower so that Salara can land there. You will be able to make the rite there if all goes well."

"With the baths away in the town?" Ciffolga shook her head, looking at Darna like she'd lost her mind.

"It was the best I could do. It's possible that there might be a hot spring under the hill. In any case, they won't build it for years, and I'm leaving here in the morning. You can tell whoever succeeds you, if you go to the hills."

"If anyone follows me here," Ciffolga said.

Darna nodded. "Speaking of the need for successors, has there been any word from Ara's Landing of the ambassadress?"

Ciffolga's scowl relaxed a little. "The ambassadress lived. They are looking for a successor, but we haven't heard what the oracles said about that this winter. She should be out of seclusion by now. You'll know before I do."

"I'm glad to hear that she lives."

Kinner's mother burst back in, interrupting whatever Ciffolga had been about to say.

"Riders are coming," she announced. "They're coming up the coast road, from the south provinces."

"Which one?" Darna asked.

"I don't know. They're carrying a banner; it's orange and blue."

Darna's fear must have shown. The two women rushed over to her, took her arms, and led her to the stool beside the hearth. The men from Tiadun had arrived. Ivanat had invited them, despite her warnings.

"What is it?" Kinner's mother asked.

Darna tried to think of how to explain, but she couldn't. "I can't tell you," she said, "but if it's all right with you, may I stay here until dark?" She certainly couldn't go back to the keep when they could see her in broad daylight. Even after nightfall, it would be risky.

She thought about sending a message to Kinner and having him pack the rest of her things, then meeting Nolerin on the road in the morning. She could tell him where the various plans and tools were and where she'd left her clothing, but it was too complicated; she needed to go back.

"Stay as long as you need to," Kinner's mother said. "You can sleep here."

"No, it'll be all right," she said, hoping that it was true.

Kinner's mother gave her a warm cup of tea, which settled her nerves a little. Darna kicked off her sandals to wait for the cover of night.

Now that it was spring, the sky stayed bright late. Through the cottage window, she watched the workmen amble back to their own cottages. Day settled into evening. A fisherman brought a basket full of his catch up to the keep, greeting a man going the opposite way with an empty basket balanced on his head. From her window high in the keep wall, the village had seemed almost lifeless. Watching from closer by, it was still poor and secretive but not empty.

Finally, darkness settled in. Darna thanked Kinner's mother and offered to repay her hospitality if she should ever travel to Anamat. Kinner's mother laughed at that idea and led her to the door.

"May Salara's blessing go with you," she whispered.

"And her bounty stay with you," Darna said. She spoke the ritual parting phrase reflexively, but as it came forth, she realized how ill-fitting it was. Salara was not the nurturing protector she might once have been, certainly nothing like Anara.

Kinner's mother smiled a thin smile and shut Darna out.

§

The keep loomed over the town. Darna had only just begun to feel welcome now that she was leaving, welcomed by the people of the village, at least. The keep was still cold to her, except for those hours she'd spent in the circle of Ivanat's arms, those stolen moments and foolish days. She shook the thought away. She would get some supper in the kitchen, then go to her rooms, staying as far as she could from her prince and his new guests.

She slipped in past the dirty pot in the kitchen yard and found a piece of bread on a table. She was about to start climbing the stair to her rooms when a serving maid with a tray bustled around the corner, nearly knocking her over. Intent on the path to her rooms, she didn't even look up.

"Lady Planner," the maid snapped. It was the one who usually brought her morning bread and tea. "Where have you been? They expect you in the great hall, to meet the guests from Tiadun."

"Send my excuses," Darna said. "I was in the village, seeing to a few details."

"You're to go to the hall now," the maid said. "His Highness has been plaguing me to fetch you."

"I'm very tired, setting off early." Darna eyed the stair, but the maid was still firmly blocking her way. Ivanat wanted to see her. She wanted to see him, too.

"They've opened the rooms next to you for the men from Tiadun," the maid said.

Darna looked dumbstruck, and the maid noticed.

"Well, they have to put them somewhere," the maid said. "You can hardly expect to have a whole wing of the keep to yourself, guildswoman."

"Of course they have to put them somewhere," Darna echoed. Not even her rooms would be safe. She might as well go down to the hall, if only to see Ivanat one last time. It was probably only a messenger from Tiadun, in any case.

"Hurry along, then," the maid said, and only then did Darna realize that she'd been blocking the maid's way. She stepped aside and the maid passed.

She considered going on up to her rooms to change into her better tunic for the feast, but she wasn't at all sure where she'd packed it, and if it had been packed, it might already be down in the stables. Besides, the thought of running across a Tiadun guardsman with a bounty to win in a deserted corridor – no, she would take her chances with the hall.

After the sputtering torches in the corridor, the hall seemed blazingly bright. The sounds of dozens of shouted conversations filled the air. Darna stopped just outside the doorway to observe from the shadows.

Ivanat had not offered his guests the good Helanum wine but had left them slurping local ale. The delegation from Tiadun consisted of four young men, one of whom was seated next to Harzet, not quite at Ivanat's right hand. Like Darna, he was red-haired, but the resemblance ended there. He was tall and broad-shouldered, with thick dark eyebrows and a slightly crooked nose. It made him look disgruntled, or perhaps his stomach pained him, or he needed to urinate but didn't want to excuse himself and miss any of the conversation between Ivanat and the Ganatean on his other side, a conversation he was straining to understand, apparently without success. The red-haired man touched Harzet on the shoulder and said something into his ear. The Cerean leaned back and said something – probably in Cerean – which made the big red-haired man look even more put out.

The man appeared to be a little younger than she, though it was hard to tell. He looked enough like her alleged father that he might be her cousin. He was too close. She could make do with the bread in her pocket and let Ivanat keep asking for her all night. She turned to go, but as she turned, her nose crashed into a large tray carried between two servants. The bread on it rolled to one side and the maid scrambled to catch it as it fell.

"Pardon me!" Darna said. She staggered back and into the light of the feasting hall, her hand clutching her sore nose. There, she gathered herself together, leaning on her stick to regain her balance. Behind her, the clamor of conversation ebbed. She looked into the hushed room – straight into her cousin's squinting face. The chewing seemed to stop. He leaned over to ask Harzet something.

Harzet waved dismissively as he replied, all while using his other hand to summon a serving girl to refill their glasses. Darna backed into the shadows again, but she'd been seen. Kinner rushed over to her.

"I got your message, but I didn't have time to reply, to tell you to hurry. There's a seat for you at the high board," Kinner said. "You should have come earlier."

Darna was just as glad she hadn't. Ivanat was watching her, but then he turned back to the Ganatean, deep in some topic that probably had nothing to do with Tiadun.

"I'm afraid I'm feeling a little faint," Darna said.

"You'll be all right," Kinner said cheerily. He led her up to the table. "They've roasted a goose, not enough time to roast a pig, but it's still good and there's some left. Cakes, too, I think. They'll be late, though. His Highness wasn't expecting these new guests yet. The messengers must be very fast."

Darna nodded, not really listening as she felt her insides churn. A servant gestured to Harzet, who in turn told the red-haired man from Tiadun to move aside. The servant placed a seat between them. Darna sat. Ivanat smiled at her as if there were no trouble between them at all.

"Lady Planner," Harzet said, his smile cold. "May I present Lord Hedrin of Tiadun. He tells me that he is next in line to the throne of your home province."

"Your home province?" Lord Hedrin asked smoothly.

"Oh, I'm afraid not, you must be mistaken," Darna said, wishing that she could stab Harzet. "My home is Anamat."

"Even so, I am pleased to make your acquaintance, Lady Planner," Lord Hedrin of Tiadun said. He reached for her hand, as if to shake it in the Cerean manner. Darna let him take it. She had a freckle on the back of one hand. She noticed that he had one too.

"I'm sorry I was late," Darna said, directing her comment mostly to Harzet. "Preparations, you know."

"Of course," Harzet said. His gaze flicked back and forth between Darna and her cousin.

"What do you know of our poor province?" Lord Hedrin asked. Darna wondered if he was armed. She wished that she had a good hunting knife, even if she wouldn't know what to do with it.

"Very little," Harzet said, "only that some of my countrymen have taken an interest in it. Tell me, is red hair common in the south of Theranis?"

"Not particularly."

"Not that I know of," Darna said to herself. It wasn't common enough, that was sure.

"Tiadun is a fine place, I think," Lord Hedrin said, puffing up his big chest. "It will be finer still when my father is confirmed in his rule at Midsummer and he can begin enacting some reforms, not too different from what we hear of here in Slaradun."

Darna seethed inside. The destruction of the temples, this dubious alliance with foreigners, and creeping in to steal the lifeblood of the dragons.

A servant set a full trencher in front of her and she took care to keep her mouth full so that she was spared the trouble of answering any questions that might be directed at her. She nodded here and there, avoiding looking at her cousin as much as possible. As the cakes came out from the kitchen, she rose from her seat.

"I'm afraid I must take my leave," she said to Harzet. "I still have matters to attend to before my departure."

"Everything has been taken care of," Harzet assured her. "I will see you at your leave-taking."

She smiled and nodded. Then she felt a tug at her back. She was forced to turn to face Lord Hedrin, young, drunk, and not quite stupid enough.

"You'll be going back to Anamat, then, cousin?" he said in an undertone.

"I'll go where I will," Darna said, yanking herself away.

Ivanat was trying to call her over, but she ignored him and tried to hurry away, but she got stuck behind a servant clearing away a heavy tray, so she heard the exchange between Hedrin and Harzet as she tried to escape.

"Strange girl, that," Lord Hedrin was saying. "Not very talkative."

"Not tonight, no," Harzet said thoughtfully. "You called her cousin?"

"Only a fellow southerner, I think," Lord Hedrin said. "Anamat priestess, too, I'd say."

Darna reached the safety of the corridor. Not really safety, but it would have to do.

§

Chapter Ten

Back at her rooms, she attempted to bar the door. She didn't have a good latch, but the worktable pushed across it would alert her to any intruders and possibly slow them down some. She had almost gotten the table into place when she heard footsteps in the hall, light, familiar footsteps. She hastily pulled the table back to let Kinner in.

"Lady Planner," he said. "You rushed away, and I was afraid that you were not feeling well. Will you be able to ride in the morning?"

"I will."

"His Highness said that you might stay. He might ask your advice on the matter of Tiadun."

"No!" Darna put up a hand in an all-but-forgotten gesture, as if to ward off a blow. "I'm sorry," she said, lowering her hand. "I must go. If he insists I stay, tell him that he will regret it."

"I don't understand," Kinner said. "And what's this with the table?"

"It's nothing," Darna said. She looked around at the boxes and saddlebags. "Perhaps we should have these taken down to the stables tonight."

Kinner was still standing in the doorway.

"Your mother invited me to stay the night in her house," she said. "I think I'd like to."

Kinner stepped inside. "But why would you stay at my mother's house?"

Darna shrugged. "She helped me to find some herbs I had need of. We talked about things."

"She is well liked in the village, but she can't come up to the keep anymore, not since the new prince came back. The old one didn't like her either, but at least he let her come when she was needed. She almost didn't let me come here to work for the prince, even though I'm useless to the fishermen."

"Well, you're here now." Poor Kinner didn't really belong in either the keep or the village. "You might be happier in Anamat," she suggested.

"No, not Anamat! I'd miss my mother, and I do much better here in the keep than I did trying to fish or mending nets on the shore. I got very sick in the boats, but I like the work here most days, and Harzet doesn't seem to mind me like he does you."

"It's because you're a boy. He doesn't even like the maidservants, as far as I can see." Darna cast her eyes around the room and listened for the sound of anyone coming up the corridor.

"Do you need help with the table?" Kinner asked. "Getting it back to its place?"

Darna eyed the door uneasily. "I'd rather not... Do you think that one of the Enomeans could stay here to rouse me at first light?"

"I'll ask about that," Kinner said. "Shall I ask our prince?"

"Don't trouble him with it," Darna said quickly. She felt like pointing out that he was not *her* prince, not any longer, though surely Kinner understood that already.

"Is it the Tiadun men?" Kinner asked. "They're our guests. I'm sure they won't trouble you."

"They don't know where my rooms are, do they?" Darna asked.

"I wouldn't think so. I'll mention that you'd like someone to come rouse you."

"Just before first light," Darna said. Kinner didn't understand and she couldn't risk explaining it to him. If word got out, it would only confirm her cousin's suspicions. They were only suspicions. He wouldn't try to kill her unless he was sure, would he?

The rain lashed against the shutters, drowning out any sounds that might have drifted up from the feast in the great hall. Her dinner sat like a stone in her belly. She shoved the table across the door, then crawled into bed to rest, if not to sleep, keeping her stick in her hand.

§

She'd fallen asleep, like a fool. The table crashed in the next room and scraped across the floor as someone pushed it on in and tripped over a packed bag.

"Packing, eh? Thought you could get away," the man slurred. He was on his feet again in no time. He was young and fit, and the fact that he was clearly a bit drunk didn't seem to slow him down. She hoped that at least it would make him clumsy. Otherwise...

She had no idea what time of the night it was. She'd been deeply asleep. She couldn't hear anyone moving except for the menace in the next room.

"Where are you, cousin?" he said, speaking more clearly. "I'm sure you're in here."

Darna flattened herself against the wall, holding her stick with a rigid grasp. She knew from long-ago experience that she'd be better off in a fight if she were not so afraid, but she was terrified and she couldn't stop herself from shaking. She looked over to where the little shrine to Salara had been. It was gone now, packed away by the servants along with everything else. They wouldn't want the prince to see it. She reached for Salara with her mind but found nothing.

"Come on out to play," Hedrin chuckled. "You think you can challenge us, you mistake of a village priestess. She's not even alive. I'm just as glad my uncle never knew you."

Her father had known her a little. Darna had never liked him, not even after she'd learned that he might have sired her, but she liked this cousin of hers much less.

"You're all oafs," she grumbled.

"Ah, that's better; there you are." His footsteps advanced toward her. She raised her stick. He stepped through the doorway and she brought it down hard.

Well, as hard as she could manage. Not hard enough, as it turned out.

Hedrin cried out, then he laughed and snatched the end of the stick, which was still pointed at him. He twisted it out of her grip.

"Can't have that," he said. "That stung a bit. I didn't like it."

He had liquor on his breath, as well as the ale. Darna backed away, but he lunged after her.

"I can't have you screaming," he said, wrestling her down. He somehow got both of her arms behind her back and pinned them with one hand – his hands really were much larger than hers. He got his other arm around her neck.

"Last words?"

"You killed Tiada."

He snorted. "I killed Terenet, and I'm not sorry for it, either. He was a fool. If you don't exist, no one can prove that he sired a child."

"Plenty of people know I exist," Darna gasped.

Hedrin's grip tightened. She struggled for air.

"Time to finish this, then."

He had to let go with one hand to reach his knife. She jerked herself away as well as she could, but she didn't get far. He tripped her and stepped on her to keep her still. She didn't think screaming would help, but it was all she had. She couldn't get up, and even if she did, she wouldn't be able to run, so she let out the biggest scream she could muster.

It came out as a squeak.

"Shut up."

She heard the blade slide out of its sheath, but then she saw the flicker of reflected torchlight on the wall and heard footsteps, with more footfalls following them.

"What's this?" It was Ivanat, the prince himself. Darna turned to look at him. In the torchlight, she could see that Hedrin had sheathed his knife.

"Just a little rough play. Some women like that," Hedrin said. His voice was calm. He laughed a little.

"I did not invite you to take my women."

"Yours? Oh, I thought she was an Anamat guildswoman."

Darna managed to get up off the floor. "And I am, but..." Her teeth were chattering. She shook her head. Ivanat's eyes flicked between her and the smug man who'd been about to knife her.

"You did not invite him in?"

Darna shook her head and swallowed. "He broke down the door. I had the table across it."

"I was awake and in the courtyard. I heard the crash, and I came."

Three guardsmen stood behind the prince. At Ivanat's signal, two of them took Hedrin's arms while the third patted down his sides, coming up with three sharp daggers and a small club.

"Why do you do this?" Ivanat asked him.

Hedrin didn't answer but cursed Darna instead: "Bitch."

Darna took a step farther away before she addressed Hedrin. "Earlier, you called me cousin. I didn't think you would kill on a suspicion, I thought you would want to be sure. I see that I was wrong."

"You're his cousin?"

Harzet spat in her direction, but the projectile fell short. "She claims to be my uncle's daughter."

"Other people claim that I am," Darna said.

"She could stand in our way."

"In your way, maybe," Ivanat said. "Not in mine." He nodded to the guards. "Take him to the holding room, and his men to the cellar. Lock them there and say nothing of what you've heard here."

The guards nodded and went out.

In the distance, outside the shutters, the birds began to sing.

"I should leave," Darna said. "I need to leave now."

"It's still night. Stay. I can protect you."

Darna shook her head. "You can't. They know I'm here now. I need to leave."

He crossed the room and wrapped his arms around her. She shook until she cried, and he rocked her against his shoulder. After a while, he stiffened. Her tears subsided.

"I never cry," she said.

"I don't mind, but maybe you're right that you should go. I'll see you down to the stables. It's almost morning."

Darna nodded.

"Before you go, though, tell me: are you really the old prince of Tiadun's daughter?"

"As far as anyone can know. They say I look like him, and the priestess who bore me said I was. His mistress was barren. She didn't know that I existed until the prince was on his deathbed. She wants me to challenge Calar's rule. I don't want anything to do with Tiadun, but he can't be allowed to rule it, and it's worse if he's just the puppet of some Cerean duke. He had my father killed, though Hedrin there claims that he was the one to shoot the fatal arrow."

"Did Lord Hedrin know you were here in Slaradun?"

"Not until I saw him last night, and I don't think he was sure even then."

"I'm sorry," Ivanat said. "I've failed you, as I feared I would. We'll hold the Tiadun men until your escort returns from Anamat. It would be as well if he were killed, but I can't. Politics."

"I wouldn't mind if you did."

"The cost would be heavy."

"I need to get out of this room," Darna said. She kept feeling that choke hold on her throat, hearing the blade slide out of its sheath and Hedrin's derisive laughter. And now Ivanat was saying that he wouldn't kill Hedrin. She'd never known his name until that night, or if she had, she'd blocked it out.

Ivanat helped her put on her sandals – her hands were still shaking too much to do it herself. He could do that, even if he wouldn't avenge her. He helped her down the stairs. Outside, the dawn was just beginning to lighten the sky, but torches ringed the main courtyard, making it bright. Ivanat pulled her back into the shadows and embraced her one last time.

"A safe journey to you," he said. "Harzet is there. I think you will be safe for now. If you think it would be prudent, I can send more men with you."

The thought of more of those surly guards around her was less than reassuring. Any of them might have learned of the price on her head from the Tiadun men, and it wouldn't take long to piece it together. "No," she said. "Use them here to keep the Tiadun men in your holding cells until I'm well away. I hope Hedrin rots there."

"He wouldn't have tried to kill you if he didn't think you were a threat. If you come back here, you must marry me."

"I must?" That was one of the most absurd things she'd heard all morning. "What about your princess from Ganat?"

"I'll find some way out of that. Maybe you're right; maybe the trade will be enough for them."

He looked over her shoulder. Following his gaze, she spotted Harzet emerging from the prince's tower. He was carrying a purse, shifting it from hand to hand as if it might burn him. It looked quite heavy.

Ivanat let go of her, and when she looked back for him, he was gone. She walked out into the circle of torchlight where Harzet waited for her. He seemed strangely calm.

"Your payment." He tossed the purse to her.

Darna had to drop her stick to catch it. It was even heavier than she'd thought it would be. From the way it moved and the rub of the pieces against each other inside, she could tell that it was more Cerean gold than Theranian beads. She grunted her thanks to Harzet and turned her attention back to the periphery of the courtyard. She didn't see anyone waiting in the shadows. She could just hear the rough noises of the armsmen shutting the Tiadun men into their temporary prisons.

"It seems you'll have little enough time to enjoy it," Harzet said.

"If I can get back to Anamat, I'll survive," Darna said, as much to reassure herself as anything else.

"I'm sorry for what happened tonight."

"Are you, now? I didn't think you cared for me."

Harzet sighed. "Ivanat does, though, or did, and now I see that you are a person of some importance in this land."

"I'm not, really," Darna said. "It's just an accident of birth."

"And a little hunting accident. In Cerea, we believe that things happen for reasons, especially parentage. I don't care if you don't believe in your own importance; it's clear enough to me now."

Darna shrugged and looked for the horses at the stable door, wishing that she were away.

"I apologize for not recognizing your worth sooner. I'm sorry that I kept you from Ivanat, too." He allowed himself a rueful smile. "If you weren't a whore of the dragons, you would have been a good match for him."

Darna shook her head. "Is nearly getting killed what it took you to admit that much?"

Harzet didn't answer that. "Just accept it," he said instead.

"I will; I do. I'm sorry to say I didn't like you much either."

"That's fair enough, but let's not part as enemies. I am sorry that I took you for an overreaching commoner. I underestimated your importance. I'll keep our new prisoners here for as long as is needed."

"Thank you for that, I suppose, though for myself, I'd rather I were a commoner. Thank...thank His Highness, too."

"I will," Harzet said. "I'll go see that the cellar is well locked and that it stays that way." He hurried away before she could answer.

Behind her, Darna heard the clomp of hooves on stone. She turned to see Nolerin leading two horses and a pack donkey out from the stables. She'd never been so glad to see a horse in her life.

"Would you want to wear this again?" he asked, holding out the turban.

"Yes," Darna said, "I believe that would be prudent."

Her hands shook too much to do the wrap herself, so Nolerin helped her. Once it was on, they rode out of Slaradun Keep and through the still-sleeping village

"What was there before this?" Nolerin asked her as they passed the new tavern.

Darna hadn't realized where they were. She felt like she was moving in a haze. She looked up at the raw new tavern with its snoring guests, and hoped that its baths really were still hidden underneath.

"The temple," Darna said with a sigh. "Ivanat had it razed."

Nolerin shook his head. "Heedless. I do not agree with your religion, this worship of the worms of the earth, but in Anamat, the temples are very beautiful."

"They are," Darna said, glad to be on her way back. "I think that this one must have been a sight to see, too. It was made of the yellow marble, and from what I saw in the rubble, the craftsmanship was very fine."

"Do you mind if we stop at sunrise?" Nolerin asked.

Darna looked back over her shoulder at the keep. No one was following them, not yet. "A short stop," she said.

"I know, you need to be on your way, but a prayer to Farseer would not go amiss."

"Farseer didn't help my father," she said to herself.

"Your father? Was he a devotee?"

"I don't really know, but he took instruction from one of your priests for years. It wasn't right. He abandoned Tiada, the dragon of his lands."

"He should have honored his own god," Nolerin said, "but Farseer is my god, and so..."

Darna decided that it would be safe enough. If Nolerin's prayers could lend them some protection, then why not? "I'd like to go to the top of that hill again, to look back at the place once more before I go," she said, looking up to the place where Ivanat had given her the pendant. She still had it around her neck, but now she reached into her pocket and fished out Myril's more ragged charm. She would wear it against her skin once more, beside the precious dragon stone.

"That hill? It is a holy place?" Nolerin was asking as they passed the last of the houses. Darna could hear someone inside it, cracking wood for a fire.

"Why do you ask?"

"We always build our temples in such places, hills on plains."

"The prince and I planned to build a pavilion there someday," she said, thinking that she would never see it happen, not with her own eyes.

"That would be good," Nolerin said. "Not enough to appease Farseer or your dragons, but something."

"I've heard that Farseer is worshiped with blood sacrifice, with the death of small things."

Nolerin stroked his horse's neck and slowed to ride beside Darna. "That is the way, with some priests and many warriors, but we do not all worship him so. For us, for the farmers and herdsmen, he is the sun, bringing light and heat." He chuckled to himself. "He would do well to visit this land more, but in Enomae, the heat is as often a curse as a blessing, so we worship his consort, too. She has no name but Shade. We make our prayers at dawn, because it is the time of their meeting."

It was not like the worship of the dragons, where the meeting was between petitioner and priestess, or between human and dragon, but the way Nolerin described it made it sound far more agreeable than the cult of vole-slaughtering her father had told her about. She could almost see how it made sense after a fashion. She didn't speak again until they reached the foot of the hill.

"Wait," she said. "If I told you that this hill is sacred to Salara, would you still go there to say your prayers to Shade and Farseer?"

Nolerin turned in the saddle to face her, looking at her carefully before answering. "Why not?" he said. "Their realm is the sky; your dragons rule the earth. They are not at war, nor are our nations, not yet. Besides, I've done nothing to offend Salara, unlike –" He stopped himself, then shook his head and went on. "– unlike your lord prince," he said, jerking his chin back toward the keep. "He plans to mine the dragon's sacred hills, or so the Ganateans say. I heard the guardsmen talking about it. They still think I don't understand their speech. They wanted to buy protective amulets from the priestess in the village, but she wouldn't sell any to them. They were angry with her."

She should have known that all the prince's foreigners wanted were the dragon stones. That was what the foreigners usually wanted, and there was no denying that Ivanat was in league with them. Besides that, he could hardly be expected to defend the dragon who was supposed to destroy him. He never would have defended Salara, either because he didn't believe that the dragon existed or because he feared for his own life.

"I should have known. If I'd realized it fully, I might have been able to stop him."

"You can't now, and it was probably too late long before you came here." Nolerin took her reins. "The men from Ganat have him under their power. You wouldn't have been banished if they did not."

"And if I go back, I die. How inconvenient." She laughed at herself. Her death would make things so much easier for Ivanat, for his Ganateans, and for Calar. If only to spite them, she needed to go on living.

Darna thought of Kinner going back and forth between the keep and his mother's house. Kinner's mother surely knew all that was going on. The village still lay shuttered against the night, shuttered against itself. As sad and angry as Ciffolga was, the villagers sheltered her, and if the priestess fled, they would not betray her.

"We'd better go on," Darna said with a sigh.

"Let us go to the top of the hill, then," Nolerin said. "The sun is rising."

§

For one glorious red-gold moment at dawn, the sun broke through under the clouds. The sun – or the face of Farseer, as Nolerin called it – hid from them after that, all through that day and the beginning of the next. It didn't break through the clouds again until they reached the border shrine. There, Darna laid out her offering while Nolerin gazed at the sun.

All through that first day's ride, she'd been thinking of Ciffolga in her dingy room. Her life there was not easy. She might have been better off running for the hills, into bandit country. Too many men knew where to find her, and if the prince's men came for her, it would be hard to escape them. Too many knew where to find the temple in the hills, too. Darna did not believe that it was deserted – Ciffolga's word was better than Ivanat's when it came to the occupants of hidden temples.

They could see the long road stretching away below them, all but empty on its way to the keep. All they had to worry about now were bandits, and the worst they would do would be to steal her beads and Cerean gold. They usually let men go with their lives, and if needed, she could convince them that she was a priestess. The horses would be safe from them too – as devotees of Na, bandits kept no animals, not even hunting dogs, and they certainly would not want foreign beasts.

"Do you think you'll be safe here for the rest of the day if I take a walk into the forest?" she asked Nolerin.

His eyes widened with alarm. "Where are you going?"

"There is a temple not far from here, a very old one. I'd like to see it for myself," Darna said.

"But is it safe for you to go into these woods alone?"

Darna shook her head. "Not entirely, but I believe these woods are guarded by the dragon. It will be at least as safe as the road ahead."

Nolerin looked out across the clouded fields of Slaradun. The road looked like a muddy river in the green grass, unpopulated except for a few farmers with their oxcarts near the villages.

"I have my orders to return you to your guild in Anamat," he said after a while. "They wouldn't want to hear of delays, but they are not here, and the road measures its own time. I will wait here with the horses and kill any who would follow you, but for my peace, I pray that you'll return before night."

He patted a long, slender pack that hung behind him, and for the first time, Darna realized that Nolerin was an archer as well as a horseman.

"I didn't know you could do that. I can't ask you to do that for me." It seemed wrong, somehow, that this foreigner would kill to protect her. Ivanat hadn't done that.

"Your prince had a province to hold," he said, as if reading her thoughts. "I have nothing more valuable than a friend."

Darna felt a tug in her throat and turned away before he could see the tears. "I don't have anything to value above friendship either," she said, but she was not sure that it was true anymore. "Thank you."

She went to the roadside shrine that marked the border, its poor statue of Salara as clean and bright as it could be. She looked into the carved dragon's eyes, then she closed her own eyes and felt the land spread out around her, sensing the trail that led into the woods. It started a little distance down the road, a strong thread of a trail, ancient but neglected. Its current would be easy enough to follow, even if it was overgrown.

When she looked up, Nolerin was already taking the packs off the donkey. "I will wait here and make a camp," he said. "I think the bandits will not trouble me in this holy spot, with the sun shining down."

"I'll try to return by dusk, but I will certainly come back before the morning light, one way or another."

"You can follow a trail in the dark?"

"I used to be able to," she said, feeling her old senses coming back to her as she prepared to set out alone. "At least, I could when I was in the city. It will be different here in these woods, but I think I'll be able to make my way along."

She went back along the road until she reached a scraggly bush just below the shrine. There she found the trail. It was clear as day and marked by a line of dark green plants, their leaves almost black in the shade, like Salara's wings. She unwrapped her headdress and draped the cloth over her shoulders like a cape, then set out along the faint trail. Soon, the green plants parted to show stepping-stones, but the feeling of the trail gave Darna a stronger sense of the path than the stones did, and sometimes she veered away from their course as she went. It was an ancient, once-well-traveled path.

She didn't hurry. She didn't want to lose her footing on the sometimes-slick stones, but also she did not want to come up to the temple too suddenly, to startle whoever was hiding there. Bandits might have taken the place, but a solitary priestess might not welcome an unknown visitor in such an isolated spot. The woods were quiet, far quieter than the roads. On the road, there was the constant clomp and snort of the horses, and the obligation to chatter with her fellow travelers from time to time. It was hard to let her thoughts settle, even in Nolerin's easy company.

On that forest trail, it felt as if no person ever crossed the path of another, as if she might be entirely alone in the world. She enjoyed the solitude. No one was watching her. She adjusted her gait so that it felt more comfortable but not quite as dignified. The birds in the forest wouldn't care how she walked.

Most of the path's paving stones were made of plain gray granite, but around midday, she found one of marble, white Anamat marble, carved at the edges. A little farther on, a yellow marble stone peeked out from the undergrowth. A bird squawked away into the trees. At last, the trees thinned and she found herself in a clearing, facing what could only be a temple. It was no larger than a farmer's cottage, but it was exquisite.

It was, as she'd guessed, built from the same yellow marble as the temple in the village had been. Here, whether from age or just from the dark shade of the forest, the stones had an orange tint, like fire or rust. The temple's roof was a patchwork of chipped, red-glazed tiles, plain mud tiles, and – even shabbier – a few roughhewn wood shingles patched hastily on. It did not look abandoned, but it did seem to be in very poor repair. Vines twined up the columns of its porch, and no curtain hung across the dark doorway. The presentation stage was strewn with old leaves and twigs.

Darna heard nothing but water and wind. A spring burbled out from a spout, splashing into a beautiful bowl of yellow marble fringed with moss before it spilled over the edge and ran away into a clear channel, down the hill into a sparkling stream beneath the windblown trees. The water channel had been well maintained. Darna cupped her hands under the falling water and drank.

When she looked up, someone was standing on the porch. It was the same priestess she'd met at Midwinter, at the border tournament with Helanum.

Darna turned and bowed to her. "Greetings, Blessed One," she said.

"Why do you come here? Did he send you to try to shoo me away?" the priestess asked. "He hasn't even given you a decent robe. No respect for my station."

Darna looked down at her clothing. She was dressed as herself, as a simple guildswoman. Her tunic wasn't new, and certainly not fine enough to serve as priestess garb, even if it had been the right color. Then again, the priestess before her was wearing robes more threadbare than Ciffolga's were.

"He thinks that this temple was abandoned," Darna said.

The priestess snorted. "Then how did he summon me to the tournament?"

Darna backed away. "I don't believe that he did summon you. You just went on your own, to make a show of strength to the Helanum priestess, just as the tournament fighters did."

The priestess wrinkled her nose. "Go away, then, and don't tell him I'm here, waiting for his folly. I thought you were one of the men from the hills, splashing around in my fountain, but no, you're just the prince's bed slave."

"I am not," Darna said. "He was simply my lover, and as a guildswoman or as a former priestess, there's no reason not to take a lover."

"When he banishes me, your fellow priestess? Get out of my sight. You went willingly to that dragon-denying prince, did you?"

"I did, and I'm sure that you've let dragon-blind men into the rite, too. We all have, haven't we? Besides, I didn't pretend that the prince was honoring Salara. I haven't corrupted the rite with him, at least." Darna suspected that this priestess would not have refused the prince if he'd asked, that she was mostly angry because he hadn't asked, because he ignored her existence except to try to banish her from the land. The fact that the prince had seen Salara was not something she was ready to tell, not to this priestess, at least.

"I have left the lowlands; you're still whore to them," the priestess said.

"You sound as bad as the Cereans, and yet you're cursing one of your own kind," Darna said. "The prince wants his foreign bride and her tribute, not a priestess, not even a fallen one."

"Na's curse on that foreign bride, then." The priestess tilted her head then nodded to Darna. "Go on."

Darna had tried very hard not to think too much about the woman Ivanat would be taking as consort or wife. At least she'd had her pleasure with him, and shown him the dragon, which was more than this reclusive priestess could say.

"I only came to bring you a warning," Darna said.

"You would betray your own lover?" The priestess sounded scornful, doubling back on herself.

"I care for Salara too."

"Oh, do you?" the priestess glared at her. After a long time, she turned into the temple, gesturing for Darna to follow.

The temple's interior was just as shabby as its roof. She could see why Ivanat had thought it abandoned. Old drapes lay piled in the corners, dusty and rotting. A mouse scurried across the room, but one thin strip of mosaicked floor had been swept clean, and fresh incense burned somewhere deeper inside the temple, which felt bigger on the inside than it had looked from the outside. Darna felt the pendant on her chest heat up, the dragon stone Ivanat had given her, the one that had belonged to his grandmother. It knew this place. The priestess didn't seem to notice its light escaping through the weave of her tunic. She didn't look at Darna at all.

The foyer in these small temples served as a public sanctuary, where anyone might leave an offering, just as they would at a roadside shrine. This one felt different from others Darna had seen, but she couldn't pinpoint what made it feel so strange. The priestess stopped in the center of the room so that the light from its dingy clerestories poured down on her. It was truly a well-designed temple for that trick to work despite the layered grime.

"Stop there, come no further, and tell me what you came to say," the priestess said.

Darna drew her hand away from the wall, where she'd been about to brush away the dirt to see the painting underneath.

"I didn't mean to overstep; it's just that this is a very fine temple," she said.

"Used to be," the priestess countered. "You didn't come to tell me that."

"No, you're right," Darna said. "There are two things." She wondered which to begin with, and decided to start with the lesser problem.

"Ciffolga, the priestess in the village –"

"I know who she is."

"The men in the keep, some of the guardsmen, want her to make them charms to ward off the bad luck when they come into the hills."

"Well, she shouldn't be speaking to them, let alone making charms for them."

"I'm only telling you what I heard," Darna said. "She told me herself that she only sees men from the village, not from the keep, but men do go back and forth. Ciffolga may be in danger."

"Well, she's a fool if she thinks she isn't. That's not news." The priestess sighed. "So, what else is it? What do they want these charms for?"

"Ciffolga asked me to warn you that the prince plans to mine in these hills, to dig for the dragon stones."

"He's certainly come nosing around here with his cursed foreign beasts often enough that he's probably up to something. Even his father, fool though he was, knew not to cross Salara, knew better than to wound the flesh of the dragon." The priestess gave Darna a sidelong look then stepped out of her patch of light, walking over to a niche in the wall where a statue should have stood.

"He took this one," she said. "Perhaps he only plans to raid this temple, to raze it, as he did the others. Perhaps he'll leave the dragon alone."

Darna saw the plinth where the statue had sat. What had he done with it? She certainly hadn't seen it in the keep. Could he have hidden it in his bedchamber, just as so many of his subjects hid their own shrines, or had he sent it with Harzet as tribute to Ganat? That had to be what he'd used it for.

"The prince has invited allies from Ganat to help turn his fishing village into a trading port. They may not always do as he says."

"Foreigners can't be trusted. Even the fool prince should know that much."

Darna took a deep breath. "So, you see, it's not only him you have to worry about."

The priestess rounded on Darna. "What do you expect me to do about it? I'm just one frail woman. I can't stop them. I probably couldn't even stop them with the dragon at my back, and the bandits can only fight so many. Besides, they say that the dragon's gems are in the prince's realm, and the bandits stay to Na's land when they can. I can't do anything about it; you've wasted your time coming here. Get out!"

Darna squared her shoulders. "Think of something!"

"No. You're the one who bedded this traitor. Yes, I heard you in his tent at Midwinter, and don't tell me you were making the rite." The priestess paused to spit on the floor. "You tell him to stop them, and if he can't, may Na shake him off."

The priestess's curse echoed. Darna took a deep breath and backed out onto the porch. After the dim, cobwebbed interior of the temple, the shade outside seemed bright. Out of the corner of her eye, Darna saw a dark green dragonlet fade into the undergrowth.

"Salara hasn't been seen for years," the priestess said.

"Yes, he has," Darna said.

"I don't believe you." The priestess had followed her outside. Her voice softened a little once her feet were on common dirt. "I believe you, that the foreigners will come to dig. They did it in Tiadun; they'll do it here."

"They didn't get much of what they came for in Tiadun, but they did kill the dragon," Darna said.

"I heard no such thing. Besides, a dragon can't be killed."

Darna shrugged. Tiada was gone. "They say that dragons join the deepest stream instead of dying. Maybe it's different, but as far as Tiadun is concerned, their realm dragon is gone."

"Take your tale to the Aralel, if you're going back to that corrupted city. I'll keep to the hills, myself."

"Take it to the Aralel?"

"Yes. She'll tell you you're no priestess anymore, and maybe you'll believe her, if you won't take my word for it."

"She's never told me that yet, and I don't think she'll start now," Darna said. "Besides, the threat to Salara would be the same whether I'm a priestess or not." She began to walk toward the trail.

"Stop," the priestess said, hurrying after her. "If you're going to Anamat, there's a shorter trail. You can get back to the main road by sundown."

Darna hadn't sensed it, but then, she'd been intent on the trail she *had* found. She was too unfamiliar with the wild, wooded terrain to sound out all its paths.

"I'll show you," the priestess said, leading her up behind the temple.

"Thank you," Darna said. "Na's blessing on you, too. I hadn't thought to take this to the Aralel. Now I see that it's the thing to do."

If anyone had the power to stop Ivanat's reckless, dragon-killing schemes, it would be the Aralel, or the governor, if the governor would ever exert himself to do such a thing. The thought came to her that maybe Thorat and his apprentice girl could help somehow. She shivered, as if someone had thrown a bucket of water over her.

"What is it?" the priestess said. "You got a prophecy?"

The old priestess might have been more than half-mad, but she wasn't blind.

"Not much of one," Darna said. "I don't have that gift, so I wouldn't say so."

"You be careful with those visions; they're tricky," said the priestess. She pointed Darna onto the trail. "Go along there. The way is clear enough. It comes out just a bit upslope from the border shrine. Get your whore's self back to Anamat."

As Darna walked away up the forest path, she realized that the priestess had not given her a blessing, not even a gesture. Oh, well, she'd gotten that far without much help from Salara's priestesses. She wouldn't have minded, except that it made her doubt the priestess's goodwill. Living alone in a temple on the edge of bandit country must have been strange, alone with only her solitude and those close but powerful temple walls to shelter her.

In the early evening, Darna arrived back at the road. She thought that she saw Salara in the sunset, but she wasn't sure. Again, and again, she was never quite sure.

§

Chapter Eleven

They camped beside the lake halfway across the mountains and reached the edge of Anamat valley the following evening. It had taken much less time to make the crossing than it had with the whole train of the prince and his followers. Darna was glad that she hadn't had to go alone, on foot. She wondered why no bandits attacked as they crossed the mountains. They would have been an easy mark – two unimposing travelers on horseback with full packs, neither of them visibly a priestess. They were unarmed except for Nolerin's bow, which might be enough of a deterrent. In any case, it was better to be robbed in the mountains than to sit in Slaradun, waiting for Hedrin to break out and try to kill her again. Bandits, at least, were better known as thieves than as murderers.

Darna's heart lifted at the sight of Anamat's gold-roofed temples gleaming in the last light of the setting sun. She let out a long, contented sigh. If assassins lurked in the city, they could hardly be more determined than the one she'd faced already. Ivanat would not be there to protect her, but in Anamat, she had other allies, and more of them.

"It is a pretty city, but it cannot compare to the splendor of Calandria," Nolerin said. "Is it safe for you to return? The city could hide more of the ones you fear."

"It might, but it's home, and Slaradun isn't safe either."

"Why did that man attack you in your rooms?"

She was glad that he'd waited until they were within sight of their destination to ask her that, where Anara's dragonlets could protect her. "I think I'll get down and walk for a bit," she said. Once her feet had gotten the feel of the earth beneath her, she gave Nolerin something of an answer.

"The new ruler of Tiadun wants me dead," she said. "He thinks that I can threaten his claim to that poor throne, but I have no wish to take his place as regent."

"You are...not only an honest tradeswoman, though. You did your work, but you are also something else."

They were winding down the road, getting closer to the shrine, closer to Anara.

"No, I'm not only a guildswoman," Darna said. "I was also a priestess, and before that a thief and a scavenger. Before I came to Anamat, I was a young servant at Tiadun Keep, and a child in a village. The old prince might have been my father, but it never mattered to me, not until this. Now it means only that there are men plotting to kill me."

"We have a legend about someone like you, in Enomae," Nolerin said.

"You do?" Darna said. "How could there have been someone like me in Enomae?"

"Well, not much like you," Nolerin admitted. "He was black as night, skin as well as hair, and he was called the hidden prince. I'm sure he was never a priestess, or even a priest, but they say that he will come again when Calandria falls, and that he will be born into the poorest peasant hut. Do you have no such legends here?"

"No, I don't think so, but our legends are many and I don't know all of them," Darna said. "Here in Theranis, the princes are always in service to the dragons, or at least that was how it was supposed to be. They were supposed to win the right to rule from the priestesses, not only because they were born of the right sire or of a keep mistress." She thought back to what the elder priestesses had taught the novices about the history of Theranis, as well as little bits Myril had mentioned from time to time. "Some time, about a hundred years ago, there was a sudden change in Anamat. I don't know what caused it, but at that point, the work the guilds created grew rougher, less beautiful. Also around that time, the princes began to bring in Cerean tutors, to learn foreign ways, and to ensure that their sons always took the throne."

"Does a prince's daughter ever rule?" Nolerin asked.

"No, but she can prove that a prince had sired a child and should not have been overthrown. They say it was a hunting accident, but everyone knows that it was far too convenient for Calar to have his brother out of the way. He must have convinced his Cerean allies that he would take the throne next, because my father had no children."

"Apart from yourself."

"My father didn't try to acknowledge me until I was half-grown, and even then it was a secret known only to a few, most of them priestesses sworn to secrecy. Not even his mistress knew. You can think what you like of our priestesses, but we do keep our secrets. In theory, a daughter could rule as keep mistress and there might be no prince of Tiadun at all, but that would give all the power to the dragons, so the princes and the governor have never allowed such a thing to happen."

"But you could do that, could you not?" Nolerin asked.

"No. Our dragon is dead."

Nolerin dismounted and came to walk beside her, letting the tired horses lag behind. He tipped his head as the border shrine came back into sight.

"Your god has died?"

Darna nodded.

Nolerin stopped. "I am so sorry to hear that. I cannot imagine your grief."

Darna swallowed and blinked back tears. The thought of Tiada's death came to her as if she hadn't truly felt it before, suddenly and hard. "I haven't been able to mourn her as I should," she said quietly. "Perhaps when I return to Anamat, I'll be able to. I don't know."

"Only if you stay alive," Nolerin said. "Let's make camp a little distance from the road tonight. We don't need to make a fire, I think? We can buy morning bread in the next village, and I think that you should not be seen with your hair." He gestured to her turban.

Darna agreed, and they made camp that night in a clearing behind the shrine. Nolerin prayed to Farseer, either not realizing or not caring that the place was sacred to the dragons, and for some reason, Darna didn't think that the dragonlets took offense. Maybe her father had not been such a fool to seek out Enomaean allies after all, even if their horses shied from dragonlets.

§

The road rolled down into the plain surrounding Anamat, winding through pastures and fields, orchards and villages. They rested the next night at a large tavern in one of the villages, where they kept to the shadows of the taproom. Darna overheard villagers saying that the trading season was busy already, busier than usual. Ships from Cerea, Enomae, and Ganat had come, but there were also rumors of boats from farther away, from cold lands trading in furs and powerful medicinal herbs. Though Darna's headdress drew a few curious glances, no one pried, and no one seemed to recognize her.

They set out later than they'd intended to the next morning. As they approached the west gate, the bells rang out to signal the midday rest.

"What is this? Why do they close so soon?" Nolerin asked as the farmers covered their baskets and stowed their wares away.

"It's the midday rest – surely you noticed it when you were here before. Even in Slaradun, they stop work at midday."

"I was mostly in the governor's palace when I was here at Midsummer. I did see that at Slaradun, but I thought it was only the custom of the countryside. In Calandria, the markets are open day and night, never stopping."

"But when do they sleep in Calandria?" Darna asked.

"Never!" Nolerin said, but he laughed at the thought. "They take it in turns." He slowed as they approached a stall that was still open, selling bread and soup. Some of the farmers were gathering there, along with other travelers who hadn't reached the gates in time. "Shall we stop here?"

They'd breakfasted late, and the soup smelled thin and bland. Darna thought that she might be able to creep in under the wall, but Nolerin and the horses wouldn't be able to follow her.

"If you don't mind, we could go in by one of the other gates," Darna suggested. "I should go to one of the places on the far side of the city first, and I can reach it sooner that way."

"As you wish," Nolerin said, looking longingly at the hot bowls of soup.

"The fare is better inside the walls," Darna assured him. "It will be worth the wait."

They circled the city. A gaggle of mercenaries rested under a broad, solitary tree near the palace gate while their horses grazed in the pastures just beyond. Nolerin and Darna urged their horses on past the temptations of the green pasture and the promise of fodder in the palace stables. The mercenaries yawned and scratched their bellies, paying no heed to the two turbaned travelers.

When they were safely out of earshot, Nolerin looked to Darna. "Are you quite sure you'll be safe?" he asked.

Darna shook her head. "I'm not sure at all. I do need to deliver these plans to the guildhall, though, and there's another message I intend to deliver."

They were passing through the orchards, pink and white with blossoms. Nolerin reached into his pocket and brought out a small, clear disc of crystal that Darna hadn't seen before.

"What is that?" she asked.

"A priest gave it to me, to consult at crossroads when I traveled," he said. "I am no augur, but my mind is uneasy. I do not like the thought of you going back to the guildhall. I can't say why."

"I should read the signs for myself," Darna said, "but perhaps you're right to be uneasy. I won't go there directly but to another place, a safer place." Not that the temple would be safe forever, but she had promised to speak with the Aralel, and she did want to see if Iola was well.

She rode along a little while longer in silence, listening to the creak of the saddle and feeling the sway of the horse beneath her. She would not see any dragonlets to point her along the way, not from horseback, and yet now she felt quite secure on top of the hoofed beast. She was not quite willing to give up her perch to go tapping along the ground. She would just have to think it through and not wait for signs from Anara – or from Farseer, for that matter.

She ought to go to the guildhall, but Tevan would be there, and she did not want to see him. He would gloat over her failure to complete the year in Slaradun. Worse, he might expect her to take him as a lover again. Besides, there might be armsmen lurking in the street outside the guildhall, waiting for her.

"Did you meet the planner who was supposed to have gone to Slaradun?" she asked Nolerin.

"No, I didn't."

"He is a little older than me, a little broader, and a good bit taller," Darna said. "His name is Tevan, and you should deliver the planning documents to him. Tell him that I've gone to visit my home village."

"You are asking me to tell him an untruth?"

"It's more of a misdirection. I'll be in the city, but it is a sort of village within the city, and from there I'll send a message to the guild master. He will know where to find me."

"And where will that be?" Nolerin asked.

"The temple," Darna said. "I can reach it unseen, but I must leave you here."

They'd arrived at the culvert just before the northeast gate's market. The gates wouldn't be open yet, but Darna gave Nolerin directions to the guildhall, telling him where to find the best food and ale in that quarter.

"I would prefer to see you safely to your destination," Nolerin said.

Darna shook her head. She guided the horse into a hidden spot in a stand of trees. There, she unwrapped her headdress and handed it to Nolerin.

"Keep it," he said. "You might yet need it, and I would like to know that you have it."

"Thank you." Darna folded the long cloth and fit it into the top of her bag, a bag that carried only a few pieces of parchment, her beads from the work in Slaradun, and a few other tokens. The pendant Ivanat had given her fell away from her chest as she leaned over, gleaming in the sunlight. She looked at it, then at Nolerin. She almost wanted to give it to him, but not quite. It was the one thing she had left from Ivanat that wasn't only inflated payment for her work as a planner.

She rummaged in the bag until her hand touched the small cedarwood box she carried her incense in. Myril had given it to her years before, the Midwinter after they'd both moved from their guildhalls into their own quarters.

"Here," Darna said, handing it to him. "It's for incense. Take it."

"Thank you, Lady Planner," Nolerin said. "I hope that we will meet again."

He had always kept some distance between them, physically, helping Darna onto the horse only as much as she needed, but now he embraced her with a friendly, affectionate hug. It held no trace of longing in it, a sisterly sort of hug.

"You are - I hadn't thought of it before, but -" She'd never felt drawn to him, sexually, but it was only now that she realized he felt no desire for women.

"Never mind that," Nolerin said. "It is a crime among my countrymen. Don't speak of it."

"I won't," Darna promised. "I don't know if we'll meet again, but if you find that you need help, leave a message for me with the priestess at the back gate of the temple of Ara's Landing. I don't know that I'll stay there, but I'm sure that someone there will know how to get a message to me."

"Only if it is safe for you, sister of my travels," Nolerin said.

"I may never be safe again," Darna said. "I don't think I ever really was safe. Maybe it's no loss if I look at it that way."

"It is, though," Nolerin said. "It is a loss, to be known, to be hunted. Hide well."

"I'll try," Darna promised.

Inside the city, the bells began to ring. The gates would be opening soon, bringing travelers back onto the road. Darna gave Nolerin one more parting hug, then hurried away into the culvert. She disappeared into the hidden ways of Anamat, the ways she had known so long ago and that would always welcome her, as long as the city lived.

§

She emerged just upstream of the old bridge, and from there she had to go through the public ways to reach the side house. It was a short stretch, and she could hope to cross the distance unobserved. She *was* unobserved by ordinary people, but she hadn't counted on Myril, who was waiting for her at the corner.

"Darna," Myril whispered. "Thank the winged ones you're alive. Why have you come back so soon? No, don't tell me here. I couldn't see beyond the mountains, but I heard you today at gate closing."

"They found me in Slaradun, but I got free of them, and they won't follow soon." Darna squeezed Myril's outstretched hands. "How did you know I would come here?"

"The temple is almost the safest place in the city, but the old Grandmother is gone. You'll need to be introduced to the new one."

"She died? I thought she could go on like that forever."

Myril nodded. "The new Grandmother was a hermit for dozens of years." She paused to listen.

Darna could hear only the shouts of scrapplings back on the main thoroughfare and the clatter of cartwheels, but Myril heard much more.

"Come," she said. "The way is clear."

They ducked into the blind alley that led to the side house. The oppressive air of the temple seemed extended out into the alley. The feeling there reminded Darna of the stifling round of ritual and of dissembling to petitioners. They'd had to try to please the men while also pretending to be the voice of the dragons, but most times, the dragons said nothing.

"Maybe I'd better just stay at your place," Darna said.

"It's not safe enough," Myril said. "Besides, you have business here, don't you?"

"How is she?" Darna asked.

Myril bit her lip. "Iola is as well as can be expected, but you'll see for yourself soon enough. We'd better get inside."

The side house's sitting room was the same as ever, still musty and dim with its cobwebbed window and the old woman sitting there, waiting. This one was not quite so old. She sat straighter in her chair than the old Grandmother had, and her eyes were not yet clouded with cataracts.

"Who's this?" she demanded of Myril.

"A guildswoman, formerly of this temple, seeking sanctuary."

Darna opened her mouth to protest, and if it had been anyone other than Myril saying those words, she most likely would have objected, but Myril knew what she was doing.

"She smells of horse."

"I have been riding a horse these past few days," Darna said. "I needed to, to cross the mountains." She indicated her bad leg, but the old priestess still looked at her skeptically.

"You are aligning yourself with foreigners?"

Darna hesitated. "Not with foreign powers, no, though I do not count all foreigners as enemies. I may not be a priestess anymore, but I still owe all my loyalty to the dragons."

"Humph. Once a priestess, always a priestess," the old woman said. "Go on in."

§

The Aralel was busy, as usual, so Darna and Myril sat on the bench outside her receiving room, sipping tea and eating good temple bread while they waited. The bread wasn't as good as it had been. Something had changed.

"How is Geta?" Darna asked. Geta was the old priestess who'd overseen the kitchens and the baking of the bread since before Darna and Myril were scrapplings.

"Not well," Myril said. "She's in the infirmary. She doesn't have the strength to go into the hills."

"No wonder the bread isn't the same," Darna said, picking at her loaf. "Still, it's better than the bread in Slaradun was." She took another bite – it was really very good, if you didn't compare it to what it had been a year before. "Who's taken over for her in the kitchens?"

"Illaya, of all people," Myril said. "The palace reaches into the temple more and more, and it doesn't bode well for our arts."

"Remind me; who was she?"

Myril chuckled. "Of course, you weren't there," she said. "You should know her; she might be able to help you. She was the old governor's mistress. I was sent to fetch her down to the temple after Parnet banished her. At first, I think she went to the hills, but since then she's come back to stay."

Darna stared off into the distance. "You could have had that place."

Myril slapped her hand, startling Darna back to the present. "Are you prophesying now?"

"Not really." Darna was quick to deny it, but Myril would know the truth no matter what her words were. "What about you?"

"I can steady myself in the temple more easily now. I've had to come and go quite a bit, since Iola..."

"How is she?"

"You'll see for yourself."

At least she was alive. When Myril asked Darna about her work in Slaradun, she told her a little about the plans for the trading post there, the breakwater and the new dock they'd already built, and that the temple had been razed before she'd arrived. She didn't care who overheard that. It was there for anyone to see if they bothered to travel so far.

Myril closed her eyes, imagining the destruction.

"But Salara still lives?" she asked.

"After a fashion," Darna said. "Salara is...different."

Myril turned to look at her more directly. "You've changed too. It's not just the scent of horse, or the ability to see a little more than you did before. What happened to you there?"

"I can't say, not here," Darna said, thinking of the knife sliding out of its sheath in the dark, thinking of all the ears that might have been listening.

Myril squeezed her hand. "I'm sorry I was wrong about it being safe there, but it's not just that. You had a lover there. You were a priestess."

"Yes and no. I'm not a priestess."

Myril couldn't reply to that because just then, the Aralel arrived, coming up the stairs with Sunna at her back. Sunna had been their mentor when they were novices, but now she wore a guardsman's tunic rather than priestess robes and carried a sword at her side. Darna jumped to her feet.

"Come inside, both of you," the Aralel said as Darna and Myril made their obeisances. "Sunna will carry the news to the other concerned parties."

Sunna's wry smile was the same as ever, even if her clothes were different. She looked a little tired, but then she always had, though Darna hadn't known what obligations she had outside the temple.

"Sunna is training some of the younger priestesses to bear arms," the Aralel said. "The ambassadress said that we must learn, that we cannot count on the princes and the governor for protection."

Darna could have told them that without asking the dragons, but the Aralel was the most powerful priestess in the land, and she had to decide things her own way.

"Not that we should have ever have trusted them," the Aralel said as she settled down behind her desk.

As they all sat, two young priestesses arrived with an ewer of wine and a platter of cheeses and bread, as well as the ubiquitous temple tea. Darna reached for the tea, but Sunna passed her the wine instead.

"You'll need this," she said. "No holding back."

"You still are," Darna said.

"Shush, both of you." The Aralel looked as worried and distracted as Darna had ever seen her. In the almost-a-year since she'd been gone, the Aralel's hair had gone from steely gray to mostly white. As soon as the two young priestesses had backed out, the Aralel turned to Darna.

"Tell us about Slaradun," she said. "You took the prince as a lover?"

Myril gasped and Sunna's sword clattered. Darna froze, the cup of wine halfway to her lips.

She took a deep drink before she answered. "I did, but it's not widely known."

"Iola told me," the Aralel said. "She sensed it on her return journey; she said that the sacrifice of his seed was what opened the gate at last. They had needed it, the dragons."

"Oh." Ivanat wouldn't like to know that. It was good that she couldn't tell him.

"You have done us a great service in that, but we know little else. Tell me."

On Midwinter night, Darna had simply been overtaken by lust and curiosity. She'd only reached out to Salara as an afterthought, almost, though she had thought of doing it before that night's moon rose. She missed Ivanat, but she could hardly tell the Aralel that. She didn't have anything to say about him that the elder priestess would want to hear, and she didn't want to talk about the quick joy of falling into his embrace, of his kisses when no one was looking. She drank from her cup and tried to think of something else to say.

"Well, to begin with, he razed the temple in the village, but that was before I came, and you must know that already."

The Aralel shook her head. "The one in the village, as well as the one in the keep? The yellow marble one?"

Darna nodded. "I saw some pieces on the ground. The priestess who remains there takes audiences in an old storeroom hung with drapes, in secret. They say that the baths are still intact, underneath, but I haven't seen them."

"Are there any other temples left?"

Darna thought back to her journey. "If there are any in the villages, they are so well hidden that no one knows where they are, and the roadside shrines are badly neglected. I only met one other priestess, besides the one remaining in the village by the keep. She appeared at the Midwinter games, but not at the prince's bidding. I didn't see her again until I took a detour to find a half-ruined temple in the hills, near the border."

The Aralel gave Sunna a significant look. "First, tell me about the Midwinter games," she said to Darna.

She left out as much as she possibly could. She said nothing of joining the prince on the ground under the trees, or of their tour to the quarry after their Midwinter meeting at the border. It had not been the kind of relationship a priestess was supposed to have with a petitioner.

"So, you were in his tent, rather than in the temple, but it worked anyway," the Aralel said. "That speaks well to your skill and power as a priestess."

"I'm not much of a priestess, and I didn't go to him as one," Darna said. "Mostly not, at least, though I did know that Iola needed all of us to help her back to the surface."

"She owes you her life."

Darna shook her head. "It was only a little part of it, no more than a passing thought. I'm glad it was enough, but I... I'm surprised."

The Aralel frowned. "You must have done something. Don't deny it."

Darna looked away. "I don't think I did, not as much as you're giving me credit for."

The Aralel nodded to Sunna, who checked the door, then filled all of their cups with wine again, except for Myril, who drank only tea.

"Will he come to her this Midsummer?" the Aralel asked. "He didn't last year."

"I would be very surprised if he did. He might not even come to Anamat for the Governor's Council." She shivered. Would the Ganateans, or Harzet, let him come?

The Aralel sat back. She picked up one of the scrolls from her desk and set it down again, then ran her fingers through her almost entirely white hair. "You two, go outside."

Myril stood. She and Sunna went out, leaving Darna alone with the Aralel.

"You've always denied that you're a priestess, and believe me, I understand why. We all feel like impostors sometimes. Even your friend Iola might have had a twinge of worry from time to time."

"Surely, *you* don't," Darna said. The idea of the Aralel feeling any self-doubt seemed absurd.

"Oh, I do, or at least I did when I was young, before I flew to the heart of the earth." The Aralel had been ambassadress in her youth. It was sometimes hard to remember that there'd been other ambassadresses before Iola. "When I came back," the Aralel continued, "I'd seen enough to know that the little I had was enough, would have to be enough. I only flew the one time, and I'm just as glad it was only once, but it taught me what I needed to know.

"Look at me, Darna. I think it can teach you what you need to know, too."

It took Darna a long moment to understand what the Aralel was asking of her. "But I can't!" she said. "I'm not strong enough. I never have been."

"You feel the gaps in the earth, the dragons' ways. If anyone can go down into it and come back again, it's you."

"Me? What about Iola?"

The Aralel shook her head. "She's very weak. She looks well enough on her good days, but those are few, and even then I can sense that... Well, prophecy was never my strongest skill, no more than it was yours, but times are changing. Unless we can rally all of the princes to send their offerings, I fear that the change will go too far."

The wine churned in Darna's stomach. She wished she hadn't drunk so much. She set her cup down. "So, you think that if I am in the ambassadress's chamber, the prince of Slaradun will come?"

Others would come, too, perhaps including Calar, who would surely want to kill her even more if she were ambassadress. Then again, she might be able to turn the other princes against him. It was almost tempting, but it was absurd to think that she could take Iola's place.

"I do," the Aralel said, still thinking of Slaradun. "Don't you think so?"

Darna shook her head. "He wouldn't, not even for me, perhaps especially not for me. Ivanat spent most of his life among foreigners, learning their ways and their fears. You don't understand how much he hates and fears our temples, even though..."

"Even though what?" the Aralel prompted her.

"He isn't dragon-blind. Soon before I left, we both saw Salara early one morning, in the sunrise."

"I see. And how is she?"

"Salara has changed. She's longer, stretched out. She's the shape of Na, not like the statues I've seen of her or of any other realm dragon."

The Aralel sat stock-still, staring at Darna. "Oh," she said after a while. "I didn't know that." She took a deep breath. "So, Salara has changed, changed from female to male. I had heard that it could happen, it's part of hermit lore, but no dragon has ever changed, not since Ara and Enat landed." She took a quick breath. "Na doesn't like humankind, especially not princes. I wonder: will Salara be the same?"

"I don't know, but there was a prophecy..." It had been a prophecy for Ivanat, but the Aralel was a better judge of prophecies than anyone, despite saying that she wasn't a prophet herself. "The prince's grandmother foretold that the dragon would destroy him."

The Aralel nodded. "I don't see why Salara wouldn't. It's the nature of male dragons to destroy princes."

"Could he live if he left the province?" Darna asked.

"Did you like him as well as all that?" the Aralel asked, but she didn't wait for an answer. "He could, if he goes soon, but what is the worth of a life in exile, especially for a prince? It is better for him to die at the dragon's will."

Darna opened her mouth to protest, but she couldn't think of any good argument, so she changed the subject.

"There's another matter," she said. "I can't go under the earth, because I need to challenge my uncle for the rule of Tiadun."

"Now you acknowledge your birth?"

Darna sighed. "If they're willing to kill me for it, with their own hands, I don't have much choice. I don't like to think that Tiada, or even my father, won't be avenged."

The Aralel squinted at her.

"My cousin, named Hedrin, he came as an emissary from Tiadun to Slaradun, to discuss their foreign trade and treaties. He recognized me. He came into my room that night and..." It was still too hard to talk about.

The Aralel got up from her seat and tried, in her stiff, over-powerful way, to comfort Darna. Darna clenched her teeth and fought back the tears with anger. "He didn't know who I was, not for sure. And worse, after the noise brought Ivanat and his guards running and he'd been about to knife me, he said that some women like it like that." She shuddered. "I'm no delicate lover, but how can he say –"

The Aralel shushed her. "Some men say these things. Most don't mean them like that, but this? We won't welcome would-be murderers."

"He claims he's the one that killed my father. I didn't care before, but now I do."

"Of course you do, now that you see it for yourself. Very well, then, you certainly can't go under the earth if you might be heir to Tiadun. You have too much to attend to here. We'll help you with this matter of Tiadun however we can."

"You should, against dragon slayers."

The Aralel shook her head. "The prince's kin weren't the ones to send Tiada to the deepest stream."

"They invited them in. That's just as bad, isn't it?"

"Rest assured we will help you as much as we can. The first thing is that we'll find a place for you to stay here in the temple, somewhere safe."

"Thank you." Darna stood. "What about the ambassadress?"

"You may see Iola tomorrow morning and explain all this to her yourself. She will not be flying again, no matter what she thinks."

"But then who will?"

"You ask too many questions, Darna. It's not always good to know these things, and some questions don't have ready answers. With Salara changed, there's far too much unknown. The augurs and I will consult the signs. They should have seen this." The Aralel's voice turned deep, heavy. "Now go, and tell Sunna to make sure to guard you well."

§

Chapter Twelve

S unna ushered her through the temple, hurrying past the elders so fast that Darna scarcely had time to see who was there, let alone exchange greetings with any of them. The interview with the Aralel had been enough talk already, but it still felt strange to be rushed through. In the peresi's garden, though, she was all too happy to ignore everyone. The only two peresi Darna saw there looked young, almost too young.

"They're new," Sunna said as she fumbled for her key at the ambassadress's gate. "Young, but no younger than you were. It's just that it's been years since you were that age, and it looks younger every year." She said it as if she was trying to convince herself, too. Darna did feel old at the sight of the younger priestesses, but it was disheartening to realize how predictable that feeling was.

Sunna finally fished out her key and unlocked the ambassadress's gate. No one was standing guard.

"There," she said as the gate clanked shut behind them. "Let's see if the Most Blessed One is awake."

Sunna hurried to Iola's doorway, but Darna took her time. The garden, beautiful any time of year, was in full flower and as well tended as she'd ever seen it. Its earth fairly exploded with late-spring flowers, all colors of the rainbow. An elder priestess was sitting on the porch – not much of a guard, but the ring of walls made it feel safe anyway, despite its lack of human guards.

Iola was sleeping, so Sunna showed Darna to the bath. Its every surface shone like pearls. The sheer beauty of the space made her forget whatever it was she'd been about to ask.

"Towels are over there," Sunna said, brusque as ever. "I'll see you when you're done."

Darna hadn't bathed properly since Midwinter, and that had been rushed. She splashed off the worst of the dust with a bucket, then she sank into the steaming waters, letting all the aches and pains of her long rides back and forth over the mountains ease away, not to mention everything in between. Priestesses bathed often, to wash away the scent and the feeling of the men who had touched them, to make them new again, to return them to themselves and to the dragons in case the rite hadn't been perfect. It was never perfect, possibly not even for the ambassadress. It troubled Darna that she'd been allowed into Iola's own baths, but she pushed that thought to the back of her mind. If she soaked there long enough, it might be as if Ivanat had never been, as if Hedrin hadn't had his foot on her neck only days before.

After a long while, she tipped her head back to look up at the dome as it turned golden in the late-afternoon light. The bath was magical; it had to be, to wash away all the things the ambassadress's petitioners brought with them. If Iola had no successor, then perhaps it didn't matter that the bath was supposed to be for the ambassadress alone. If there was no ambassadress, it was better that someone use it a little. Still, it was one thing for the temples in the provinces to lose their strict adherence to tradition, but this place was supposed to be the model for them all. What else had changed in the time she'd been away?

Darna let the water buoy her up She spun slowly on its surface. Reflected sunlight poured over her and shimmered on the ripples surrounding her. As the light faded, she put her feet down and walked out of the bath. Back in the outer chamber, she found that a second nook had been prepared as a sleeping place, with a bed brought in from some other part of the temple. It had the look of an infirmary bed, but she fell into it and slept.

§

The air outside was loud with the birds of morning when she woke, and Iola was sitting beside her, waiting in a circle of lamplight. Even in the dim light, through sleepy eyes, Darna could see how thin she'd gotten.

"Thank you," Iola said before she'd said good morning.

"For what?" Darna asked, but she didn't expect an answer.

Iola rose to her feet, grimacing as her knees creaked. She grabbed the wall for support. "I'll bring you tea," she said.

"No, no, sit. I'll get it." Darna found a plain robe folded on the table by her head and pulled it on, then took up her stick. Her body's aches hadn't all melted away in the bath, and she didn't move very quickly, but Iola looked near collapse. The elder priestess who'd been at the doorway the afternoon before was still keeping watch.

"Back inside with you!" she scolded. "You shouldn't be here."

"I know that better than anyone," Darna said, "but the Aralel -"

The elder priestess brushed her excuses away. "You'll be hungry, I expect. It will be yesterday's bread, but I'll see that it gets here soon." She took up her cane and hobbled to the gate. Darna heard a small bell ring, then turned her attention back to the ambassadress.

Iola was standing behind her, halfway between the door and the disused offering place. She had no cane to lean on but looked as if she needed one.

"Come on, let's sit," Darna urged. She loaned Iola an arm, and together they hobbled to Iola's sleeping nook, which was better appointed than Darna's makeshift one.

There *was* something magical about the place. It seemed that they were in a world unto itself, with the offering place and Anara's statue safely distant but only steps away if they were needed.

"I'm sorry about Tiada," Iola said.

"There was nothing else you could have done. I'm sure you did everything you could."

Iola bobbed her head noncommittally. "I don't know. It was almost as if she was gone."

"Almost?"

"Even among the dragons, she existed only as an echo, and with Salara's ties to the surface so weak, I didn't think I would return. I thought it was the end, especially when Anara came to take me back. We – I don't think I can describe the journey back to the surface, but I felt like it was crushing me, squeezing not only my breath but my bones, too."

"You're very thin," Darna said.

"I know." Iola stared off into the distance.

"Salara was thin, too," Darna thought aloud.

"How strange. When I was under the earth, Salara was fat, round. I thought that she might be about to bear an egg. I'd never heard of a dragon actually laying an egg. They live so long, it must be generations and generations of humankind in between any birth or death of a dragon. But maybe I was wrong. You say that she was thin?"

"Long, at least, and so far away that I can't really say, but Salara's visible form was shaped more like Na than like any of the realm dragons."

"And yet you lured her up again."

"Or him. I don't know. Na's male, or at least we speak of him as male."

"The free dragon. That's what Thorat says the bandits call him. As if only men can be free." Iola gazed wistfully at the windows above, but before they could say more, their breakfast arrived.

Darna ate with the hunger of a scrappling while the elder priestess stood over them, watching their every movement, rushing in to help when Iola's cup shook dangerously in her hand.

"You must drink," the elder said, urging Iola to her tea. It smelled of something strong and medicinal, some obscure herb, no doubt. "Her Holiness is coming to speak with you about the succession again." The elder glanced at Darna.

Darna shook her head and the bread went dry in her mouth. Iola cocked her head.

"No," Darna said. "We spoke of it, but I don't think –"

"The augurs met," the elder said.

Another noise at the gate announced the Aralel's arrival. The elder hurried out to greet her, then Darna heard more voices coming from the direction of the bath. Iola reached out hurriedly to ring a small bell. The voices in the baths stilled.

"What's that?" Darna asked, alarmed.

"Thorat, but he's not alone," Iola whispered.

Outside, the Aralel was dismissing the elder priestess and sending for a fresh platter of tea and cakes. As soon as the gate clanged shut, Iola rang her bell again. At the signal, someone in the bath let out a long-held breath. Whoever was there stirred into motion again.

Thorat entered, followed by an old and rather disgruntled-looking woman in a laborer's tunic – or, rather, a guardsman's tunic. Sunna brought up the rear. They all stank of canal water.

"Who's this?" the old woman asked, indicating Darna with a flick of her wrist. She didn't move like an old woman.

"She's the one who brought the news of Salara," Sunna said.

"And she's an old friend," Thorat added.

Iola was staring at the old woman, ignoring Thorat.

"Who are you?" Darna asked her, awed that anyone could eclipse Thorat in Iola's eyes.

The old woman looked steadily at her for a long moment before she answered. Maybe she wasn't so old, only prematurely grizzled. "The Aralel's equal," she said at last.

That didn't answer anything. Darna glanced to Sunna in hopes that she would provide another clue, but then, behind her, Iola stood.

"Lady Enatel, I am most honored." Iola swept a shaky curtsy. Thorat and Sunna rushed to her sides to help her back down to the seat. Enatel. Like Aralel. Enat had an heir, had established an order as the priestesses had. How had she never realized before that such a thing must exist? Just as Iola was a priestess and a follower of Ara, so Thorat must be in Enat's realm. Nothing else made sense. Ara and Enat had greeted the dragons together, and Enat had been Ara's protector and the guardian of the dragons. He would have had followers and successors, but she'd never heard them spoken of, certainly not in their temple history classes. Then again, there was a lot left out of those lessons.

"I see," the Enatel said. "You're the ambassadress I've heard so much about. You look like you've had a hard time of it."

Iola shook her head. "I've seen the dragons and dwelt with them. That is all that matters to me."

Darna glanced at Thorat, who was doing an admirable job of not looking too heartsick. Just then, the Aralel entered, with Myril at her heels, bearing a sheaf of parchment and writing implements.

"Your Grace," the Aralel said, inclining her head slightly to the Enatel.

"You know I don't like titles, Nalani, or should I say Your Holiness?" The Enatel raised an eyebrow, still looking none too pleased.

"It makes no difference to me, Sovara," the Aralel said. "I won't be held back by formalities. Myril, Sunna, get stools for everyone. We'll gather around Iola's table. She needs to preserve her strength. Darna, you can sit beside her."

"I'm not going down," Darna said. Sitting beside Iola might make the others think that she was taking the ambassadress's place. The Aralel was arranging people to suggest a way forward, planting a seed for what she would say later. That was the way with her.

"Forget that I suggested it," the Aralel said. "We must discuss what's here on the surface before sending anyone to her death in the deeper realm."

Darna was not reassured much. Sunna grunted as if she would have said something but thought better of it. She and Thorat brought seats for the Enatel and the Aralel, then for themselves, while Myril produced a seat and set up a small table for her parchments. She carried an empty tray out to the garden and Sunna went with her, whispering something.

Iola sipped a cup of tea and leaned back against her pillows as the others took their seats.

"Why do you all come to me now?" Iola asked. "I don't think I've seen so many here together before."

"It has to do with Tiada, and with Salara, as I understand," the Enatel said. She inclined her head to the Aralel.

"I have told my fellow elders that we are discussing the succession. They're under the impression that we're discussing who will follow Iola in the ambassadress's chamber, and when. I'm rather more concerned with whether we should replace her at all, whether we can have an ambassadress anymore."

The Enatel nodded at that. "I'm surprised that you've managed to send a girl down to the dragons every year for so long, corrupt as the temples are. Can any of your younger women see the dragons without their clazan?"

The Aralel stiffened at the mention of the forbidden drug. It helped induce trance, but often left a priestess sick to her stomach for most of the following day. "Some can, but not many, it's true. I understand that one of yours can, though."

"She's made her choice," Thorat said. "She's not becoming a priestess."

"That's hardly your choice to make, young man," the Aralel said.

"It's all right," Iola said. "I'll go again. Eppie doesn't have to."

"But you'll die," Thorat said.

Darna looked back and forth between the two of them. She was sure that they were still in love with each other, yet Thorat's fear didn't seem to matter to Iola. She reached for his hand.

"I'll have to die some time anyway," Iola said. "Better among the dragons."

"No," the Aralel said. She stopped Iola and Thorat's reaching hands with a gesture, and they both sat back, chastened. "As your superior in this temple, I will not permit you to fly again. If anyone flies, it will be one the dragons have not carried before. That is what the oracles have decreed, though they found no one fit to fly. But that is not what we must discuss this morning."

She stopped then as Myril and Sunna returned with two groaning trays, then went back to fetch pitchers of tea and a stack of cups. Darna helped Iola play hostess, and it was only after all were served that the conversation turned back to the matters at hand. Darna was seated next to Iola; Thorat edged his stool closer to her on the other side. The Enatel sat opposite Iola, flanked by Thorat and Sunna, and the Aralel sat between Darna and Sunna. Myril looked on from her perch behind the Aralel.

"Tell us again about Slaradun," the Aralel said. "Are there any priestesses left there?"

"Hardly any; why?" Darna asked.

"If, indeed, Salara has become male, they would have to be hermits, only taking the dragon as a lover," the Aralel said. "The hermit priestesses in the hills only have Na."

Thorat shook his head. "It's not true, though, about the bandit priestesses."

"The hermit priestesses are bandits?" Iola asked, looking shocked.

"They're still priestesses, as far as I can tell, but they're not chaste to Na alone," Thorat said.

"How do they draw Na into their bodies if both the dragon and the petitioner are male?" Iola asked eagerly.

"I don't know," Thorat said. Iola's disappointment was plain on her face, but they clasped hands again. When they touched, it seemed that everyone else in the room faded away, that all their talk meant nothing. They'd always been like that, but it had been a very long time since Darna had been there to see it. Instead of feeling her old jealousy, she thought back to her times with Ivanat, especially that last time when they'd been in her own chamber with its makeshift shrine, when they'd both seen Salara. She wasn't sure what it had been, if not just the common lusty sex she'd thought it was.

"I think it might be the same, whether the dragon is male or female," Darna said after a silence. "I'm not sure it makes that much difference. It feels different, but the priestess's actions might be the same."

"It does, though. It means a great deal." The Aralel looked at Thorat, then to the Enatel. "Does he need to be here?" she asked.

The Enatel crossed her arms over her chest. "Yes, he does. He was at Tiadun, the leader of that mission, such as it was."

"The leader?" Darna echoed.

"That mission failed," the Aralel pointed out.

"I know that as well as anyone," Thorat said. "It's my fault."

The Enatel shook her head. "It may have been, or maybe there was nothing he could have done. The attack on Tiada's gate tells us as much as we know about the way the foreigners are moving in, about what they want and how the dragon -"

"Don't say it." Iola broke in. She was shaking.

The Enatel looked down at the ambassadress pityingly and went on. "They find allies in the prince's courts, they arrange trade agreements, then they want to go to the hills and break the dragons' veins. I still hope that we learned something there which could help elsewhere. *We* are sworn to protect the dragons, while you merely collect tribute."

"The foreigners aren't all the same," Darna said, but no one seemed to hear her.

"We're also sworn to protect the heirs of Ara," Sunna said tiredly as she took a cake.

The Enatel harrumphed, seemingly indifferent to the delicacies in front of her. She and the Aralel frowned at each other while the younger people helped themselves to pastries - including Iola, who did not look particularly young just then. Darna sank her teeth into a meat pie and closed her eyes to savor it.

She was on her third bite when the Aralel broke away from the Enatel's locked gaze. "We priestesses have retained our position thanks to our close relationship with the rulers of this land, and with the common people. You Defenders failed to save the stone of Anara. Because the common people were scarcely aware of your existence, the rulers could simply sweep you away as if you had never been. I am sorry for that, but it is not my fault. I am grateful that you managed to go on in secret. We need you now."

The Enatel scoffed. "For all the favors you've shown us."

"There have been some," the Aralel said.

Darna set down her pastry. "Can someone please explain to me what all of this is about?" Everyone else around the table seemed to know who these Defenders were.

"I'd like to hear it again too," Iola said. "Thorat explained it to me once, but I don't remember everything about the darkest night."

"We will not repeat the whole sorry tale," the Aralel said, "but I think that Sunna can explain it briefly enough."

Sunna sat down, rubbed her face with her hands, and cracked her knuckles. "All right, well, this is it, Darna, Iola." She hesitated. "Do you know that spot in the temple forecourt where the stones are broken?"

Darna nodded. Iola did not, but Sunna went on anyway.

"There used to be a plinth there with a very large dragon stone on top of it. One Midsummer about a hundred years ago, some Cereans stole it. We – the Defenders of the Dragons – were supposed to be guarding it, but there was a tournament. We were winning, as usual, so we stayed at the fields instead of hurrying back to the temple as we should have. By the time the sons of Enat got here, it was too late. After that failure, the governor and the Council of Princes disbanded us – or, rather, our predecessors – and dismissed us from their service." She paused.

"Enat's sons?" Darna asked.

"Before our fall, and for some time after, all of the Defenders were men," the Enatel explained. "But times change, and not all girls who see dragons want to be walled in a temple all their days."

That much, Darna could agree with heartily.

"May I continue?" Thorat asked. Sunna gave him the nod. "After that, the remaining Defenders went into the hills and became bandits. Eventually, some returned to Anamat and built a secret training hall over the place where our hall and sacred shrine had been. It's been there ever since; we've never really gone away."

"There are very few of us now, far too few to be of any practical help in defending the dragons, let alone the temples," the Enatel said. "I do as well as I can, but we lack the means to watch all of the gates, let alone to drive the foreign raiders off when they do attack, as they did in Tiadun. We have some chance of keeping the hills free. There, we are on familiar terrain and the attackers are not, but it is a slim advantage."

Darna felt, again, the chill of the absence of Tiada. For all that it had been over a decade since she'd seen the dragon in person, it was so much worse to know that Tiada was gone under the earth forever.

"And now, Slaradun. Salara..." The Aralel's voice trailed off. "We hear worrying stories from Naramun and Seiganum, too. Well, you tell the story, Darna."

Darna had known everyone around the table for many years, with the exception of the Enatel, who smirked as she waited. Darna smirked back.

She launched into the story of how she'd taken the place of the planner who was hired to plan the city at Slaradun, and how, quite by accident, she'd let the prince seduce her, or she'd seduced him, she wasn't sure which, but she made no pretense that she'd done it for the dragons' sake, or for Iola's. She had wanted to see Salara, too, whatever Ivanat's charms might have been. She wasn't sure what to say about the prophecy that the dragon would destroy him, so she left it out.

"Slaradun isn't as barren as everyone in the city thinks it is," Darna concluded. "The Ganateans seem to think it's worth acquiring some influence there, and at considerable expense. The prince can't build this city of his with Slaradun's resources alone."

"He might have robbed from the temple before he destroyed it," Iola said.

The Aralel gave Iola a look that made her wilt back into the cushions like a scolded child. "I'm sure he did," the Aralel said, "but Darna's right; that alone would not be enough." She let a long silence settle over the table, then she turned to Darna.

"There were some differences between your account yesterday and what you told us just now, but nothing to change the essence of the story. Is it possible that you might be able to persuade this prince of Slaradun to abandon his foreign allies, to turn him back to the ways of the dragons?"

It was so absurd that Darna couldn't even laugh. She set her cup down. "I can't. You must see that I can't, even if I lived long enough to try. Besides, would it make any difference if Salara is already male, becoming a wild dragon like Na?"

"Highly unlikely," the Enatel said, "but possible. Not very possible, though."

"I do think it might be the same," Iola said. "It might not matter. Na is different from the others, but not so different, and I thought that Salara was still female. Perhaps I was wrong."

"If Salara is still herself, though, and the prince returns to her worship, it's possible that the province will belong to the dragon and her – or his – people again," the Aralel said. "Otherwise, the Ganateans will conquer it as the Cereans are trying to take Tiadun. It will not go well for the villagers or for the men in the keep. You should go back there," she told Darna.

"To Slaradun?"

"No, to Tiadun," the Aralel said.

"And have my uncle kill me?"

"Who is your uncle?" the Enatel asked.

"Calar of Tiadun," Thorat explained. "She'd be the rightful heir of the old prince, by blood, if she were male."

"That would be a help, or would have been. It would not bring Tiada back, though." The Enatel turned to Thorat. "Go to Salara's gate. Take Eppie, maybe Sunna. The rest of us will meet you when we can."

"Sunna needs to stay here in the temple," the Aralel said. "Midsummer is too close, and the girls must learn as much as they can. She's all we have for a militia leader."

The Enatel sighed. "That may be. It raises our chances of failure to near inevitable, unless this newly male dragon has become more like Na than a realm dragon."

Myril, silent until then behind her scratching stylus, gasped. Darna tried to leap up to steady her, but Sunna was faster. Darna sat again. Was Salara like Na? She'd said it herself, but she didn't know what that meant, not really. She needed to go back, to find out. That would be better than sitting idly by in Anamat, waiting for someone to knife her in the dark again.

"I'll go," Darna said. "I'll go back, but you shouldn't hope for much."

"It's too dangerous for you now," Myril said faintly.

"My would-be assassins are imprisoned in the keep. I'll stay to the hills. I might survive."

"I'm not worried about that," Myril said, but Darna ignored her and no one else seemed to hear.

Iola leaned forward. "I could talk to them, to Na and Salara, when I go down under the earth."

"You will not go under the earth again," the Aralel said. "Hear me this time! You are too weak, and unless the portents change, no one will go at all."

Darna had suspected that this was coming, but it was still shocking to hear it said so plainly.

"We will carry on as usual," the Aralel said, "but when Midsummer comes, you will simply go into seclusion here, as the rumors say that you already do."

"The priesshood is over," Sunna said. "I don't know why I bother."

"You bother because it is all we have left," the Aralel said.

"It's true," the Enatel agreed. "We have the dragons, but we have to live in the human realm, too. This pomp and ceremony will have to be enough, even if no one can make the journey. Your spirit isn't strong enough, never mind the rest of you."

"But I –"

"Quiet." The Aralel laid her hand on Iola's arm. "The Enatel understands these things too. You may wish to go, but there's no one to replace you if you don't return. You will not return if you go this Midsummer, unless the tide changes entirely."

Iola reached for Thorat. "You will try to change it for me, won't you?"

Thorat nodded. "I'll try."

§

Darna stayed in Iola's chamber for the rest of the day. The ambassadress took no petitioners; she hadn't taken any since her return from the dragons' realm, not even Thorat.

She stayed in her sleeping nook in what looked like a deep sulk, while Darna fretted and paced, fussing with her cane.

Finally, when dusk was falling, Sunna returned. "Come with me," she said to Darna. "Your guild master is here, and one of your fellows. I think it's your lover boy."

Darna's heart sank. She still did not want to see Tevan.

Sure enough, it was Tevan. He met her at the door of the counting room. "Look, Darna, I'm sorry, I didn't expect you back so soon and I –" He shook his head.

"Go on, tell me," Darna said.

"I met this other woman. She's very young, just new to the city, but we're going to be living together." He broke off again, as if it were all too hard to say.

Darna almost laughed to see what effort it took him to get the words out when they meant so little to her, when whatever had been between them felt like it was so far away in her past. "It's all right. It was over. We should have ended it long ago."

"No, we shouldn't have, I see that now, but...but wait, you don't mind?"

"No, I don't. I take it this means you won't be replacing me in Slaradun?"

Tevan shook his head and the guild master cleared his throat. "I don't know who, if anyone, will replace you. We'll discuss it inside."

Sunna ushered them into the dimly lit chamber and went to stand guard outside, probably listening to every word. Darna didn't really mind. She'd always relied on Sunna for so much.

"Any replacement will have to wait until Midsummer, or later, when the prince comes to Anamat again," the guild master said. "I will need to discuss these plans with him myself. I do not think they can be carried out."

"They work perfectly with the contours of the land there," Darna said. "You should see it for yourself."

The guild master smiled. "I don't doubt you, they're fine plans, quite fine, really; it's just that...a city of that scale is almost a sacrilege."

Darna shook her head. "Not 'almost.' It's an affront to the dragons, but a sensible enough plan if you look at it in any other way."

"I take it the prince didn't see it that way?"

"He liked the plans well enough."

"Then why were you sent back to Anamat so soon?" the guild master asked. He stood and looked down his long nose at her, his broad old shoulders square against the small window behind him.

Darna jerked her head in Tevan's direction.

"Leave us," the guild master told him.

After the door had closed behind him, the guild master raised his eyebrows at Darna. "Well, did you have some soured love affair there, then?"

Darna sighed. "I did. You should know that the prince of Slaradun would cross the dragons any way he could. I could say more of him, but the real trouble for me now is that Calar of Tiadun wants me dead. His son arrived and realized who I was. He tried to murder me that night."

The guild master stood aghast for a moment. "He tried to kill you?"

Darna nodded.

"I don't understand why."

"It's because I'm proof – though not very good proof – that his brother was not barren and therefore shouldn't have been usurped. That's the main reason he felt he could take the throne and convince the people of Tiadun that it was his right." She shuddered inside. "I have to leave the city again before his henchmen find me. They found me all the way out in Slaradun. I'll have to leave the guild."

"That's not up to you. You can't just leave the guild."

"I can't stay here."

"I didn't say that you had to stay in Anamat," the guild master said gently. "I can only assure you that when, or if, this threat passes, you will always have a home with us."

"Thank you," Darna said. "That means more to me than you can imagine."

"Don't underestimate my imagination," the guild master said. "Go where you need to go, and don't tell me where it is. We'll cover your tracks as well as we're able. Shall I say it was a jealous lover?"

"It's as good a story as any," Darna said. "Say whatever you think they will believe."

§

Chapter Thirteen

When Sunna returned, she was carrying Darna's pack and a long, hooded cloak. They said nothing until they passed through the side house and were out on the streets again. "Thorat's making arrangements for the journey," she said. "I was wondering, though; how did you cross the mountains? Surely, you weren't alone."

Darna shook her head. "I rode horseback. I know it's a sacrilege, but it got me here."

"Do you suppose you can walk back?"

Darna paused where she stood, at the intersection just up from the bridge, on the temple side. The bath had helped, but even the short walk across town was making her back tired. She shook her head. "I hadn't really thought about how I was going to get back."

"Well, think fast," Sunna said. "You're supposed to set out from Raina's house at dawn."

They walked on. Halfway across the bridge, Darna had a thought.

"I could ride back with Nolerin," she said.

"Who's Nolerin?"

Darna almost wished she hadn't mentioned it. Sunna would hate Nolerin just because he was an Enomaean and a foreigner, and so would the others. Nolerin had no business getting caught up in this plot, but he *would* be going back to Slaradun soon, and with a spare horse, a horse that had gotten used to her.

"He's an Enomaean horse handler," she said. "He brought me back here from Slaradun, and he has to return the horses, so he'll probably be going back."

Sunna hurried after her. "That might do," she said, somewhat to Darna's surprise. "I'll talk to Thorat and the Enatel. We'll see if we can make it worth his while." There was a hint of threat in her voice.

"You can't kill him. He might be Enomaean, but he's done nothing to harm the dragons."

"Oh, his life will be safe enough. Wait, though." Sunna caught her by the arm. "Darna?" Her voice had a hesitant tone to it.

They were almost at Myril's place now. Myril would hear whatever they said. Surely, Sunna realized that, too.

"What is it?"

"If you don't want to answer, you don't have to, but what was he like? The prince, not the Enomaean."

Darna was glad that night had fallen and that the torchlight along the street was dim, because she was fairly sure that she was blushing. "It was nice while it lasted. I didn't think of it as being a priestess."

"I just wondered. I've never really taken a lover like that, not for more than a night or two. I'm too busy playing go-between, and I have too many secrets."

"I probably shouldn't have done it either. I guess I have secrets too, not that I'm keeping them very well." She glanced up ahead to where Myril was emerging from her door.

"I'll walk with you," Myril said. "I have herbs to trade with Raina." She and Sunna moved into position, walking behind Darna on either side and talking with one another.

"She wants to go on the horse that brought her back here," Sunna said.

"I see," Myril said. "That might not be a bad idea."

"Na wouldn't like it," Sunna said.

"I don't know what to think about that," Myril said, "but so far, Darna's contact with horses hasn't done any damage to her dragonsight."

"Stop talking like I'm not here," Darna grumbled.

"Shh!" Myril said.

Darna didn't need warning twice. None of them said anything more until they reached Raina's farmhouse, also known as the Gone Duck Inn. Once there, they busied themselves with preparations for the night and for the journey to come.

Darna woke to the sight of Myril sitting beside her bed and holding a steaming bowl, which she handed to Darna. It held a sort of sweet tea similar to temple tea.

"This will wake you and give you strength for the journey," Myril said. "I've repacked your things, and I made you a fresh bundle of herbs." Darna took the small cloth bag from her. "I added another warding charm. It should help keep them from finding you. It's a little bit like the one from last summer."

"Should I wear both?"

"No, give me the old one."

Darna reached for the worn string around her neck. As she did so, the gold chain of Ivanat's grandmother's pendant caught the light.

"What's that?" Myril asked.

Darna put her hand over the pendant but did not bring it out from under her tunic. She'd kept it hidden when she was in the temple, too. "It was a gift from the prince, in Slaradun. It belonged to his grandmother, who was a priestess. At least he didn't give this to the foreigners."

"You'll have a piece of Salara to guide and guard you, then," Myril said. "Between that and my charm, I think maybe you'll come through all right."

"And I'll have Thorat," Darna said. She was glad that he would be traveling with her.

"Having him is not how I'd describe it. He has to guard the gate before protecting you."

"Still, it will be reassuring."

Myril nodded agreement, then she went to the doorway and listened. "He should be here by now, but come on, let's breakfast."

Raina's children and fosterlings were gathered around the kitchen table. Many of them were the older offspring of priestesses, come to lodge at Raina's house and learn to farm. Soon after the bowls were cleared away, Thorat and Eppie arrived with Nolerin, the two horses, and the donkey. The children scurried from their places to gawk at the foreigner and his beasts from a safe distance. Nolerin crouched to speak with one of the bolder boys at eye level. Darna watched from the doorway.

"They won't hurt you," Nolerin told the boy, "just don't startle them from behind. One of them kicked me when I was about your size, and I never went behind that horse again, kept face to face with him after that."

The boy's eyes went wide. "You can talk?" he said.

Nolerin chuckled. "I had to learn, but yes, I can a little."

By that time, the morning's traffic had begun to roll by on the road outside. Nolerin and Thorat kept a careful distance apart, and Darna could tell that they didn't like each other yet.

"We should go, I think," Darna said. She took her head wrap out of her pack and began to put it on.

"What are you doing with that?" Thorat asked, horrified.

"It's a disguise," Darna said. "Besides, the horses don't like my hair."

Thorat shivered. "It's uncanny. I don't like it."

Eppie shrugged. "As long as it works, right?" she asked Thorat pointedly. She gave Raina a wry smile, and Darna wondered if any of them knew where they were going, exactly.

"Maybe we should travel separately," Thorat said, eying the horses.

"Don't be ridiculous," Myril said. "You're traveling together."

Thorat shook his head. "But we can't show him...where we're going."

"I am merely guiding the horses back to their master," Nolerin said. For the first time since they'd left Slaradun together, Darna noticed his strange, simpering accent. It was as if he affected that voice only to reassure his employers of his subservience.

"So, we'll leave you at the road?" Thorat asked.

"I can walk from near the border," Darna said. She turned to Nolerin. "It'll be good to have a couple of swords by our side, as well as your bow, in case the bandits attack."

"They won't," Eppie said.

"How can you be sure?" Nolerin asked her. He'd dropped the simpering attitude, and his eyes narrowed.

"We just know," Thorat said.

"It's because you're a priestess," Eppie said, obviously recognizing the inadequacy of Thorat's response. "They can just tell. Come on, let's get out of here."

They set out into the busy road, traveling in increasingly companionable silence as the days went on, broken only by small talk about the practicalities of finding campsites and the like. A few days later, they reached the far side of the mountains, where the road wound down toward Slaradun. They reached the sudden gap in the rocks that showed them the long spread of the coastline, fading away into the misty distance.

"I think we should part here," Darna said, drawing her mount to a halt. She'd learned how to do that much at least, and she was beginning to rather enjoy riding, even though it meant that she had no chance at all of seeing dragonlets while the horse stood between her and the earth.

"Why not go on to your border shrine?" Nolerin asked.

They were on a particularly steep and rocky stretch of road, not at all a good halting point. Thorat and Eppie looked inclined to agree with Nolerin, but Darna held up her hand.

"If we go on, it's more likely that we'll be seen by the people in the next village. Nolerin isn't supposed to be traveling with anyone else, and it will be safer for him, and for me, if he goes on alone from here. It would be best if we're not seen together."

"Or seen at all," Eppie agreed.

Thorat offered to help her dismount, but Darna waved him away. The horses had not gotten used to Eppie and Thorat, and their distrust was mutual. Darna wasn't sure whether it was the pair's gleaming weapons, their association with the dragons, or something else. She dismounted on her own and handed the reins to Nolerin, who looped them over his arm and reached down to clasp her hands.

"Take the rest of the provisions," he said. "I'll buy what I need in the next village."

Thorat thanked him and went to unstrap Raina's bag, still half full, from the uncomplaining donkey.

"Is there a path here?" Eppie asked Darna.

Darna nodded, then squeezed Nolerin's hands. "I don't know if we'll meet again," she said, "but if we do, I hope it will be as friends."

"Always," Nolerin said. "Besides, it may not be long. I do not think I can stay in this cold, wet place. I will go back to Calandria, but before that, I hope to see you in Anamat."

"Perhaps," Darna said, not saying *if I survive*, though that was what she was thinking. "Go on now. Keep yourself safe, and these cursed beasts, too." She patted her horse affectionately on the rump.

Nolerin stopped short in alarm, but when he saw that Darna was smiling, he smiled too. "To meet again in Anamat!" he said. He urged the horses forward, out of sight around the bend in the path.

Darna raised her hand in farewell.

§

After Nolerin had gone, Darna searched the hillside for a triangle of three dark rocks. The pattern was so subtle that Darna was not entirely sure it had been made intentionally, and a person would have to know exactly what they were looking for to recognize it. She remembered where the trail was, but she looked for the stones anyway. They were there, and they still pointed directly at the trail.

"This way," she said to Thorat and Eppie.

She didn't hear what Thorat had been about to say, but she did hear the "oompf" as Eppie elbowed him.

"She's been here before, all right," Eppie said. "And you're the one who says that she always knows where she's going. We won't have to go looking for little flowers this time."

"What flowers?" Darna asked.

Thorat sighed. "I shouldn't be telling you this."

"Well, you'll have to tell me something if I'm going to be any help to you." They'd given her no more hints about who the Defenders were, or what they did, as they crossed the hills. They hadn't even practiced their swordwork for fear that Nolerin would steal their secrets.

"Sovara said you could tell her. Besides, it's not likely we'll live through this one, too," Eppie said. They'd all been thinking that, but only Eppie seemed willing to say it.

"I'll tell you as we go," Thorat said as he came up beside her. "Every dragon has her characteristic plant," he began.

"Or his," Darna said. "Salara's a he now."

"Or his. It grows thickest closest to the gate, which is where –"

"It's where the dragon goes down to the chambered earth, I know," Darna said. "Like Anara's, on her island, only most of them are in the foothills. We were taught this in the temple, though I'd say most priestesses don't think much about it."

"Fine, but did you know that the dragons' stones are thicker in the ground as you get closer to the gate?"

"I did, but that's something I learned in the planners' guild," Darna said. "That's how we know where to stop digging when we're looking for marble or the like." She paused to lift a branch out of her way. The knowledge was a guild secret, but any quarryman might have discovered it at some point and seen the profit in selling that secret to foreign traders. "It's not much of a secret anymore, is it?"

"No, I suppose not," Thorat said. "Maybe we don't have any secrets left worth keeping at all."

"We do, though," Eppie said. "There's the shrine and the fighting techniques."

"People could find the shrine some day, or steal our techniques," Thorat said. "Besides, the bandits have those too."

"The bandits are... Is that another secret?" Eppie asked.

"You seemed pretty sure about them not attacking priestesses," Darna commented. "Feeling kindly toward them these days?"

Thorat didn't answer that. "I don't think we do have anything to tell you, then." Whether or not all his secrets had been laid bare, he didn't seem to think there was anything more to tell her.

The slopes to the west were covered with tall, straight trees. One of Slaradun's prime trade goods, they were a source of good timber for boats' masts and the frames of wooden buildings. Other than that, there was little to note along the trail that led them to the back of the neglected temple.

"Wait here," Darna said.

"I'm coming with you," Thorat insisted. "It doesn't feel safe."

Darna wanted to listen without anyone breathing down her neck. She didn't really want Thorat trailing after her like a body guard, though she knew as well as he did that she needed one.

Eppie raised her eyebrows. "Well?"

Darna held up a hand for silence, then closed her eyes and listened as well as she could. She heard no one. "I don't think anyone's here," she said. "Let's go see."

All three of them circled around to the front, where the water still spilled merrily out of its spout and the vines still climbed the columns of the porch. Darna took a deep breath. The smell of neglect had deepened over the past quarter-moon. The air was stagnant, and the dust inside had settled more deeply. A new cobweb hung in the entry arch, and the clear trail inside the doorway, where the priestess had walked, was covered with a thin coat of dust too.

"I think she's gone," Darna said. "There was a priestess here when I passed on the way back to Anamat, but she's gone now. It's abandoned." She shivered, as Myril often did when she skirted the edge of a trance, but everything she'd said had been quite ordinary. Thorat and Eppie hadn't heard her - they'd gone to get a drink from the waterspout.

"You're here," Thorat said, coming back to the porch. "We could try to summon Salara."

She looked at him, into his eyes. She knew what he was suggesting. She hadn't thought that he would ever be the one to say it, to propose making the rite with her. It was only because Iola wasn't there, or because Iola couldn't. He still didn't want to do this, not really, and she didn't want to draw him in that way either. She'd always wanted to before, ever since she'd first met him, when she barely knew what she was desiring. This was different. Now she didn't want him any more than he'd ever wanted her. Even though she knew it wasn't supposed to matter, she felt in her aching bones that it simply wouldn't work.

"No," she said. "I won't make the rite in this temple unless it's with the prince of Slaradun. If anyone can summon Salara, it's him." Not that he would *want* to summon Salara. She wasn't even sure that she did. After all, it would probably kill him. The thought turned her stomach.

"I don't know if I can do this," she said.

"You can." Eppie clapped her on the shoulder.

Darna shook her head. "Meeting the dragon... It could destroy him."

"It might not, though?" Thorat asked.

"I really don't know," Darna said, "but I can't think of what else to do."

"Well," Eppie said. "You can hardly use him to summon Salara if you can't get your hands on the prince." She looked down the hill, into the thick of the greening forest. "We'd better go find him, then, hadn't we?"

§

"You're sure you don't want to?" Thorat asked, after Eppie had left on her scouting expedition. The two of them were making camp.

"I'm sure," Darna said. "You don't really want to either; you just think that you should."

Thorat looked at her oddly and shook his head. "Why do you think that this dragon-hating prince can summon Salara better than I can?"

"He's not dragon-blind, and he's seen her – him – before. Besides, it's what feels right."

"You sound so much like Myril today," he said. "Usually, it's hard for me to believe you're a priestess, but not now."

"It's hard for me to believe it, too, and it's certainly not how I've thought of myself," Darna said. She walked over to the porch and ran her hand along one of the columns there, pushing away the dark leaves of the vine. "Look at this," she said, pointing out a carving of leaves. They were so well carved, so natural that the real leaves beside them looked like pale imitations of that ancient art. "It's beautiful work. We don't have anything better in Anamat, not outside Ara's Landing. Only little bits inside it are as good as this. Strange, that Slaradun would have such fine stonework, hidden away in these mountains."

Thorat came over to look. "It's nice, but I don't know anything about stone carving. Do you think it's very old?"

Darna nodded. "Maybe from the time of Ara and Enat. If there were anything older, I would think this could be it, but they were the first."

"They hadn't built a city in Enat's lifetime," Thorat pointed out. Even he knew that much history.

"I don't know," Darna said. "This temple's been here a long time, anyway." She didn't want to think too much about the past, though. "It's been here long enough that it's not going to fall down tonight. Let's make camp on the porch."

Thorat walked a small circle through the woods around the temple, returning with a few very early berries and a handful of firewood. While he laid the fire and searched for more tinder, Darna went inside. She found no signs that the priestess planned to return. The room where she'd slept and made the rite – if she'd done that much – was bare except for a tattered mattress ripped open at the side. She hadn't even left a robe behind. Darna found a needle and thread in her pack and sewed the mattress back together, then had Thorat drag it out to the porch. They might as well be comfortable for their last few nights, and the mattress was wide enough for all three of them together. She wondered how long she would have to wait for the prince to come, and if he would come to her at all. Alone, thinking about it, she couldn't imagine how she might be able to lure him there from so far away. She wasn't ready to go back to the keep. Even if the Tiadun men were still safely jailed, which she wasn't at all sure they would be, word of the price on her head had probably spread.

Darna leaned back against the porch wall and looked out at the purple-and-orange sunset sky through the trees. When it was dark, she went to sit beside the crackling fire with Thorat. They listened for sounds of Eppie's return. For a long while, they heard only birds.

"Hey!" Eppie appeared at the edge of the clearing, behind the waterspout. "You didn't hear me coming, did you?"

"No, I didn't," Thorat said. He sounded as if he'd been as far off in reverie as Darna had been. "You've gotten good at that, going silently."

"I didn't hear you either," Darna said. "What did you find?"

Eppie sauntered over to the fireside, taking a piece of hard bread out of the bag on her way. She sat down, tore off a bite, and reached for a cup of water before she reported.

"There's a village straight downhill from here," she said. "It's pretty small, not much to look at. About a dozen...no, closer to two dozen houses, but they're all small except for two of them on the market square."

"Two large houses?" Darna said. "Most villages in Slaradun just have one large one for the chieftain."

"It was probably like that until not long ago. One of them looks really new, like someone decided they needed a tavern all of a sudden."

Thorat leaned forward to stir the fire. "Go on," he said.

"Well, instead of going in, because it's an awful small place and I don't know where the next village is, I went on another scout-around, keeping to the edge of the forest. Sure enough, down the road a little way, there was a new clearing with some lean-tos and a couple of men standing around, grumbling at each other about something."

"Couldn't you hear them?" Thorat said.

Eppie shook her head and pushed the hair out of her face. "I could hear them all right, just couldn't understand them. I think they were Ganateans."

"Just Ganateans? No local men?" Darna asked. That wasn't good.

"As far as I could see. I hung around for a bit, but then it was getting dark, so I started to head uphill, thinking I'd head back to this place, but then..." Eppie looked off into the distance, eyes sparking in the firelight. "So, they had this trail, and I thought it was heading this way, but then I got up it a ways and thought it was off the mark a bit. I've got a pretty good sense of direction, but before I went off into the woods, I thought I'd see where the trail went."

She stopped and looked down at her hands, then she went on in a whisper. "It was the gate. It led right to the gate. I had no idea what I was going to see there. It wasn't like Tiada's gate at all; it was huge, big enough for a dragon to go in and out of easily, and it was open and glowing in the dark. I don't think you'd see the glow in daytime, it was faint and sort of greenish, but it was beautiful in its way." She sighed. "I stayed there for a while, then it seemed like the light was fading and I thought I'd better get back here, so here I am. There's a trail from there to here. I fell off it a couple of times, but in the morning, we'll have no trouble following it."

"So, no looking for little plants this time?" Thorat asked.

Eppie shook her head. "No, not this time. They know the way straight to it. I can't see any way we could stop them." She looked to Darna. "Not unless you can come up with something."

"I'll try," Darna said. "I don't know what I can do either, but I'll try."

§

Darna woke to the light of the sun coming up over the mountains and the sound of Eppie snoring beside her. Thorat was across the clearing, blowing on a small fire to get it started.

"Is that a good idea?" Darna asked. "Won't they see the smoke?"

"Good morning to you, too." Thorat's eyes were drooping, as if he hadn't slept at all.

She got up and went over to stand beside him. "Did you keep watch all night?"

Thorat shook his head. "No, but I woke up before dawn and had another look around. Eppie's right; the gate's wide open."

Roused by the sound of her name, Eppie broke off her snoring and yawned. "Of course I'm right," she said sleepily. "Do we have tea?"

"In a minute," Thorat said. "You're supposed to be the apprentice here."

"Stop bickering," Darna said. She could hear how tired they both felt. Oddly, she felt as well as she had in ages, as if sleeping on the temple porch had somehow restored her. "I'd like to go see this gate too."

"We'll come with you," Thorat said.

"No," Darna said, a little surprised at the conviction in her response. "I'll go alone. I may not be as quiet in the woods as Eppie is, but the men from the keep will be loud enough that they won't catch me by surprise if I do cross their path, which I probably won't. You two find out what's happening with those Ganateans and in the village. We can meet back here at midday."

Thorat seemed as if he was about to say something in protest, to take command of the situation, but then just nodded. "We'll do that, then."

The trail behind the waterspout was as clear as anything, just as Eppie had said it would be. It wove between the tall trees in a steady flow, the underbrush parting around it as if it were a stream. Its ground was well enough trodden to provide good footing for Darna's stick. A few spring flowers bloomed here and there in the undergrowth, common yellow dandelions and bluets, nothing to particularly point the way to the dragon unless it was the dark herb on the south side of some of the evergreens. It didn't look like much, but Darna didn't think she'd seen a plant like it in Anamat or in Tiadun. She wasn't sure, though; she'd never paid much attention to herbs, not like Myril. She wished she could tell Myril that they'd made it this far.

After a little while, Darna sensed a change. It was nothing visible, more like the sense that had always led her into the hidden ways of Anamat, but louder. The hidden ways were lightly traced by dragonlets' paths, echoes of dragon energy coursing through the town, but this feeling was more like a slow flood, quiet but deeper and stronger. It tugged like a river under her feet, drawing her on toward the gate. The place must have been obvious to anyone with a trace of dragonsight, any feeling for the dragons at all. How had it ever become secret or been considered a hidden place when she could sense it so clearly?

Abruptly, the flow of energy stopped, leaving Darna on an ordinary path again with only paving stones to mark the way. The trees loomed overhead, indifferent to her presence. That dark leafy plant she'd noticed now grew on all sides of the tree trunks rather than pointing in one direction. The air felt warmer – not surprising, since it was late in the morning and even in cloudy Slaradun, the sun did rise. What was surprising was the suddenness of the change, coming on all at once as the feeling of the current beneath her feet disappeared, leaving her in its quiet eddies.

The only sounds were the breeze in the dark-boughed treetops and a distant trill of birdsong. Darna walked on along the narrow path. She pushed past a low bough of rhododendron and arrived.

The gate sparkled, it shone. It was unlike anything she'd ever seen and, despite Eppie's description, not at all what she'd expected. It was not hidden now, if it ever had been. The ground was rocky and bare, but with gems of the dragon lying all around among the ordinary rocks. They shone and pulsed with their own light as the sun bore down on them. They formed a path up into the hillside, into a great, open maw of glistening, toothy gems. It was brilliant even in the light of day, clearer than Anara's gate hidden inside that manmade tower on its distant islet. This was a full, open conduit between the chambered heart of the earth and its living skin, the surface of Theranis. It looked raw, as if it had recently exploded, had been blown open by a blast of heat and life. That blast would have consumed anything and anyone in its path, dragon-blessed or -cursed alike.

Darna wondered if the men of Ganat understood what they were doing at all. Standing in this place would spark their fear of the dragons, make it seem entirely reasonable and well-founded. Surely, they must understand that taking these gems would make their lives forfeit to Salara, who would come to defend his own, whether humans fought beside him or not. The pendant hanging from her neck burned hot between her breasts, so hot that Myril's packet of herbs began to steam.

She was so transfixed by the sight of the gate that she didn't see Ivanat coming until he had stepped into the clearing.

"You?" he said. "You're supposed to be in Anamat. It's not safe here."

With some effort, she pulled her gaze away from the dragon's gate. "Ivanat," she said. "My prince. It's not safe for you here, either."

"You don't need to warn me. I know the curse better than anyone." He hesitated where he stood, as if unsure that she was really there. He looked the same as he'd been before – after all, it had been less than a half-moon since she'd left his keep, but it felt like far longer, and she had not known that they would ever meet again. Darna stepped toward him, but he held up a both hands as if to hold her back. "The others are coming," he said. "They'll be here in a moment. You should go. The Tiadun men are still locked at the keep, but the others would know who you are now."

"I'm gone," she said, stepping back onto the shadowed path. "No one needs to know that I'm here. No one but you."

"Why did you return to me?" he asked.

Darna heard the clumsy crash of men behind him, making their way up the new-trampled path. "Meet me here at midnight," she said.

She left before he had the chance to answer, hurrying back into the cover of the forest, past the sticky, leathery leaves of the rhododendron into the empty gap until she reached the dragon's current again. It pulled her back toward the gate, but she waded against it all the way back to the yellow temple.

§

Chapter Fourteen

The joints between the stones were smooth, even after all this time, as perfect as a human hand could make them. Darna wondered what tales the temple could have told if it had a voice of its own, what memories had been lost with its priestesses, those who'd died long ago or the madwoman who'd left it only a few days before. She wandered around its perimeter. She'd never seen a place so well rooted to its site, not even Ara's Landing itself. It was ancient; it felt older than the oldest temples of Anamat city itself, but she had no way of being sure of its age. She wondered if the place was recorded at her guildhall. Surely it must be, but she'd never heard of it. Was this the place that Ara and Enat had fled to in the first generation of Theranis? Or had there been someone here before, to teach them the dragons' ways?

She didn't hear Thorat and Eppie returning, whether because they walked so quietly or because she was so deep in reverie. Apparently, they hadn't noticed her, either.

"I told you not to go in," Thorat was telling Eppie.

"How was I supposed to know he'd recognize me, or that he'd be there?"

"Who recognized you?" Darna said, coming around the corner of the temple.

"That boy, the prince's page," Eppie said with a sigh.

"Kinner?"

"That's the one," Eppie said. "It was almost two years ago, and we hardly said anything to each other; I only asked him where to find the privy."

Thorat sat down by their fire pit and started to break up twigs. "I did tell her to stay out of the village."

"We had to know what was happening somehow," Eppie said. "So, I went in and looked around."

Darna crouched beside the fire and helped Thorat tear up dry bits for tinder while Eppie paced.

"She did find out that they're set on mining, starting tomorrow or the next day, dependent on the weather," Thorat said.

Darna looked at the darkening sky. "It looks like rain, but then, it always does here in Slaradun."

Eppie gathered some larger branches from the edge of the woods and brought them to the fire. "He asked what I was doing here. He knew I didn't belong here. I said there was a merchant caravan I was traveling with over the mountains and then I got lost."

"Not much of a story."

"I *know*," Eppie said. "I didn't have time to think."

"And what did Kinner say? How was he?"

Eppie shrugged. "He looked just as nervous as I remember him from that night when we took the seal back, maybe worse. He said that he was there with the prince, but then he just stopped, like he didn't know what else to say."

"The Ganateans are more than he bargained for, I'd say," Thorat said. "There are dozens of them. A whole shipload of them, maybe a hundred. They seem to have their own ruler with them, and your prince of Slaradun only has a dozen men, plus the villagers. Even if you can sway him..."

"More must have come since I left," Darna said. "Do they look like a trade delegation?"

"If the Cereans in Tiadun were a trade delegation, then this is half an army," Thorat said. "Their leader has a lot of men at his command. With luck, and maybe a little landslide,

Eppie and I might be able to fend off a dozen of them, but not a hundred."

A hundred men. Darna wondered how many ships had come. She wished she hadn't built that breakwater. She hoped it would fall to the bottom of the bay rather than harbor these foreigners. She should have known that this would happen. She needed to see Ivanat again.

Eppie looked over her shoulder as if some spy from the Ganatean camp might have followed her up through the woods. "We're going to set their horses loose, and the donkeys, too," she said. "I don't know what else we can do."

"A few traps around the gate, maybe?" Thorat suggested.

"Something like that." Eppie looked glum.

The temple's vines seemed to be pulling it down; its silence felt like a reproach.

"Anyway, I'm hungry," Eppie said, breaking the lull. "We might as well eat while we can."

Darna hadn't thought of food, but now that Eppie mentioned it, she realized that she hadn't eaten much that morning. They trundled out most of the rest of their provisions from Anamat.

"We can buy more in one of the villages tomorrow, if we're still alive and if the Ganateans haven't eaten it all," Thorat said. "We might as well eat everything."

"Save a little," Darna said. "Let's not give up yet. One of us might yet walk away, and they'll have emptied the villages."

Thorat agreed that this was prudent, if overly optimistic, so they ate only enough to keep them going through the rest of the day.

"I'll go back in the night to see if there's anything I can do as a priestess."

"It's too dangerous," Thorat said.

"That's not for you to say," Darna said.

Thorat frowned at her. "We're supposed to keep the priestesses safe, too."

"The dragons first, though," Darna said. "Besides –"

"Don't pretend you're not a priestess."

Eppie elbowed him. "She's right, though; it's her choice, priestess or not. I know I wouldn't want to stay here sitting on my hands."

Darna wondered if she should thank Eppie for sending her into the dragon's mouth. Well, she was going to go anyway. They all were. She only hoped that Ivanat would come too, so that she could see him one more time before the end.

§

Clouds blanketed the sky, making the night warm and dark as a womb. Darna made her way to the gate, using her stick like a dowsing rod to feel the path and follow its course along the hillside. The dragon was under the earth; she could feel it in her bones. She was glad for her solitude, glad that she didn't have to find the words for what she knew. Instead, she simply let the current in the earth carry her up to the jagged mouth in the hill, into the teeth of the dragon's gate. There, she spread out her cloak and sat, taking one last sip of water before she settled down to wait.

Once upon a time, she'd been taught how to court a trance to open her mind to the thoughts of the dragons. She'd only gone through the motions then. Most priestesses couldn't trance, could see neither the future nor the other realm, at least not without clazan to push them along. Even the drug hadn't worked for her, back in the temple, but at this gate it might be different. She tried to remember those long-ago lessons, to apply them in earnest for the first time.

Her mind stayed stubbornly on the surface of the earth, but as she sat in the dark, alone in the path of the dragon, she listened to the world around her, quieting her own mind as well as she could. Eventually, she heard something like fish climbing up the mountain streams to spawn, yearning toward something they could scarcely remember. It was as indistinct as the voices of dragonlets, but it was something.

A light rain fell, too gentle to penetrate her thick wool cloak. It misted the edges of the clearing, shimmering in the ghostly light of the gate as it fell. With the stars clouded over, the gate had paled to scarcely more than a firefly's glow, its light extending only to the nearest of the trees. From time to time, the light would brighten, then fade again. Once, it flared so bright that Darna looked up, hoping that Ivanat had come, but he had not.

Time flowed by. It was some time late in the moonless dark of the night when he came at last. She stood to greet him, holding her hands out as in an invocation. He was the prince of the land. He had never been anointed by his priestesses, but he'd come to her at last.

"You are one," he said. "Hedrin told me, when I had him alone, that you'd been trained at the temple in Anamat. He doesn't understand my view on the matter. He thought that I'd been angry about his sacrilege, for violating a priestess."

"Never mind about that now. Salara is near," Darna said. When she looked at Ivanat, she could no longer hear the rushing current under the earth.

"I should have known you were a priestess. I should have sent you away before you made me remember the dragon."

Darna shook her head. "I couldn't have made you remember what you didn't know already."

"Still, I thought about it after you left, after I realized that you were the daughter of an anointed prince." He chuckled softly to himself. "I was recognized as my father's heir in Anamat, but by their rules, I'm not a prince either. I haven't been blessed by the priestesses. We're not supposed to rule except by your grace and the grace of the dragons."

A rushing sound welled up in her ears, like a waterfall, but then it faded again and she heard only the faint whir of insects in the night.

"Do you still fear the prophecy that Salara will destroy you?"

Ivanat looked over his shoulder, back toward the lowlands of his realm and the dreary keep above its poor little town.

"I don't know anymore; I only know that I must face it. It followed me across the seas; it dragged me back here to this wretched place. After this year and a half since I took up the throne, I find that I don't even belong there until a priestess spreads her legs for me. It's absurd, or maybe it isn't. Tell me, did you anoint me ruler of this land without my knowing it?"

"No, I never came to you as a priestess."

"You didn't tell me that you were of royal blood, at least as royal as my mewling bride."

"Has she come?"

Ivanat nodded. "It's too late now. The Ganateans want the stones before they pry her away from her nursemaid and let me join her."

"She's not so young as all that, is she?"

"She'd seen sixteen summers when I met her two years ago, but for all her years, she seems like a child, and a rather dull child at that. She's not stupid, just incurious. I can't desire her since I've known you, and even if I did, the Ganateans wanted to ensure that we were safe from the dragon's curses before the marriage rites, and I find that I'm glad of the delay. I don't even know that they plan to keep their end of the bargain anymore."

Darna could picture the girl in the keep, cow-eyed and lovely but dull and afraid. No sheltered girl like that could be a match for Ivanat.

She smiled a rueful smile. "You're not safe, not from the Ganateans and not from Salara. I heard how many of them there were. I don't think you expected that."

"No, but I should have. By the time Harzet saw their third ship, it was too late to turn them back. He's trying to see if they've broken their contract, but he doesn't have much hope for it, or that they'll respect the contract if it no longer suits their purposes."

"I'm sorry for that," Darna said. "Maybe I should have told you that I was a priestess, though I didn't consider myself one anymore. It was never what I wanted to be, and I was never very good at it. Now, though, I think that we should summon Salara. I can hear him. Do you want to meet him again?"

Ivanat looked at the cave mouth, brighter now but not so bright as to blot out all of the stars. He shone in its reflected light.

"I don't want to take my fear to the grave with me. If I don't face this prophecy, I'll have it following me forever. What if the dragon destroys me? At least I'll have tried to be the land's prince, which is what I thought I was doing all along."

"Shall we call Salara up, then?" Darna asked again. She took a step toward him and, after a moment's hesitation, he nodded and extended his arms to her.

"The ground is very rocky."

"I don't mind."

"You could marry me instead," Ivanat said.

"It's too late for that. Besides, I only ever wanted to be a guildswoman of Anamat. Now I have to be a priestess again instead."

They searched the ground for a smooth spot, but the only one was right in the mouth of the gate itself, a patch more sandy than rocky.

"Is this what you really want, to face Salara?" Darna asked. "You could still sail away with the Ganateans."

The earth trembled beneath her feet, just a little. If she hadn't been standing still, she wouldn't have noticed. Ivanat felt it, too.

"If I'd meant to sail away, I would have done it before I led them here. Maybe I would have taken you with me, to see the worlds across the seas."

"I'd have liked that, but maybe now we can see the heart of our own world, if I can play priestess to you after all."

With that, Darna shook off her cloak and stretched herself out in the pattern of the dance, feeling the long-unpracticed movements coming to life again. It felt wrong. She turned her back on Ivanat, turned to face the gate. She could feel Salara coming. She wouldn't even need to take Ivanat into the rite, the dragon was coming already, but if they did lie down together in Salara's name, at least the dragon would know him as the prince.

"You're bright," he said when she turned to face him again. "It's like you're on fire."

He was too, but she shushed him. The time for words was gone. She reached her mind out to the dragon, who was trembling and straining up through the earth beneath them. Her arms went out to feel the air around, the forest and the hills. Ivanat faced her, naked now, as she was. He reached toward her, let his hands come to rest on her shoulders.

As they touched, a current ran through them, like lightning, like dragonfire. It was already accomplished, but she drew him down to the ground and into her body to consecrate the bond, to cement him to the pulse of the dragon.

"Do they all – Have all the princes done this?"

Darna shook her head. "Not like this, I think. It's not the time for words."

The sand was warm beneath her back and he was like a fever in her. The dragon came, step on step and pulse on pulse, wings beating on a wind that blew out from the dragonways, over the earth and all the way up to the stars.

When she opened her eyes, Salara was there, coiling around them. *Go on*, the dragon seemed to say. *Go on and give us your life.* Whether Ivanat heard Salara or not, whether he understood or not, he did go on. Darna embraced and rocked the power of prince and dragon together while Salara circled above, snaking down ever closer.

Ivanat saw the dragon at the last moment, just as his offering spilled into her. It was complete, as complete as it could be. The newly anointed prince slumped onto her, his priestess. She *was* a priestess now, at least in this. She felt his weight on her like a blanket, but it did not come to rest. The dragon reached in, put one hot claw between them, and rolled the prince aside.

Ivanat startled awake and tried to escape but the dragon overwhelmed him, lifted him in a clawed grasp. The prince strained in a bewildered attempt to shake off the scaly force encircling him. He pushed and elbowed and reached for the sword that was not at his hip, then raised his empty fist to strike.

Salara stared him down, mesmerized him, hypnotized him. That, or the dragon became him. He went slack under the dragon's power, then Salara laid him down on the sand.

He was still alive – Darna could see the pulse in his neck and the rise and fall of his chest – but before she could reach him to wrap her arms around him for the last time, Salara's gaze was on her. A hot wind swirled around the dragon, breaking over her like a wave, searing her.

She did not so much hear the dragon as sense his intent.

Dance for me. I would take his place in your rite.

Darna shook herself. She did not feel like dancing. She wanted Ivanat.

You owe us your life.

She turned to the dragon. *And you owe me this prince.*

Perhaps. Dance.

So she did, and the power of the dragon flowed into her through the soles of her feet, animating her beyond anything she'd felt before. It was not like the dances she remembered from the temple. A music seemed to come from nowhere, from deep inside her childhood memories when Tiada had flown to her side and made her live instead of dying. She did owe the dragons her life, but she was not ready to lose it, not yet, no more than she was ready to lose Ivanat.

You must live for us, Salara said.

Darna missed Ivanat's touch, but the dragon was on her too soon to move back to the human realm.

Salara's wings made a tent around her, blocking out the world beyond his reach, until he was all she could see, all she could think. Salara burned into her with that power she'd once felt only as traces in the stone across his land, as weak, distant echoes. Here, now, the source of that power pressed down on her, sundering her from everything that was familiar. She reached into Salara as she had into her human lover. In that touch, the skin and scales between them fell away. She dreamed the dragon's dreams, she felt the land as he did, as her own body. She was the furrows in its soil, the roots of its trees, the feet and hooves tromping its roads, the waters lapping its shores. She felt the spine of the land, hard against her back, pulling away. Then she felt the land slough down around her like an old skin falling from a snake. She was bonded with the dragon as he took flight, filling her. They soared over the trees, through the cold clouds into the starlit night, into the heavens.

No one should fly with a dragon and live, she thought; *no wonder so many of the old ambassadresses had died.* Salara arched up like so many statues of dragons, but close and hot like the fire of a thousand suns. She was cool in the heat of it, like ice. She felt the dragon ripple around her like waves in the water, herself like a falling rock. She had no names for what the dragon did to her. It was a thing of a creature that can live a million years, a thing beyond her imagining, beyond her senses. It was as if she'd dissolved in its power and was no more.

When Salara cast her aside, she floated down like a feather through the air. She fell back into her body on the living earth, to the sandy, shimmering place where she'd lain before the dragon took her, when she was human. Ivanat was gone. The mountainside rocked her down into its hard embrace, and she knew no more.

§

A sound woke her, or maybe she was not awake. She could hear, but she could not feel. Her body was there; she could sense its presence, but it seemed far away. Nothing hurt. What was that sound? The snap of a twig? The breaking of a mind? The gate had gone dark and cold, becoming a mere cave in the hillside. Darna turned her head to look around, feeling stiff with cold, or was it only that her body and mind were so far apart? Dawn lit the clearing with the common light of the sun, dimmed by the ever-present clouds. The dragon stones did not glow now, but they still caught the morning light, as any common crystal would, a faint echo of what she'd seen in the night.

It should not have been possible to live through that, through the waves of Salara's power. Now she could hear, but she could not stand or move except to turn her head, as if she'd been remade from stone, a graven image of a fallen priestess, but oh, how she had fallen! She had fallen beyond the stars.

Another sound brought her back to the clearing before the gate. It was the clatter of armed men crashing through the underbrush, making their way clumsily up the path. She saw Ivanat, standing like a bonfire in the middle of the rocky clearing. She wanted to cry out to him, but her voice was as frozen as her limbs. He still glowed. Even from behind, she could see it, as if all the light of the dragon stones had gone into his body to animate it. He walked toward the edge of the clearing and picked up his sword. He was still naked, but the power of the dragon was like a cloth around him, translucent like Iola's veils, and more mesmerizing. Salara's strength fiowed through him, taking away all that was human except for his form and his voice.

The sound came again, much closer. Someone barked out a command in Ganatean, which must have been "Halt!" to judge by the way the clatter slowed and stilled, and the way one solitary set of footsteps came marching on, alone. Away on the other side, she heard someone else approach along the path from the temple. A fiash came from the trees, burnished metal among the dark boughs.

Darna tried again to move, and this time, her inert, rock-like arms shivered to life. Maybe the dragon's power had left her not quite empty. Perhaps she would have some strength if only she were not too dizzy to stand. She felt light, disoriented, and a disconcerting absence of pain. She felt as if she was fioating through the air. Was she alive? She wasn't sure. She reached for her cloak and pulled it up over her shoulders. Her skin felt strange too. Her tunic lay off to one side, scorched and shredded, its threads blowing away in the morning breeze. The edge of the forest seemed to have drawn farther away; the rocky clearing looked like a vast wasteland stretching between her and the shelter of the trees. It was so hard to move, hard to imagine ever leaving this place where a dragon had made its claim on her.

A shudder wracked her body and suddenly she felt able to move again, not like the creature of stone and earth she must have become in the dragon's arms...in his claws, under his wings, beneath his belly. Darna stood. Now the changes in the clearing around the gate seemed less significant. The only difference now was in Ivanat, who moved steadily toward the approaching men. He looked too different, too strangely powerful. She edged toward the path to the temple, keeping him in her sight.

She had almost reached the cover of the bushes when Harzet broke through from the end of the Ganateans' path. He might have seen her - she wasn't sure - but if he did, he ignored her. How could one see anything but Ivanat, striding forward with the light in his eyes and his sword at the ready?

"Friend, are you yourself?" Harzet asked him in Cerean.

The sound that Ivanat made was not a human sound. The Ganateans behind Harzet quailed. Some ran, but others recovered and edged closer.

Darna stepped into the shade, if she was indeed stepping. She scarcely felt her feet on the ground. Perhaps she was only a ghost, and her life, too, animated Ivanat. She willed him to speak, to tell them –

"Go! Down with you all! Down the mountain! Down to the depths of the sea you go!" He roared and lunged forward with a fierce, swift power. The Ganateans scattered before him.

Harzet stood his ground. He shouted after Ivanat. "Wake, damn you! You are possessed, cursed!" His voice cracked.

Ivanat turned. "I was awake once," he said, in Theranian. His eyes were not his own. They gyrated in their sockets, seeing nothing.

"Will you wake?" Harzet cried.

"I was awake." Ivanat swallowed, as if he were struggling with something far too big to pass his gullet.

After that, his words made no sense, not in Theranian or Cerean, not in Ganatean or Enomaean or in any language Darna had ever heard spoken. His voice, his words, the sounds of his anguished throat grew wilder and stranger. Once, his gaze lit on Harzet for a moment and Ivanat's arm whipped out like a flash of lightning, striking him down.

Harzet rose slowly from the ground, singing softly something that might have been a lullaby. Darna strained to hear the words, to understand what Harzet was saying as he drew the dagger from his belt.

"We had a pledge," Harzet said. "I never thought to carry it out. We made our minds king of our souls; we steadied our wit with knowledge. I told you, the curse of the dragons has broken many. We have that legend, you knew it, and yet you returned to face this danger when you could have run and lived a peaceful life."

Harzet circled, dagger in his hand. Ivanat shouted to the trees, to the skies, arms upraised. He ran circles around the clearing, indifferent to the sharp rocks beneath his bare and bleeding feet, raging up at the sky.

Harzet spoke again, more loudly. "We said our minds are our whole selves. You said it. You said, 'Should any power of the earth break my mind, break my body so my might will not serve the demons of the earth.' You pledged this, and I pledged to strike you down, I pledged it, you pledged it."

The dagger trembled in Harzet's grasp. Tears rolled down his cheeks as he watched Ivanat stumble across the rocks, still bright with Salara's light.

"Give me one answer more, one clear answer, and I can spare you. They're coming back." Darna could hear them too. Some of the armed men were almost at the end of the trail. Preternatural strength or no, there was only one of Ivanat, and there were dozens of the foreigners. She felt paralyzed, as if the rocks had become one with her again. She could not move. Ivanat careened past. She felt the heat of his body, the wind of his passing, but she could not reach out to him.

"One more clear answer, one more sane word," Harzet pleaded, still not seeing her. She must be a ghost, she thought.

Ivanat made a sound that was something like a laugh. His disordered limbs united for a moment and he burst forward, not into the forest, not toward Darna or toward Harzet, but straight into the mouth of the dragon's gate.

Salara rumbled; as the body of the land, he rumbled. Harzet's dagger fiew, sinking true between Ivanat's ribs as he ran through the dragon's gate. The earth rang like a bell.

Harzet turned then to face the men from the keep and the men from beyond the seas. They were at the edge of the forest, but they had stopped there, fear in their eyes, hesitant.

"Go away; you heard him!" Harzet said.

"We came for –"

Something yanked Darna away, breaking her out of her stony stillness. She didn't hear the rest. Strong, familiar arms circled her and tugged her back into the forest. It was Thorat, looking just as he always did but now with a sword in his hand. Its hilt glowed as the gate had shone. The amulet around her neck, still there through all the tumult, sparked back to it in answer, but now its heat did not burn her. After the dragon, nothing would ever burn her again.

"Get behind me," Thorat whispered. "Get back to the temple. You're wounded."

Darna looked down at herself, naked except for the cloak. She could see no wound except for long red lines on her belly. She could see herself, and Thorat had seen her. Perhaps she was not a ghost yet, but still she felt nothing until Thorat's hand settled on her arm, his soft grip stirring life back into her, animating her as the dragon had animated Ivanat's empty shell as he fell into the mouth of the dragons' realm, joining the deepest stream.

"Hurry," Thorat urged. "Get back."

With one last look over her shoulder, Darna picked up her feet and ran. She ran, ran through the trees like a hare, like a deer, like an unbroken child. She ran.

The earth rocked beneath her. She had left her stick behind, but she did not lose her balance. She ran as she had never run before until she reached the ancient, abandoned temple.

§

As Darna's feet bounced up the steps to the porch, she felt as if she was running into stillness. She slowed. The marble tiles beneath her feet were still, not rocking. She paused to look back out at Salara's land.

The earth was folding in on itself with inexorable gravity, as if Salara were pulling his land down with him, closer to his other realm. The treetops shook. Scree rolled down the mountainsides. Through gaps in the trees, she saw land rippling like the sea and waves cresting like hills. Small animals ran for higher ground as clouds massed out of nowhere and the rains began.

§

She dreamed, and in her dream Salara spoke in words she could understand at last, saying, "Go and avenge us; go and take back Tiada's land in our names."

Those were the words ringing in her head when she woke. She was inside the temple, just inside its front portal.

Someone had dragged the mattress in, and she'd collapsed onto it. A jug and an old loaf of bread stood on the porch outside, as if in offering. She stirred herself to reach them, her body still moving easily, as if it were gliding through bathwater, but the jug was solid in her hand and the bread smelled of yeast, salt, and grain.

Outside, the world was changed, the trees askew and broken, the wind too fresh. She could not bear to look at it yet, so she carried the jug of watered wine and the loaf of bread farther back into the still-dusty temple.

She passed the shrine room where the priestess had lived, going farther and deeper into the heart of the temple, finally reaching its baths. There, she stepped into the water. It would let her be born again after the thing she had felt in the night, after the visions and after the dreams. The dragon should have killed her, or the Ganateans, or even Hedrin of Tiadun. It all should have killed her, but it had killed Ivanat instead, only not quite by the dragon's will. If he'd run away from Slaradun, he would have died anyway; and maybe Harzet was right, maybe Ivanat would not have wished to live with his mind deranged. She wasn't sure. Sometimes, the dragon-touched woke up with their minds whole again, as surely as they'd been broken before, but Harzet couldn't have known that, and it was a rare, long chance to take. It was not Harzet's fault, but Darna wished that he had never set foot on Theranis's shores, had never met Ivanat.

As she floated on the water, the whole of the night and morning played out over and over again in her mind's eye. She had been touched by a dragon again. It had been a very long time since such a thing had happened to her, and maybe the Aralel had been right; maybe the dragons weren't done with her yet. In the end, she had not screamed in broken words as Ivanat had. She wondered if she could even speak anymore. Perhaps she was mad too.

It might have been late that afternoon when Ciffolga came, the tap of her feet sending ripples of sound through the water to Darna's submerged ears. She lifted her dripping head up and blinked the water out of her eyes.

"What are you doing here?" Ciffolga asked. Her words were barely audible through Darna's waterlogged ears, but she looked angry.

Darna blinked away the image of the dark-winged dragon taking her again and shook off the sound of Ivanat's screams in her head.

"I'm taking a bath," she said, stupidly. She could talk, after all.

"I can see that." Ciffolga's robes were just as ragged as they'd been in the village, but she carried a new cloak over her arm. "I meant, what are you doing in Slaradun? You were supposed to go back to Anamat to get your replacement, or don't you remember?"

"Is that what I told you?" Darna asked. "It doesn't matter anymore. It seems I had unfinished work here."

Ciffolga's lip twitched. "There's nothing left of your so-called work. The sea took it all."

"What?" Darna asked. She'd seen water through the trees, from the temple porch, but it had all been so far away, rocking wildly in the far distance like a half-felt dream.

"You'll see, or maybe you should just stay here until the next shake brings this place down on your head. It would serve you right. I'm going to sleep on the porch; it's safer there in case this place falls in."

Darna looked up at the ceiling, firm and high as it had been in the morning, and golden in the bright, west-slanting light. She hadn't felt anything. She wondered what these shakes were. The temple felt as still as a scrying pool.

"I'm going to Anamat," Ciffolga said. "Maybe you should come with me. What's that?" she pointed to Darna's amulet, still hanging from its golden chain, nestled between her breasts, and the drenched rag of Myril's charm bundle beside it.

"These were gifts," Darna said. "I'm not ready to go back to Anamat yet."

"Fine, then. You have until morning." Ciffolga looked at her as if she were as addled as Ivanat had been. Darna's heart ached at the thought of him. A wave of pain ricocheted through her body, sharp and sudden. It was gone as quickly as it had come, just like the priestess of Slaradun village.

Darna watched Ciffolga leave. She needed longer than just one night in this stillness. Her body wasn't ready, not for such a long march. She had to stay there a little longer in this yellow-marbled womb.

§

Chapter Fifteen

Ciffolga might have come back at dawn, but if she did, Darna slept through it. She dreamed of Salara and only Salara, wrapped around a bright orb and surrounded by the fire of a hundred other dragons. Salara strained up through the narrow passages of the earth, her body growing thinner, longer, until there was a change and it was *his* body and Salara was like Na, the wild dragon, shaking the mountains from their core.

When Darna did move, she was propelled only by her body's needs. She ate, drank, and lay down to sleep on a pile of old blankets. She didn't know how much time had passed when she woke, ate again, and slept once more. The sun rose and set. She heard only the song of the running water outside and the chirping of birds in the distance, the caw of a crow, the echoing rumble of the earth.

After some days, three or four, maybe more, maybe less, a hermit priestess appeared. She came into the room where Darna rested, scanning it for anything that might be carried away, nervous of the beams above her.

"Don't worry; they won't fall," Darna said.

The hermit priestess screamed and jumped back. Darna let out a little chuckle as the woman recovered from her fright.

"I didn't see you. I thought you were just a pile of rags there in the corner." The old priestess's voice shook; her hands trembled.

Darna draped one of the blankets over her bare shoulders and sat up. "No one's called me a pile of rags in years," she said.

"I didn't mean any insult by it," the hermit priestess said, still eying Darna warily. "What are you doing in here? It could have fallen down on you."

"Not this temple," Darna said. "It's been here for a very long time, maybe since before Ara and Enat came."

"Ara and Enat never came here," the hermit priestess said, quite sure of herself. "Even that fool girl who lives in the village knows that."

"Ciffolga?" Darna asked. "Is she still here?"

"She was never here. Maybe she's dead. It's under the sea now, that village."

Darna was fairly sure that she'd seen Ciffolga, but she didn't feel like flexing her voice to argue with the hermit priestess. She hadn't looked outside since that first day, but now she remembered what Ciffolga had said. "Did anyone survive?" she asked. Maybe the sea had taken the Ganateans with it, or at least some of them.

"This place could have fallen in on you," the old hermit priestess repeated. "Who are you?"

"I don't know," Darna said. "I *was* a master planner from Anamat, so I know buildings, and this one won't fall. I came to Slaradun to help lay the foundations for a new city."

"It's all water down there. Only two of the Ganatean boats survived out of the five of them. The keep is still sticking up out of the water; you can see it from the overlook."

Eppie and Thorat had been by the gate, well above the reach of the water. Salara would not have drowned them. She wondered if they'd survived their battle with the Ganateans, and if there'd been one. Then she thought of Kinner and his mother. Kinner had come with the prince on this ill-fated mission. Closer to the hills, he might have lived. Eppie said that she'd seen him, but his mother must have still been in the village. She hoped that he was well away, at least.

"What about the fishermen and their boats?" Darna asked.

"I saw some of the lowlanders swarming up to the higher villages while the Ganateans scurried down from the hills, trying to get back to their boats. Salara's curse was faster than their feet. It's on them now; they won't trouble us anymore."

"Is it a curse, though?" Darna wondered aloud. Maybe it was something simpler, like revenge, or a change of the dragons' seasons. The peace between dragonkind and humanity had always been a fragile thing. Building a harbor for the Ganateans had strained that peace, if wasn't already broken beyond repair. She'd drawn Salara and Ivanat together, but that was probably not enough to balance her account. Guilt pressed down on her chest, guilt and mourning.

"What else would it be?" the priestess was saying. "All this hillside coming down, half the houses down to rubble in the villages, only this place standing?" She shook her head at it all, then ran her hand over the wall, feeling for cracks. Seeming satisfied that it would stand a little longer, she turned to go but stopped at the doorway and spoke again.

"You'd best come with me. Those foreigners will be back if there are any left and if greed is what's driving them. I can't imagine it would be anything else that brought them here. You'll be safer in the hills, fallen priestess like you."

Darna didn't want to leave, but she could feel her body surge up at the invitation to move again, to return to life. She also didn't want to start her new life face to face with a row of Ganatean spears or worse. She stood, bringing her blanket with her.

"I did not fall," she said. "Salara put me back down."

The hermit priestess shook her head. "Dragon-touched. There's no place for you but the hills."

Darna didn't deny it. She looked down at her belly. The amulet still hung between her breasts on its gold chain, but its dark stone lay inert and cold against her skin. Myril's bundle of herbs had dissolved in the bath, leaving only a knotted string stuck to her skin. The bright red ridges left by the edges of Salara's scales still marked her, but their color was already fading. She could still feel them, though. She would always be able to feel them. What she couldn't feel was her old familiar pain as she stood and began to walk. Her body felt newly born, as strange to her as a new lover – not that she ever intended to have one of those again, not after the dragon.

§

Darna was glad that her leg still felt whole and strong as they climbed up into Na's peaks, that whatever Salara had healed in her seemed to be staying healed, at least for a while. They followed almost-invisible trails among the rocks. They weren't paths of the dragons but only human etchings, marked by subtle signs that the hermit priestess seemed to find along the way. At nightfall, they sighted the fires of the bandit camp. Darna's stomach knotted into a sudden cramp, so sharp that it stopped her in her tracks. She held it in and tried not to cry out.

"Hurry up," the old priestess said. It was the first time she'd spoken since they'd left the yellow temple behind.

"I can't," Darna panted. "Wait." She held her belly and looked down. It felt strange to have both hands free, with no stick tucked under her elbow. Even on the rocky ground with her belly doubling over on itself, she hadn't felt the need to lean on anything. It was eerie.

Soon enough, the pain passed. "I can go on now," she said.

The hermit priestess grunted and led her on until they reached the circle of firelight. Darna barged forward and took her place between two probably flea-ridden bandits, crouching to warm her hands at the fire. A spitted goat turned slowly over its flames.

"What happened?" she asked.

"That goat fell down the mountain, broke its neck," one of the bandits said. "This is the third one we've roasted in as many days."

Darna nodded, but the old priestess who'd brought her to this place waved her back before she could speak again.

"Don't mind this one," she said. "She's dragon-touched. Thinks that yellow temple is older than Ara and Enat." She cackled at the absurdity of the idea, but no one joined her laughter.

"Who's to say it isn't?" one of them said.

"There was nothing here before Ara and Enat," the old priestess said.

"I haven't read the first chronicles," Darna said. "I don't know that."

"Have you?" one of the older men asked the priestess.

"I don't need to, to know what everyone knows."

"She doesn't sound dragon-touched to me," said one of the other old women. "Is the yellow temple still standing?"

"It is," Darna said. "It will probably outlast everyone here, dragon-touched or not." She looked around the circle slowly. There were three ancient women, including the one who'd brought her there, and about a dozen men, most of them older than she was but none as old as the women. The women were all probably old priestesses, hermits retired to the hills.

"Did the Grandmother from Ara's Landing come up here?" she asked.

"We got word that she died," one of the other two priestesses said. "She would have died here, too, but maybe not as soon. Unwholesome living down there, I say."

Darna took a deep breath. "Were any of you at Salara's gate when it fell?" she asked.

Everyone stilled. The looks of casual curiosity turned guarded.

"You weren't there," one of the men said. "I would have seen you. How did you know it fell?"

"I just knew." Darna ran her hand over the ridges on her belly. It cramped again a little, but not as badly as before. The bandits must have gone there later, after she'd run.

"It fell, all right," one of the other men said. "Crashed in on itself just as sure as it gaped wide open at Midwinter when we were wondering if it was broken, dead, and gone. Salara crashed it down on those Ganateans; she crushed them, or at least some of them. There were others who tried to get away. I saw two strangers with swords. Never saw them before. They went after some of the foreigners who ran. They were fighting against the prince's men when I left. The other Ganateans came up quick enough and we had our own losses. Bad business, all of it. Salara and her land gone."

"His land," Darna corrected. "And not quite all of it. He still has the hills, doesn't he?"

"See, she knows about the change," one of the old priestesses said.

The one who'd brought her there grunted, unimpressed. "I might have told her that, and I'm still not convinced. How can Salara be male? A realm dragon must be female."

Darna had other things on her mind. "The two strangers with swords - were they a man, about my age, and a young woman?" she asked.

"A man and a youth. The youth could have been a girl."

"Did they survive?"

"They were still fighting when we left," one of the bandits said, as if to say that they probably hadn't survived.

Darna pulled her knees up to her chest, staring at the fire as juices dripped from the spitted goat onto the smoky fire. One of the bandits cut a piece from a leg and declared it done. She discovered that she was hungry, famished. Other bandits produced a long plank and more knives to carve the unfortunate goat.

The bandit beside Darna remained sitting. "You dragon-touched or not?" he asked.

"Touched," she said. "Most definitely dragon-touched, but I don't know if I'm mad or not." While the others were occupied with the meat, she turned to ask him one more question. "Who survived in Slaradun?"

"Maybe half of the foreigners did. We came too late to drive them all back – there were too many of them – and we saw signs of some of them on the Anamat road."

"And the prince?" She'd seen it with her own eyes, but she didn't trust the memory.

The bandit spat. "Gone to his cursed grave. He was raving like one dragon-struck, then that Cerean came. Dead before the fight was on, both of them."

Darna had seen Ivanat struck down, but the bandit hadn't seen her. Maybe she'd been invisible after all, even though Thorat had seen her.

The bandit smiled a little, not a cheerful smile. "I got the Cerean myself, with an arrow."

Darna was barely listening. Harzet had killed him, who was his friend, whom he trusted more than anyone. They had been human together, too, not just whatever they were to the dragon.

"Harzet was his closest friend," Darna said aloud after a little while. "I didn't like Harzet, and he didn't like me, but they trusted each other. He was my lover."

"The Cerean?" the bandit asked.

"No, the prince. But that's done now; it's all done. Blast that Cerean to their own hells."

The bandit handed her a piece of bread and then got up, leaving her to stare into the fire until it died away to glowing coals.

§

A shout woke her, sometime around dawn. The light was misty and orange, unsettled.

The shout came again. "Stranger!"

Darna brushed the ashes and dust from her face. She looked to where the bandit was pointing, up on the hillside. A slender figure limped down, carrying two swords across her back, two good, familiar swords.

"Eppie!" Darna called.

"You know that youth?" one of the bandits said.

"One of the two from the gate?" Darna said, keeping her eyes on Eppie. "The other one..." She hurried to meet Eppie, feeling a little discomfited to notice that she still had nothing to wear except the old temple blanket and the pendant Ivanat had given her. Eppie appeared to be wounded.

The bandits were close at her heels. She wished she could talk to Eppie alone.

"Where's Thorat? Are you all right?" she asked.

"You're naked," Eppie remarked. "I'm walking, at least. Thorat's down the hill, still pretty close to the old gate, by a spring there. He got a bad cut and he was bleeding a lot, but the fever's past and he says he wants to go back to Anamat, or at least to the Eye." The Eye of Na was the lake halfway across the mountains between Anamat and Slaradun. It wouldn't be far away.

"You nursed him these past days? How many has it been?"

Eppie shrugged. "About five days, I think. I just gave him water when he could take it." Her voice sounded dismissive, but her face was gray with fatigue, her eyes haunted.

"Come to the fire," Darna said.

"It's not yours to offer," one of the bandits interjected.

Darna would have apologized, but Eppie waved her aside and spoke to the bandits first. "You know Vigda's band, from the south?" she said. Some of the bandits nodded. Eppie stood up taller, taking on an air of command that Darna wouldn't have guessed she could conjure. "We are Forlan's sword-companions. My friend is wounded by the gate, or what used to be the gate. Bring him back here. We will stay until he is well enough to walk again." She cast an appraising glance at Darna before she went on. "Then we will go with you to the meeting of the swords."

"Very well, sword maiden," one of the men said. "Show us the way."

Eppie hesitated. Her air of command fell away as quickly as a priestess's shawl. "Could I, uh, have something to eat first?" she asked.

The bandits led her back to the fire. She smiled shyly at Darna. "I thought for sure you were dead," she said. "There were Ganateans crawling all over those hills. I thought they'd be sure to hunt you down."

"I don't think they knew who I was, or even that I was there. Harzet did, but –"

"Who's Harzet?" Eppie asked.

"He was the prince's best friend. The one who killed him, saying that was what they had pledged to each other. I don't know if he'd have wanted that in the end, though. He was mad with dragonfire." Ivanat had been glorious. Dragon-touched and completely mad, but glorious.

"I'm sorry." Eppie patted Darna awkwardly on the back. "Are *you* all right?"

"I can walk without my stick now, but I don't feel quite right. Maybe I never will."

"You look better than you have in ages, but you need clothes. I wish I'd found your stick; I could have used it on the way up here. Maybe Salara gave me your limp."

"I don't think so," Darna said. "In any case, he's gone under the hills. We won't find him again on the surface of the earth, not in this lifetime."

One of the bandits stepped in front of Darna. "Say that again."

Darna thought back over what she'd just said, an utterance that had come from some wordless place within her. "Salara is gone down to the chambered earth," she said. "He won't return, not in our lifetimes, maybe never."

"How do you know that?" one of the other bandits demanded.

"I have no idea," Darna said. "Absolutely no idea."

No wonder Myril hated seeing the future.

§

It took Eppie and the bandits all day and half of the night to bring Thorat back to camp. They came in at midnight, under the light of the moon. Thorat was groaning with pain and his fever had come back, but the next morning he was better, and a quarter-moon later, he was almost well. There was an easy routine to life in the bandit camp. In between Darna's cramps, she found it restful, even pleasant. Bandit life wasn't so bad, but something was happening in her body, and it wasn't over yet. She would have to go back to Anamat, to find Gallia and go to the tribunal, to take Calar off the throne of Tiadun if he didn't kill her first. She had no idea how she would be able to avoid his assassins, before or after the tribunal.

She also needed to see Myril. If anyone could understand these strange pains, or her equally strange healing, it would be Myril. The city called to her like the moon moved the ocean tides, but she wasn't ready to go alone, not with the price still on her head. Hedrin and his men might be drowned, locked in the keep, but in the rising water, the servants would probably have released them. Even if none had survived, word had probably gotten out somehow. Hedrin himself might still be out there, along with the others hunting her, and now he knew what she looked like, that she'd survived his first attack, and probably that she'd fled back to Anamat long before Slaradun fell.

It was less than a moon before Midsummer when the bandits, along with Darna, Eppie, and Thorat, set out for what they kept calling the meeting of swords, near the Eye of Na. Thorat had recovered from his wounds well enough to make the half-day's walk, but he walked at the tail end, with two bandit men to carry him if he collapsed. Darna had overheard several mumbled conversations about this meeting of the swords, and whether or not Thorat would be able to join in, with his wounds, but Thorat insisted that he would. They still wouldn't tell her who was meeting or why.

The bandits stretched out in a long line along the track, dipping in and out of valleys where the rocks became too steep. One of the old women led the way. Darna walked in the middle of the procession, beside Eppie. She'd grown since their first meeting two years before, not so much in size as in presence. She didn't look like a scrappling anymore. Her body had settled into itself, losing its awkwardness, but she still seemed untested in some vital way. If she'd ever been broken, she hid it very well.

The trail wound through a narrow gap between the rocks and the two of them walked alone for a time with no one to overhear.

Darna chuckled. "If we weren't walking with a pack of bandits, this would be where they'd ambush us," she said, looking at the nice flat place on top of the gap. Even she could stage an ambush from that vantage point, now that her leg was strong.

Eppie eyed it, too. "I'd take the left-hand side, though."

"Why?"

"It's narrower; they wouldn't be able to get up behind you at all." Eppie slowed as they passed under its shadow. "Was it worth it, becoming a priestess?" she asked Darna suddenly.

"I don't know. You never wanted to, did you?"

Eppie shook her head.

"I didn't really want to either," Darna said, "but they dragged me in when I was half-drowned and couldn't object. Even then, I was running from Tiadun."

They crossed a patch of alpine meadow next, and their fellow travelers were still out of earshot.

"Being a priestess never meant much to me until I was at Salara's gate, but then it meant everything." There it was; she'd said it. She'd been a priestess that one time and that was all that really mattered.

"It's different at the gates," Eppie said.

"It must mean something in the lowlands, too, I just never saw the purpose there, not for myself. If I'd ever thought I would be a keep mistress, then maybe I would have paid more attention to some things they tried to teach us."

"A keep mistress?" Eppie said. "They're not priestesses, are they?"

"Most have been, since the beginning, but they change their robes and stop taking other petitioners when they ally with a prince. Half of the keep mistresses in Theranis trained at Ara's Landing, even now that it's going out of fashion. Priestesses aren't awed or cowed by the princes, or at least that's the idea. The dragons eclipse all the princes' claims on the land, and the keep mistresses are supposed to remind them of that." Darna looked back at the trail. The bandits were still far behind.

Since Slaradun's fall into the sea, they'd heard many tales of men and women struggling to keep their heads above water, of flocks being swept out to sea, and of others who'd survived by running to the top of low hills that had become small islands. In makeshift rafts, they'd flooded to the hills, and the bandits had shunted them all across the mountains to Anamat. Darna hadn't gone back to see for herself. She'd felt it in her bones, and glimpsed it that day from the temple porch. That had been more than enough. Her marks from the dragon burned every time she thought of it. "I wonder if the dragons will ever come again," she mused.

Eppie shivered. "They'll come, all right, but not in peace, I think."

Darna slapped her. Not Eppie. She didn't need that fog of prophecy on her.

Eppie slitted her eyes. "What was that for?"

"Don't go seeing the future if you can help it," Darna said. Then a stabbing pain hit her in the side and she grabbed Eppie's arm for support. It passed quickly, then she took a few deep breaths before the bandits behind them caught up.

"I need to go to Anamat, to see the healers about this pain," Darna said.

"Will you stay for the meeting of the swords?" Eppie asked.

"I'm not supposed to, am I?" Darna asked. She'd gotten the impression that whatever the bandits were talking about was supposed to be a secret from lowlanders, even lowland priestesses.

Eppie shrugged. "You should probably stay. I'll ask Sovara."

"The Enatel? She'll be there?"

Eppie nodded. She lowered her voice. "It's a sort of a reunion," she said. "I don't know if the bandits can ever keep peace among themselves, but they're on the side of the dragons, mostly. We need their help."

"They've certainly helped take care of Thorat, but it's hard to think of the bandits that way. I can see that the bandits think worse of the lowlanders than the other way around."

Behind her, one of the bandits grunted. "Precious few of your priestesses can see the free dragon."

"I haven't seen Na," Darna admitted, "but I have seen Salara, and he's seen me."

"More than most can say," the bandit said. "More than most can say."

§

The bandit trail led over a low ridge, with a sweeping view over the blue lake. It really did look like an eye, Darna thought, darker at the center as if some underwater mountain almost touched its surface. She was so transfixed by the lake that she almost didn't notice the turn in the path.

Eppie nudged her. "We're going this way." She pointed at the line of fur-clad bandits ahead of them, turning down a groove in the mountainside, a hidden track. It led to a pass so narrow that they had to edge through it sideways for a distance about equivalent to the width of a typical Anamat house. It was still like a trough after that, but they could walk normally. If there'd been any place to stand above it, they could easily have been trapped there.

The bandit behind Darna must have noticed her looking up. "Don't worry," he said. "It shouldn't fall in, and there's no chance of ambush with all of our allies coming in, keeping watch."

"All of them?" Darna asked.

The second bandit behind her chuckled. "Well, we hope they're all allies, but we know for sure they're not valley men or foreigners."

"Some valley men," Eppie said.

"Thorat and his sword-companions are honorary bandits for now."

Eppie smirked at Darna. "I don't think they'd have liked to hear that before Tiadun."

The walls of the canyon grew wider as they walked on. Darna found herself breathing more easily, and then they reached their destination.

The valley was ringed with rock cliffs higher than any Darna had seen before, except for on a very short stretch of coast to the immediate south of Tiadun Keep. It would be shaded except for a few hours in the middle of the day. A waterfall tumbled over a shorter section of cliff, and a deep pool at its base ran into a frothing stream that spiraled away into a gap between stones, into some underground waterway. Most of the valley floor was covered with low shrubs and tufted grasses, but the bandits had hacked away at that, making level areas on which to set up tents.

There were so many tents that it looked like a town of them. Most of the tents were like the ones the bandits had, rough-cut poles overlaid with furs, but a trio of cloth tents stood to one side, tents just like the ones the princes brought to their Midwinter tournaments. The resemblance to the Midwinter tournaments didn't end there, Darna realized as they made their way down to the relatively level valley floor. There was going to be a tournament field. Several people stood at the center of the valley, talking and gesticulating, pointing to one place then another, moving some stones, then arguing some more. She could see what they were trying to do, but apparently they couldn't agree on the precise dimensions.

"I think I'll go see what's going on," Darna said.

"I'd better go see if the Enatel's here yet," Eppie said quietly. "Meet me there as soon as you can."

The bandits they'd arrived with were depositing their packs in an as-yet-uncleared section of the valley, then scattering to greet the ones who'd already arrived. The old priestess who'd found Darna in the temple hurried over to her – she'd been near the front of their group.

"Don't get involved in that," she said, indicating the argument at the center of the valley. "You don't want to cross swords with Larn; I can tell you that much."

"I don't have a sword to cross with anyone," Darna pointed out.

"Don't say I didn't warn you."

Rather than going away, the old priestess tagged along at Darna's elbow, shaking her head as Darna approached the nearest of the men in the field, a tall, sturdy-looking fellow with a grizzled beard.

"Where's the cornerstone?" Darna asked.

"Over there for now," the man said. "We haven't really settled it. Whose band are you with?"

"None," Darna said.

"She's with me," the old priestess said.

"I'm a lowland priestess," Darna said, "and a full initiate of the planners' guild. I could set that stone for you."

"You fighting in the tournaments?" the man asked.

"Hardly," Darna said. "I've never even swung a sword."

"Good, then, a neutral," the man said. He raised his hand and shouted to the others. "Ho, Vigda. Here's one who can set it."

Vigda, a female bandit or a hermit priestess, crossed the field to meet them.

"Don't mind this one," said the old priestess who'd found Darna. "She's dragon-touched."

"What's your name, lowlander?" Vigda asked, ignoring the other old priestess.

"Darna, member of the Guild of Planners and formerly a priestess of Ara's Landing."

"Ara's Landing, is it?" Vigda spat on the ground, but then she looked up at Darna and smiled broadly. "I'm glad to see they haven't killed you yet." She turned away, avoiding the question Darna wanted to ask. "Come on, let's set this cornerstone."

§

Clearing and measuring out the tournament field took most of the rest of the afternoon and a great deal more argument. As the sky above grew dark, Eppie came down to call her up to the cloth tents. "It's been decided that you'll stay with us, since Sunna, Thorat, and Garren will all vouch for you," she said to Darna. "Her Grace wants a report from you."

"You'd better go, then," Vigda said, shooing her away.

"Who's Garren?" Darna asked.

"You know him; he runs that sweet shop in the West Gate market."

"The one with the nut pies?"

Eppie nodded and hurried her along. "He brought some with him, too."

Darna's mouth began to salivate at the thought. "I think I'm hungry," she said.

"Me too."

As they reached the tents, Darna glanced back to find that Vigda was still looking after her. The big bandit named Larn had come to stand beside her, placing a comforting arm over her aged-but-strong shoulders.

"There you are. Ouch!" Thorat said as Eppie opened the fiap of the largest tent.

The mountain air was fresh and clear, but inside the hot, crowded tent, the steaming tea and sticky cakes more than made up for the smell of bodies crowded close. Thorat was there, wincing as Sunna tightened his bandages, along with the Enatel, Garren the sweetmeats baker, Raina from the Gone Duck Inn, and a few men Darna didn't know but had seen around Anamat.

The Enatel rose. "I hear you called up Salara," she said to Darna.

Darna shook her head. "It could be said that the prince called him up, or that he came on his own. I only played a small part."

"A very significant part," Garren said.

Thorat pulled away from Sunna. "I don't think that Eppie and I would have made it through alive if you hadn't been there to bring Salara to the surface first."

"Here, have some tea," Sunna said, pressing a cup into Darna's hand.

"Let's sit," the Enatel said. They all found placcs in the circle, knees and shoulders touching. It was cramped, but Darna felt safe, even comfortable. "Now tell us what happened at the fall of Slaradun."

Darna looked to Thorat to begin, but he shook his head. "You were there at the beginning."

"Was I invisible?" Darna asked. "The bandits who came down to help you say that they didn't see me."

"I saw you," Eppie said, "but you were kind of thin and bright."

"Not like Ivanat was, was I?" Darna asked, then she had to explain who Ivanat was.

"No," Thorat said. "Everyone could see him. Maybe only Eppie and I could see you."

Darna took a deep breath and explained what had happened after she'd woken up at dawn. As comfortable as she felt with the assembled Defenders, she wasn't quite ready to tell how the rite had been with a dragon in attendance, and what had happened with the dragon. She might tell Myril or Iola later, then maybe Sunna or the Aralel, if she had to.

"I think the ground was shaking when Thorat came and sent me back to the temple. After that, I don't know what happened. You go on," she said to Thorat and Eppie.

Thorat and Eppie looked at each other.

"The prince ran into the gate and he died there," Thorat said. "An arrow hit the Cerean, the one who'd knifed the prince, but then he ran away."

"One of the bandits said he'd killed the Cerean," Darna added.

"Knocked him out for a bit, that's all," Eppie said. "The Ganateans were just reaching the gate when the ground started to shake more – before that, it had only been tremors. We had the higher ground and the gate at our backs, so we fell on them."

"There were about a dozen in the first wave," Thorat said. "We wounded a few of them and killed two, but when the second group came, they just ran right around us and into the cave, where they started filling sacks with the loose dragon stones. The ground was still shaking, and they were having a hard time of it, but it wasn't until they started in with their pickaxes that the gate really fell down. I don't know what happened after that."

"Thorat fainted," Eppie said. "He'd already lost a lot of blood. I dragged him away from the gate and got in one or two more stabs, but they were more interested in the stones, or in escaping with their lives, than they were in chasing after us."

"What about the bandits?" Darna asked.

Eppie shook her head. "They weren't in front of the gate. They stayed above it, shooting off arrows from behind trees. It didn't do much good."

"It didn't matter, anyway," Thorat said. "I woke up when Eppie was dragging me away. We saw them running back down to their camp. They didn't see the sea rising until later, I think."

The Enatel turned to Darna again. "What about Salara? Do you think the other realm dragons will shake off their princes?"

Darna shook her head. "As Ivanat pointed out to me, he was never anointed prince by the priestesses, so the dragons might not have recognized him as the prince. It was a land without a ruler, in a way, and the priestesses were all but gone. Salara was starved and changed –" A cramp hit Darna, but the others waited in silence for her to recover. "Tiada went silently into the deepest stream; that's what I hear. This was Salara claiming his land for the other realm. I can't say what will happen with the other dragons."

"The land isn't steady," Sunna said. "I heard about quakes and buildings falling in other provinces in the days after Slaradun fell."

"But Tiadun stands," the Enatel said.

"It stands empty," Eppie said.

The others looked at her as if she'd spoken out of turn.

"Sorry," Eppie said.

"Even so," Darna said. "I don't want to see it in the hands of the Cereans. I need to challenge Calar."

"We'll be your men-at-arms," the Enatel said. "I'll send you back to the city with Sunna and Raina, and the rest of us will be there soon."

Sunna nodded. "We'll get Tiadun back."

"In the name of the dragons, even if they're not there to see it," Darna said.

§

Three days later, Darna left the bandits and most of the Defenders in that quiet mountain valley, untouched by the tremors rippling over the provinces. They'd fought and trained and shared sword-fighting tricks, and they'd let Darna watch because she so clearly couldn't understand any of what they were doing. She learned that it was their first meeting, and there was a quiet, tentative understanding that they would all work together to drive the foreigners and their henchmen away from whatever corners of Theranis they could reach. It didn't seem quite real, but they'd pledged to take Darna's side against Calar and the Duke of the Southern Reaches, a hidden mass of what appeared to be highly trained fighters.

Sunna and Raina were escorting her back to the temporary shelter of the harbor temple. Sunna had to go back, on the Aralel's orders, and Raina had to get back to her children. Vigda went with them as far as the border shrine. She didn't say much, but Darna felt her scrutiny all the way.

"You're sure these priestesses will ally with us?" Vigda asked her.

"Iola will, and she's the ambassadress," Darna said.

"She's only a vessel, the ambassadress," Vigda said.

Sunna's expression suggested that she more than half-agreed with Vigda's assessment.

"I'm not so sure about that," Darna said, "and when she says what the dragons have told her, the Aralel and the oracles listen, even if no one else does."

Vigda sniffed. "Well, don't get yourself killed. If this tribunal happens, I'll be there. I'd like to see Calar's face. I'll rub it into the dirt myself."

"Thank you, but why?"

Vigda smiled. "For Tiada, and for my...for the death of Terenet, and for you." Then she made a shooing motion. "Go on. I'll see you in Anamat. We'll be there."

Raina opened her mouth as if to call after Vigda, but Sunna laid a hand on her arm. "Don't question that one; she's a law of her own," she said. "Besides, maybe she's not ready to see Anamat yet."

"I don't know that I am, either, but I have to," Darna said.

"You do," Raina agreed. "I can't imagine Vigda, or the rest of them, in the city."

"Forlan came," Sunna said. "I don't know why they think that now is the time to return, but maybe it is. Soon, there won't be much left to go back to."

"Why do you say that?" Darna asked

"You'll see from the next ridge," Raina said.

Darna's belly rolled, not quite cramping. They saved their breath for the climb, and then they came up to the top of the ridge.

Anamat was spread before them, the whole valley and the city, or what was left of it. The broad bay reached up farther than it ever had before. The sea was eating into the shore. Darna could see the glint of sun on water winding through the city, wider and brighter than the canals were supposed to be. She counted the ships in the harbor, or rather, on the bay. She couldn't see the breakwater at all – it was submerged under the waves. What she could see were ships, too many ships, of strange and various designs, taking on cargo and passengers and setting sail.

"What happened?"

"We had quakes, the harbor rose," Sunna said. "The temple's all right, and most of the guildhalls, but the foreigners' market is flooded and people are saying that the rest of the city will sink too. The oracles say that we'll last until Midsummer, and they're sure of that. They say the city and most of the valley will last past Midwinter, but the valley farmers aren't so sure."

"So, are you saying that it doesn't matter if the Aralel sides with me?"

"Oh, she'll take your side," Sunna said. "She knows your parentage as well as anyone in the city, and she and Gallia are plotting to overthrow Calar by any means they can. Whether it will matter in the end, I don't know."

Raina put her arm around Darna's shoulder, a firm and reassuring gesture. "We'll make sure you live long enough to take him down, and if the Enatel can be a woman, then a prince can too," she said.

"But I don't want to –"

"You didn't want to be a priestess, either," Sunna said. "Come on, let's get down to Anamat. You'll have a bandit army at your back and the lowland guardsmen will shit their pants."

Darna laughed at the image, but looking down at Anamat, she sobered again. A quarter of the city was up to its ankles in water. She would see what she could salvage, even if it was just a scrap of revenge and her own life's blood. She glimpsed a shimmer in the grass, red and gold like Anara. It was gone before she was entirely sure that it was a dragonlet, but it gave her hope, for what little that was worth.

§

Author's Note

I would like to thank the many people who helped me in the very long process of writing this series, especially the beta readers for this book, Victoria Goddard, Kira Tregoning, and Dorothy Ross. As copy editor, Richard Sheely ensured stylistic consistency far better than I could manage on my own.

Thanks also to you, the reader. Your reviews, wherever you post them, are helpful both to me and to future readers. I hope that you'll go on to the final book in this series, *Chronicles of the Last Days*. You can find it, and my other books, at my website:

http://www.ameliasmith.net